I0595029

STRIKER X

The Bold and the Deceptive
Volume 1

NEGUS LAMONT

Copyright © 2020 Negus Lamont
All rights reserved
ISBN Print: 978-0-920583-20-3
Masani Press
Toronto, Ontario

This manuscript is dedicated to all those who seek wisdom. May you find the hidden meaning within.

Disclaimer

This is a work of fiction. Names, characters, businesses, places, events, locales, and incidents are either the products of the author's imagination or used in a fictitious manner. Any resemblance to actual persons, living or dead, or actual events is purely coincidental.

CONTENTS

CHAPTER 1
CLASSIFICATION: STRIKER

Suppose I were to tell you there are things in this world that even your ancestors don't understand—places that have no explanation, and people that hide their true intentions. Suppose I were to tell you my story: one filled with the things that go bump in the night and thunder by day. I wonder if then I would be understood, perhaps even heralded as a hero. My name is Vex, and this is my side of the story.

When the blue sunray struck my visor, I know it is time to rise. I glance up at the sun and feel it mock me as only my deceased sister had ever done. Another day, another monster to hunt. Perhaps today is the day my guts end up on the ground, and not my prey's. That would be a perfectly viable solution to the mundane existence that has become my life. By the time the morning buzzer goes off, I am already fully dressed in my battlesuit.

Poking my head out of the tent marked "X," I am met with the distinct smell of cinnamon. A rarity on this cesspool of a planet.

"Navigator."

"I keep telling you, Vex, it's ok to call me by my first name. It's Allison, in case you forgot."

"Navigator," I repeat.

"Yes, Vex. I'm here, as always."

"How are the oxygen levels of the planet, and what's for the breaking-of-fast?"

"Oxygen is at 1.5, the same level it was yesterday, the day before, and the day before that. Breakfast for striker classification is cornmeal porridge with a dash of cinnamon and hard dough bread."

"Copy that."

"Navigator on standby."

Approaching the communal dining area, my eyes lock onto the giant pot of cornmeal porridge for strikers. Increasing the frequency of my strides, I approach as if stalking prey, each step carefully laid on the ground with silent zeal. When I reach the front of the line, a heaping portion is poured for me, along with two servings of bread. A meal for a champion if there ever was one.

As usual, I hear my troupe calling me over to sit with them. Pretending not to hear them, I sit in my usual spot in the corner of the large dining tent. It's a good spot. A spot that allows me to analyze the group that made it to the lush planet known as Marda.

In the distance is the number-two-ranked striker Tyrant with his troupe, a group as cutthroat as he is. I've had a few run-ins with him on my hunts. With his reinforced battle-suit, destructive phenome, and assortment of grenade and rocket launchers, he is a force to be reckoned with. I'm proud to say that I've stolen a couple of his kills. One would suppose that would make us rivals, though he doesn't pay me any mind most of the time. He is too focused on the mysterious Chaos.

My eyes survey the area to locate Chaos, but she is nowhere to be found. As the top-ranking striker in the Interplanetary Galactic Force Eclectic Division, or the IGF, she has certain privileges. The first is to be served her breaking of the fast in her troupe's quarters.

What purpose a troupe's quarters have, I wouldn't know. Never been, nor do I have plans to visit. My time is better used...

"Allison to Vex, Allison to Vex."

"Go ahead."

"An A-grade Sea Hound has been spotted approximately fifteen kilometers northwest from your location. Conditions are highly hostile, will need underwater attachments."

"Copy that."

"And Vex."

"Yeah?"

"Good luck."

"Yeah. Copy that."

After activating the thrusters on my sky board, I return to my tent to see that it has been ransacked for the third time this year. Fortunately for me, my underwater attachments were left untouched. I'll have to track down the culprit one of these days, but right now the priority is keeping my rank on that leaderboard. While putting them on, I begin my journey towards the location of this new form of monster. How these monsters keep popping up—and why—no one knows. All I know is that it's my job to eliminate them as they appear. The navigator would have marked my hunting area on the map so the other strikers know that it's my territory. To enter another striker's territory without permission usually activates a kill on sight protocol. Not something someone wants on their back when hunting.

Hovering over the webbed tracks of the Sea Hound, I disengage my sky board. With a tap of my wrist, the chip is activated, displaying a screen with the profile of this wild beast. The computer relays the notes on the Sea Hound.

This monster is an amphibian that can stay on land for prolonged periods of time due to the thick scales that cover its body. Once the scales have become saturated with sunlight it will return to the sea, where it is twice as fast and twice as deadly. Weakness: Although it has no eyes to see with, its senses are sharp. Hunts strictly by scent and sound.

The scent of some type of fungus fills my lungs while I carefully lay every step down in silence. My approach is steady yet swift. Nothing will be left to chance. The plasma rifle in my hands is primed to eliminate anything that stands against me. I clasp the grip gently, sure to keep my eyes alert and my breathing on pace. Tiny critters scatter as I near the hot spot.

Large pools of water cause me to divert my steps. Going around a large puddle, I notice several bubbles emerging. I roll backwards just as a webbed claw nicks my visor, lifting my hood in the process.

Before me stands a four-legged beast about my size. The blue-and-green creature has fins atop its head and back, with a long green tail. The front legs are muscular, with sharp fins at the back for slicing. This beast is C-grade at best. Nonetheless it will meet its demise at the end of my plasma rifle.

I raise the weapon to eye level and fire a three-shot burst. The pleasant buzzing sound of the plasma beams fill my ears. The first two beams strike the hound on the nose, the third on the neck. It drops to the ground with a whining noise.

"How anticlimactic," I whisper. "Navigator! What kind of nonsense was this? Get your head in the rankings. That was barely a C-grade beast. How am I supposed to pass that scoundrel Tyrant when you're sending me on missions like these?"

"Still detecting life forms in your territory, picking up on an A-grade Sea Hound deeper within, maybe near the edge."

"That's more like it. Send in the scav to pick up the teeth and the fins. Might as well get what we can from that kill."

I check my right wrist to see the time before my territory is up for grabs and take a deep breath. More than twenty minutes left—plenty of time. I arrive at an open clearing with four massive puddles. Instinctively, I pull out my flutter bomb: a handheld bomb with wings and motion detectors. If there was anything in my arsenal that could fish out the amphibious beast, this would be it.

After tossing the flutter bomb in a nearby pool of water, a wave of shivers wash over me. They are followed by an eerie thought.

Run.

Shaking off the ridiculous thought, I crouch down on one knee and wait for the bomb to maneuver its way through the underground waterways. All I can hope is that this beast arrives, and arrives soon.

I wait some more.

Finally, I hear a thunderous roar that shakes me to my core. The ground shudders; cracks form in the mud. Ripples in the largest puddle are followed by a massive beast four times my person. The creature shoots a large blast of water in my direction just as I unleash a barrage of plasma bullets.

The frigid water overwhelms the plasma energy, striking me in the chest. I'm thrown in the air and land with a loud thud. Sharp pain shoots through my right shoulder. I get up sluggishly when the Sea Hound jumps into the air. I look up to see the shadow looming over me. Silently I curse my luck that I would need such assistance on this mission, but I place my fingers to my temple and summon my phenome.

A large fox made of wind shadow, with a glowing tail and glowing claws, emerges from a realm supposedly constructed by my own psyche. Tirade launches herself at the Sea Hound, gripping it by the throat. While the two are entangled, I gather my senses and pull out my psionic blades. With one in each hand I charge forward, wary of the Sea Hound's lashing tail.

I jam my two blades into the back of the Sea Hound's neck, and it dashes backwards into the water. Dragging Tirade and myself with it. Underwater the beast increases its speed to the point that I feel sick. I manage to hold on, knowing that my life hangs on by a sliver, as it has many times before.

My thoughts buzz, leaving my instincts to seize the day. Removing both blades, I take two flutter bombs and jam them in the holes the blades left. Pushing off, I activate them prematurely, causing a massive explosion under water. I watch as the Sea Hound squirms its way to the opening, as though that could make a difference. The beast climbs on land as if it were running away from me.

Such peculiar behavior.

Stalking my prey, my blades have no room for mercy. Slinking towards the neck of the beast, I caress its scales and whisper the words I have said on many occasions. Words that have no meaning to me, yet which we are trained to say.

"Thou fought bravely; may you find peace in death where life could not."

CHAPTER 2
CLASSIFICATION: SCAVENGER

"Here, baby, blow on Runnymede's dice for me. My old lungs have a way of acting up." I watch the observer with the large bosom bend to blow on my dice. Would that she could blow on something else.

"Dehehehe." I laugh loudly and throw the dice on the table. It isn't until the dice show snake eyes that I realize my luck is poor, just like my scavenger pockets.

"Ah wells, you win some, you lose some." As I get up to leave, another member of the crowd sits down to test his luck at Wagner's Tale: a gambling game half luck and half skill.

Swift as my bones allow, I move towards the exit of the gamblers tent, eyeing the credit collectors. One large bulky female with biceps the size of my head, and an equally menacing male with legs made of steel. Supposedly, they were former strikers—and they seem unaware of little old me. I swipe a handful of delta chips from one of the tables, making use of my sleight of hand. I follow that up by bumping into a female patron with youthful green eyes. Not much of a looker, but she dressed well.

"Oh my, the ancestors must have placed an angelic being at my side. Would I be a fool to fall for you under such circumstances?"

She blushes and smiles. I caress her wrist ever so slightly, removing the plated watch. The exit is in near sight when I feel the sudden grip of a youthful fellow.

"Oh, what's wrong with you, young snapper?"

"You."

"Me?"

"You're the face of the ain't shit brigade. Stealing from a lovely woman like her is like failing to take down one of the monsters we work so hard to hunt." His grip tightens, and he demands I return the watch.

When face to face with such an embarrassing situation, I have few options. I'm not a fighter like Vex, nor am I reputable member of society like Tash. Heck, I'm not even an intelligent sprout like Allison. But I am stubborn like an ox, with the cunning of a fox to match. I am not the bum that many take me for.

"Ouch, ouch! My wrist!" I bellow. Dropping to the floor, I hold my back and writhe around, screaming at the top of my lungs.

The credit collectors rush over to investigate. On their arrival, I do my best to keep a straight face.

"What's going on here?" asked the female.

I let the young fellow talk his way into my trap.

"This poor excuse for a man stole that woman's watch. I was merely having words with him about returning it."

"What have you to say about these accusations?"

"How gruesome the young have become these days! I'm but an old scavenger. Someone that none pay any mind except on this day. And for what? A watch that *he* stole, among other things. I merely asked him to return the items he stole from the good people of Marda. But what can an old feeble man like me do against such vigor? He grabbed my wrist and struck me on my back for my efforts."

"What? You lie," says the young man.

While biting back a grin: "Check his pockets. I bet you will find a whole assortment of stolen items."

The male debt collector reaches into the bloke's pockets to remove a vintage watch, an ID Authenticator, several watermarked chips, and the dried tongue of a razorbeak.

"You have some explaining to do." The female analyzes the contents further. "The watch and the watermarked chips, you may be able to explain away. But you aren't a blacksmith, nor are you a striker. So what are you doing with an ID Authenticator or the tongue of a razorbeak?"

I watch his face of confusion and dismay as he is taken away to Marda's holding cells. A poor excuse for a prison center, supposedly a makeshift fighting pit.

"Better you than me," I mumble.

Smiling at my sleight of hand, I pull out of my left pocket the small pyramid I plucked from the bloke. Raising it to eye level to analyze it makes my mouth water. *My credit troubles are over.* My senses tell me that it is a device of some sort, transparent with a purple ball suspended inside. In any case, my rumbling stomach calls me. After a full night of gambling, it would take a stampede of stingbats to keep me away from the breakfast tent.

Making my way to the breakfast tent, I am slapped with the aroma of cinnamon. *I suppose the strikers are having cornmeal porridge this morning. Lucky bastards.* While lining up like the regular schmuck that I am, I see from the corner of my eye Vex cutting the striker line as usual. *Would that I had the balls to do that.* I watch as Allison and Tash engage in their usual futile attempt to beckon Vex over. *Such sad sops.* I beam into the server's eyes, hoping for more than the usual large spoonful of muck that is usually served to the scavenger class. He beams back knowingly.

Plop is the sound the muck makes when it hits an empty bowl. I look down to see grey muck this time. A welcome change from the white muck. Approaching the two ladies of our troupe, I notice a certain change in their demeanor. Not that I care. I'm used to being in places where I'm not wanted. Sitting down with my legs crossed, I catch the eye of someone putting powder in a large bowl of porridge. Not that it's my concern. People die every day. If the monsters don't get you... the psychopaths will.

"Runnymede!"

I snap back to attention.

"Yes, Allison dear?"

"When was the last time you showered?"

"Well you're the navigator. Navigate the timeline."

"I'd estimate about seven days or so."

"Right on the nose." I stretch and stealthily take a whiff of my own aroma, only to wish I hadn't. "What can I say. Remembering to shower is not my strong suit."

"Among other things," says Allison.

I take a spoonful of muck and put it on my tongue. The taste lashes my tongue three times over, as usual. First bitter, then sour, then a distinct tangy taste to finish. Not something that I would recommend to my worst enemy. I glance over to see the navigator eating something deep fried and dipped in sugar, while the blacksmith is eating steak and eggs.

I buckle myself up for a reaction to something completely taboo; a full night of gambling has me on edge.

"You guys wouldn't mind sharing, would you?"

The look of horror on Allison's face is priceless. For once the ever-talkative navigator is speechless. The ever-so-silent Tash burst into a fit of laughter. After all these years, I thought she was mute.

I make my exit with a grumble, heading to more welcoming company. The other scavengers. As I sit down to eat my muck, I pull up the death toll list using the console on my wrist. Another scavenger dead and gone.

People die every day.

Speeding on my hovercycle, I raise both hands off the steering pegs just as the motorbike hits a bump, threatening to throw me off. I chuckle to myself, dodging puddle after puddle to pull up on a C-grade Sea Hound. I quickly saw off the teeth and the fins with my multipurpose scavengers' tool.

There is the eerie sensation that I'm being watched.

I finish scavenging the remaining fins, being sure not to miss an inch. To die during a scavenge is as dishonorable a death as one of my classification could ever find—only running away from a scavenge is worse. Checking the battle feed, I notice the beast that Vex is hunting has taken the battle underwater. Water battles are not that boy's strong suit. He's a bit slow to the swim. Wondering if I'll be working for a new striker soon enough, I turn around just in time to see a baby Sea Hound approach the mother's carcass.

Although I wasn't the one to end this creature's life, a twinge of guilt fills my heart. Why do we hunt these beasts, who show up in the most obscure places on their planet? Why the harsh judgement against lesser entities? What purpose does all this serve? Questions such as these could get a scavenger like myself killed—or even worse, disappeared.

I snap back to reality to notice the baby Sea Hound has deemed me its enemy. It growls at me with sharp teeth. I turn my multipurpose tool to fire torch. The blazing flame causes the Sea Hound to run away and hop back into the puddle where it came from.

Finally, I get the call.

"Allison to Runnymede."

"Yeah, yeah. I see the battle feed. On my way."

Without bothering to look at the feed, I know Vex has conquered his greatest foe to date. He isn't the third-ranking striker in the division for nothing. The monsters seem to be getting more challenging with every planet we travel to.

Whether that is by design or sheer coincidence, no one knows.

What I do know is that I'll be better off when I "retire" at seventy. Three more years to go, and I will have served my people well. The only honorable death available to one of my kind.

"Allison to Vex and Runnymede."

"Go ahead."

"We have a distress call from an adjacent territory. It seems Chaos is being overwhelmed by Sea Hounds and needs assistance. Do we want to take the mission?"

Shit, if she's being overwhelmed and I'm the closest scavenger, that means I will have to go. Could need minor medical assistance.

There was a long string of silence.

"What class of Sea Hound?" asks Vex.

"Fifty-percent chance of there being a S-grade Sea Hound."

"I like those odds. Scavenger, rendezvous at the hot spot."

"Curses."

"What was that, scavenger?"

"See you there."

"Copy that."

CHAPTER 3
CLASSIFICATION: STRIKER

The first step into Chaos' territory nearly results in impalement. I catch my foot but a few centimeters away from a thin string stretched across two large trees. If triggered, a few sharpened branches would have found their way into my neck. It might not have been a killing blow, but would have been quite dishonorable, nonetheless.

Rifle at the ready, my steps move sluggishly through the hostile territory. The carcasses of several A+ grade Sea Hounds litter the area.

How did she kill so many?

Their scent fills my lungs: a mixture of blood and salty socks. As I progress through her territory, the once-semi-solid mud gives way to softer water-soaked grassland. The trees only serve to dampen the little light that was shining through. Just as my visor adjusts to night vision, a tiny smiley face travels over the ground, arrives in front of me, and explodes at my feet.

I hear the distinct sound of an explosive sniper rifle bullet.

"Who goes there? State your name and rank." says a voice out in the distance.

"There was a distress signal in this territory..."

"You will not hear me repeat myself again. State your name and rank."

"Vex, rank three of fifty." I show my electronic badge to verify rank.

"Vex? The loner, huh? Come to steal my fallen prey as I meet my demise. How fitting that you would die like the beasts."

"That's not true."

Another round goes off at my feet. This time I feel the warmth of the explosive.

Forget this.

I turn to leave when the voice yells out. "Stop. Why have you truly come?"

"To gain honor by killing an S-grade Sea Hound while saving your behind. Such honor would make me that much closer to rank two."

"At least you speak the truth, as most would not in your situation—as vexing as the truth may be. I will allow you to assist me in taking down the S-grade Sea Hound. May whoever deals the killing blow find honor in doing so."

Sprinting to her location, I hear the rumblings of the creature, as if summoned by the very mention of its name. I arrive atop a nearby tree, noticing that Chaos' right arm is broken, and there is a large gash on her stomach. Still she remains in sniper position waiting for the beast to return.

True dedication to the art of hunting.

"I will show you how a true striker hunts," says Chaos.

I watch in awe as she whistles, causing a giant black owl to manifest. Her phenome is legendary amongst the division. The most volatile of all phenomes, yet one of the deadliest. The owl swoops down into the surrounding marshlands, hovering over the massive pool of water in the middle. Flapping its wings furiously, it lets loose a screeching sound that cracks my visor.

It isn't long until a behemoth of a Sea Hound emerges from the pool, blasting a steady stream of water at the phenome. The phenome dodges the attack with ease, while the loud crackling sound of thunder echoes out after a lightning bolt rains down on the creature. Chaos follows the owl's attack by unleashing a barrage of sniper rifle shots at the head of the Sea Hound.

"Allison to Vex."

"Go ahead."

"Now isn't the time to be impressed."

"Shit, right."

I jump down from the tree and push forward, rifle aimed at the glowing chest of the beast. After the plasma rifle does little to no damage, I take out my psionic blades and activate them. I summon Tirade to act as a distraction. The Sea Hound's tail pushes us back with one sweeping motion, even as its webbed claw strikes the owl, causing it to tumble to the ground and disappear.

The beast turns its attention to Tirade and I. Looming over us, it stomps its feet, and a large crack in the earth manifests.

I barely manage to dodge the attack by jumping to the side. I am met with a tail to the face for all my efforts. The creature tosses me high into the sky and is about to swallow me whole when another barrage of explosive sniper rounds reach its face. I tumble down, my blades aimed at the open jaw of the beast.

With both blades together, I rip through the creature from the side of its mouth all the way down its neck. Blood spurts out in every direction, covering me in the honorable essence of the kill.

I land with a hard thud, and my ribs crack upon impact. The last thing I hear before passing out is the distinct voice of my scavenger.

"Not bad, young snapper."

I awake to find that my helmet has been removed. The only person who's seen me without my helmet since I was twelve is my blacksmith. Alone in my blacksmith's tent, I await her return. A blacksmith is a striker's best friend. They provide one with their weapons, armor, phenome cards in exchange for specific parts of a kill, and major medical assistance.

The blacksmith organization is a mysterious one—even more mysterious than the secretive navigators. What they do with their kill parts, few know, and those that do are tagged under a verbiage chip preventing them from speaking on it. For as long as there has been the hunt the blacksmiths and strikers have been hand and rifle.

The tall brunette that is my blacksmith enters the tent. Her gorgeous features as always are diminished by the scowl she wears every time I show up in her camp bruised and battered. She doesn't speak much, preferring to use facial expressions and hand signals to indicate what she wants me to do.

Some people think she is mute, but I know better.

She holds my shoulder still with one hand to scan it with her clunky electronic device. She shakes her head with a grimace, turning the setting to its maximum level.

It doesn't take a medical expert to know my shoulder blade is cracked, nor that several ribs are broken. The device beam bypasses flesh and goes straight to the bone, causing a burning sensation, followed by the scent of iron. After a few minutes of agonizing pain, I regain movement in my shoulder. This process is the same for the rib cage, but twice as painful. I wince but refuse to let out a sound.

An eerie smile creeps across her face, followed by a full-out smile when she finishes.

Whether she relishes in the pain or the healing of the pain, I don't bother to ask. Feeling brand new, although a bit sore, I explain to her what I needed in exchange for the scavenged hunt.

"I'll need a full stock of flutter bombs, a new rifle—the same color with extra energy capacity—and something to decrease the distance between me and my prey. I'm thinking something like a grappling hook attachment. How much more credit do I have left after all that?"

She places her thumb, index finger, and middle fingers together, indicating that I have enough for a tattoo or basic training for Tirade. I explain that the tattoo would suffice. The thought of upgrading my phenome makes me queasy. While some strikers rely on the manifestation of their shadow self, I simply don't trust it. As far as I'm concerned, they are nearly as bad as the beasts that we hunt. Through rigorous and disciplined training, I've managed to minimize the use of it.

When I reach number one rank, it will be of my own accord, due to my own skills, and my own abilities.

The buzzing of the laser leaves marks on my shoulder; the tattoo process is a sacred one. Only strikers can tat themselves with their S-grade takedowns. It is a process usually celebrated with much fanfare amongst one's troupe. By the time she finishes the detailed design of the S-grade Sea Hound, I hear the distinct sound of gunfire, followed by the sound of a battlesuit meeting flesh.

Poking my head out, I'm met with the visage of Chaos crushing her scavenger with a large red war hammer. She looks around in a craze, breathing heavily, then stampedes towards me, dragging the massive weapon. I prepare myself lest she try her hand at my head.

According to her profile, her demeanor is edgy at best. Her speed, strength, and intelligence are all at S level. Her cunning and wisdom are a bit lower at A. Such deadly levels, in such a compact body. She is a force of nature: something created for the sole purpose of hunting.

"Come. We shall have words."

I look around to see that there is no one but me standing where she is looking. Stretching my shoulder out, I nod.

She leads me to the back of a large tent marked "Z." The night sky beams down on us all romantic-like. But I'm not foolish enough to believe this is that kind of party. In the silence preceding our conversation, I admire her armor.

It's S-level all around, from boots to helmet. All a gorgeous crimson, with a rocket pack at the back for maneuverability. A bit loud for my taste, but hell—when your name is Chaos, maybe stealth isn't that important to you.

One day I'll have S+-level gear, and then we will see who's top dog.

"Look at me. Do I look like a damsel in distress?"

"What? No, though you look like you got issues." I briefly look her in the visor. "I'd rather not get involved."

"Too late. You should have thought of that before you answered the call to action. You're one of the few I can trust on this cesspool of a planet, and I intend to make use of you."

Grinning inside my helmet, my thoughts focus on one thing. *That upgraded rifle is gonna be so elite.*

"I don't have time for this. What do you want?" I ask.

"My scavenger poisoned my porridge this morning. It slowed me down, drastically causing me to slip up. There is something going on in this planet. A scavenger turning on their striker would take a lot of credits and a lot of conditioning rewiring. I'm going to get to the bottom of this."

I sigh, and my mouth activates before my brain. "Are you sure this isn't all in your head? I mean, you do have a reputation for being a bit loony."

I feel the energy around her increase just as she strikes me in the stomach. Gasping for air, I drop to my knees. Me and my big mouth.

Chaos tilts my head back and looks me directly in the visor, as if she can see through my soul. She deactivates her screen to reveal the piercing red eyes of a light elf.

"I'll be in touch."

CHAPTER 4
CLASSIFICATION: BLACKSMITH

"Tash. Tash. Do you hear me?"

The screeching voice of another human punctures my ear drums. It's been a busy night. But it all serves a grander purpose. In honor of the Most High, I work diligently on Vex's improved weapon set. From creating the muzzle to the trigger. Making sure everything is in place. This rifle will be heavier than he is used to, but he will adapt.

"Tash!" The screeching grows closer, and I turn to see a recognizable face donning an unrecognizable expression.

I raise an eyebrow, shrugging.

"You didn't show up in the dining tent for dinner. So I brought you your meal. It smells like mashed potatoes and venison. Or something akin to venison. Why they keep feeding you guys these hearty meals is a mystery to me, but I am somewhat jealous," she says between bites of sugar dough.

I manage a meek smile before returning to my work. She will ramble on, and I will half-listen, as usual. Thank the Most High for the conscious dancehall music playing in my chip directly fed to my brain.

"Did you hear?"

I continue with my work, expecting her to continue as well.

"Of course you didn't, you were cooped up in this small tent. We lost a striker today, along with Chaos' scavenger. It was striker forty-two."

"Well," is the only response I can muster.

"I know, I know, people die every day. But what makes this so peculiar is that we have no data on what exactly killed striker forty-two. He was an up-and-coming striker, who was venturing into the highlands of this planet—the area with the giant trees to the south. One second he was seen hovering on his board, and the next there was a blank screen, followed by his screams."

Raising an eyebrow, my thoughts turn to the song playing. Light by Govana. An instant classic if there ever was one.

My steady hand attaches the plasma cartridges that will synch with Vex's energy into the rifle, locking it into place. I grin.

"Oh, splendid. That's a nice rifle. I'm sure Vex will get plenty of takedowns tomorrow. He made a significant jump with today's hunt. Quite the impressive feat, considering the gap that there once was between us and Tyrant's troupe."

I watch as she looks at the flutter bombs, then at me.

"If only he wasn't such an isolated being. It can't be healthy for him to always be by himself. I mean he doesn't even remember our names half the time."

Clearly she is distraught. I suppose one should say something to appease her pain.

"So it goes sometimes."

She lowers her head, making a double chin. I hold back a grin as the song Firm and Strong by Popcaan comes on.

"In times like this, we have to be firm and strong. Trust the process, and have faith in the Most High."

"Who is this Most High you speak of?"

I point to the ceiling of my blacksmith tent. There is the painting of a light elf with a long beard and a massive smile, glowing a bright yellow.

"That represents the Most High. The deity that we sacrifice to."

"What do you sacrifice?"

"You know? The stuff that happens to the..." I grasp my mouth as searing pain emits from the chip in my tongue.

"I'm sorry. I can't speak any more on this topic. I thought you knew already, being a navigator and all."

"We navigators know many things, but even the blacksmiths are a mystery to us." Allison lowers her head, donning an eerie expression.

"What's with that face?"

"I caused you pain."

"Pain is a part of life. Besides, my big mouth is what caused it. There are so many things I cannot speak on. I admit that it's stifling sometimes, but fortunately for me, I have music and you guys."

"What about other blacksmith friends?"

"Other blacksmiths are too uppity. Parading around with their collections, demonstrating the specimens they have acquired through the years."

"I notice you don't wear your specimens like the others. Why is that?"

I feel myself blush slightly. "You're gonna think it's stupid."

"I promise I won't."

"Well..."

"Well what?"

"Well, I'm waiting for a special specimen. I made a vow that I wouldn't wear any specimen until we have taken down the Bee Rex."

"That's, umm..."

"I know, stupid. The Bee Rex is supposed to be a mythological creature, at best extinct for over a thousand years now. But my father swore on his soul that he had a piece of one. He was a great blacksmith. One day, his striker comrade came by on the brink of death with his most valuable catch. The stinger of a Bee Rex. I mean, when they tested it, the scanner said unknown substance, but the striker promised on his life that it was a Bee Rex, or at least it matched the rumors."

"What happened then?"

Lowering my head, I manage to stifle my tears. Tears don't do anyone any good. "My father and his striker were both executed for false monster deliberation."

"What in the world?" Allison contorts her face into a sympathetic expression. As she furrows her brows, she grabs my hand.

"I will find out more about this bee and Tyrannosaurus rex combination. Above all, we will clear the name of your father and his striker. Such a dishonorable death must weigh heavy on your head and the heads of your ancestors."

I nod my head fervently during a long string of silence. Finally, I manage a meek smile.

Hope.

As any true master of any craft, I have a ritual that I must carry out for each item that I create. There is protocol, and then there is ritual. I suppose one should define the two. Protocol is a set of rules that are laid out by the IGF to make sure that each created item is up to par with industry standard. While ritual is what the Most High requires of us to remain connected. There is a large collection of blacksmiths who are designated a specific role in our division. In fact, for every striker there are one point five blacksmiths. This is done in order to keep prices fair and foster trade of specimen from hunt. It isn't uncommon for the more popular blacksmiths to be a part of several troupes.

I, on the other hand, only serve one striker, and that's Vex. I've known him since we were children. Before he was Vex the soloist. Before he was so cross, and before he was known as Vex. Known for the most takedowns without the use of his phenome. He has become something of an inspiration for people that are called try-hards. Try-hards die at a higher rate, and make for high-risk bets for the scavengers, but are viewed as must-watch TV amongst the navigators, blacksmiths, and the civilian population. The battle feed is sent directly to every civilian's console chip when we occupy a planet.

Once upon a time Vex went by his birth name, Vincent. He was a precocious child but very lazy. From birth he was designated a scavenger and wore that designation as any scavenger would. He never cared for the slew of tests and experiments thrust on us from a young age. In fact, the only thing he really cared about was playing with his phenome. Tirade was once a fun-loving manifestation of his shadow self and wanted to play with all the other phenomes, instead of fighting them. I suppose it goes to show how kindhearted Vincent was.

But it wasn't until that fateful evening that everything changed. I remember it like I remember every scratch on his armor and every scar on his body. One evening his father returned alone from a multi-troupe mission. Staggering from the woods of Saturna, Viral was rambling like a mad man and drenched in blood. He said that his scavenger was killed, along with the striker and scavenger from the three other troupes. One of which being Vincent's older sister the striker and mother the scavenger. To make matters worse, the navigators and blacksmith from each troupe were systematically murdered—save for Runnymede, who served as Viral's blacksmith at the time. Runnymede was mysteriously demoted to scavenger and has been silent on the matter ever since.

The entire situation was considered the biggest scandal of the century, and Vincent has never been the same ever since. His father, a disgraced and raving mad-man, wandered off into the woods, never to be seen again. Presumed dead. Left with nowhere else to channel his anger and disgrace, Vex became a vicious fighter seemingly overnight. Tirade went from a fun-loving pup to something near unwieldly. But for all his efforts, he has always been number three to Tyrant's two and Chaos' one. In fact, the top five strikers are so far ahead of the rest of the group that they are called the untouchables.

I tell you this story so that maybe you'll have a better understanding of his actions from here on out. As his judge, jury, and perhaps executioner, it is best that you know some of the things that even he won't tell you.

CHAPTER 5
CLASSIFICATION: STRIKER

"Why? Why? Why?!"

Stupid Tirade. Barking in my dreams. I awake with a blistering headache, covering my throbbing head. Every time I use my phenome, she comes to me in my dreams and berates me with high-pitched yelps and deep howls. When I rise once again after another night with my helmet on, part of me is disappointed that I survived that S-grade Sea Hound. It would have served for an honorable death. I suppose there is more for me to do in this miserable life.

Like every morning, I poke my head out of my tent and inhale the aroma that wafts in the air. This time my visor picks up on the scent of fresh fried dumplings and salted fish. Whoever prepares the ingredients created by the replicators seems to be on a roll these days. A small part of me is beginning to enjoy my time on this planet. At least the ingredient replicators seem to be working fine.

"Navigator."

She sighed. "Yes, Vex?"

"I believe it's supposed to be 'go ahead.'"

"Go ahead."

"How are the oxygen levels of the planet and what's for the breaking-of-fast?"

"Hmm. Actually, today the oxygen level has dipped to caution level. It would be best to take an extra oxygen tank." There is a long pause. "That wasn't… in the notes."

"I guess the all-knowing navigators aren't as perfect as they think."

"We don't think we're perfect, we just know enough on many topics to know that we know the most, while knowing little enough to know that we're not wrong."

Both of us know that entire sentence went over my head, so I tactfully change the subject.

"Breaking-of-fast?"

"Fried dumplings with spinach, salted fish, and a special fruit called ackee."

"Interesting."

After parading to the front of the line, I take a big plate and wait for the large heap of food to be placed on there. It smells absolutely delightful. After my plate is filled, I march over to my usual spot, while ignoring the call of my navigator and the wave of my blacksmith.

Halfway through my glorious meal I am joined by Chaos, fully decked out in her S-level armor. *It seems I'm not the only one who likes to start the day fully dressed and ready for a hunt.*

"I did some digging on you, Vex. Couldn't find everything that I wanted."

"So? Why are you telling me this?"

"Are you light or dark elf?"

I push my plate away. I've lost my appetite. Sneering, I move my legs to get up only for Chaos to raise a high-tech revolver slightly above table level. She lowers it back to my crotch.

"You really like making me repeat myself. Not a good thing." She looks to her left, then her right, and leans in further to whisper.

"Are you light or dark elf?"

"If you must know, I'm dark elf. What of it?"

"Hmph. Rare for your kind to make striker classification. Even rarer to be in the top ten. Quite the feat. How'd you cheat your way to the top? Probably banging someone in control of the leaderboards."

"Quiet you," I grumble. My ire is raising to an all-time high, causing my temperature and energy levels to spike."

"Oh, have I struck a nerve? I mean, what kind of dark elf barely uses his phenome? I thought you guys were supposed to be like arse and bench with your shadow selves.

Probably sleep next to your phenome. Maybe even fondle it at night."

"Shut up, I'm warning you."

"Warning me of what? What you gonna do? Ugly darkling."

I throw up my palm, shooting out the grappling spear from my wrist. The plasma tip pierces through her arm as if it were goat cheese. I yank her arm forward, making her drop the revolver. Then I slam my right fist into her visor, breaking it on impact. But by the time I wind up for another punch, she's managed to climb over the bench and wrap her legs around my neck in a triangle choke.

The already low levels of oxygen lower even more. I feel my eyes activate, burning a bright blue as I rise to my feet, then smash her through the table. Loosening her grip around my neck, she pulls out a knife and jams it into my leg. I pick her up again and fling her across the room into one of the poles holding up the tent. The tent shakes and shudders but manages to stay standing.

As she pulls out her sniper rifle, I withdraw my new rifle.

"At this range, you'll die before I do. I dare you to grace that trigger with your finger."

To my shock, this psycho freak erupts into a fit of laugher and lowers her weapon.

"Come, walk with me. We have much to discuss," says Chaos.

I'm walking with a slight limp, and Chaos asks me a question. I'm not sure whether it was intended to piss me off or calm me down.

"How's your leg?"

"Fine."

"Aww, don't be a spoilsport. I had to find out for myself if you were as good as they say you are."

"Who's they?"

"Your navigator raves about you all the time. She has quite the big mouth, but is very knowledgeable. She said if you were to actually evolve and master your phenome, you'd be top striker within a year."

"Oh, is that so? What of it?"

"Maybe number two. What's up with that, anyways? Your shadow-self give you goosebumps at night or something?"

I stay silent.

"Ahh, there it is. I figured as much. It happens to your kind more often than not. Dark elves and such. There is a higher chance of your phenome taking over your brain and turning you into a psychopath—or even worse a raving lunatic."

"I see. I didn't know that."

She laughed. "If I were to build a bridge with the things you don't know, I'd be back home by now. Every Traveler Cube that pops up, I hope it's back to Venusian. We're so far away from my home planet that I've lost contact with everyone I knew or cared about."

"That's a shame. I'm not sure where my home planet is. I just know it's a volcanic rocky planet."

"Yes, I'm sure you wouldn't."

"What's that supposed to mean?"

"Just more dark elf stuff. Have you heard about the cyber elves?"

"Cyber elves?"

"Yes. Light or dark elves that have been corrupted by the cyber realm."

"If I had, I wouldn't have repeated the question."

"My oh my, you're quite uninformed. I would have thought with a navigator like yours you'd be one of the most informed strikers. Let's just say there are bigger things going on in the IGF than just killing monsters and collecting specimens."

"I don't speak to my navigator much. Nor my blacksmith or scavenger."

"Why is that? Think you're too good for them?"

"It'll hurt more when they die. People die every day. Why not them? Why not me? Saves them the grief and saves me the trouble."

She slaps me on the back of my helmet. "Such a foolish notion. One's navigator is like the brain in that thick skull of yours. The scavenger is an extension of your hands just like your rifle, and the blacksmith is the material that puts it all together. Your troupe is supposed to be as much a part of you as any limb or organ."

"Keep your philosophy to yourself. I got this far doing it my way."

"An impressive feat, I'll give you that. But you'll get no further. We both know you feel it. You've hit a wall."

"Say more about your ask and less about your tell."

"Frankly, I'm gonna need you to watch my back out there. At least until I can find and vet a new scavenger. Also, I'm gonna need to borrow your scavenger. He will have to carry a larger haul, since the two of us will be joining forces to take down some S-grade monsters. We'll split everything sixty-forty, in my favor."

"I can take down S-grade monsters on my own. Why do I need you?"

She slaps me on the back of my helmet again.

I grumble underneath my breath.

Both hands on my shoulders, she places her helmet to my helmet. "Listen here. Finishing off a mere Sea Hound doesn't make you a tough guy. That Sea Hound was severely wounded beforehand, and you still nearly bit the bullet. There is a big jump between A-grade and A+-grade, and an even bigger jump to S. It's almost as if the monsters stop being mindless beasts to become something more sentient."

"Ha, you mean to tell me you think these creatures have minds of their own? That they what... can think?"

"I wouldn't go that far; they are mere beasts. But I'm saying I've seen some shit. That's all I'm saying."

"I'll think about it."

"Fair enough. Tomorrow we will experiment with a joint venture."

"Perhaps. I'll think about it."

While heading over to the territory of the A+ beast, I contemplate a joint venture with Chaos. *I'm not so arrogant as to think that I can't improve. But they don't call me the soloist for no reason. I don't like the thought of teaming up. Even thinking about it makes me sick.*

I'm governed by my own hand. I had to be spectacular when I didn't have a choice. But she might be right. I have been trying to surpass Tyrant for over a decade now. With every leap I make, he takes a bound.

"Navigator."

"Go ahead, Vex."

"ETA until A+ beast?"

"You're in the hotspot already. It should be visible soon."

Suddenly, I'm clotheslined off my sky board. I land with a massive thud, my brain rattling around inside my skull. The Dakar Bear jumps on top of me and begins mauling me with paws the size of my head. Between swipes, I manage to shoot my grappling spear into the beast's lower jaw. Sparks shoot out of my damaged helmet and armor. But I manage to emit a charge of my own blue energy into the wire traveling up the spear.

The Dakar Bear backs off and I watch, amazed, as it turns invisible. I stagger to my feet with rifle in hand. My vision is blurred; the light armor I'm wearing is nothing more than cloth against this beast. I turn in every direction waiting for the bear to show itself.

I cannot afford to be caught off guard again.

I hear the swishing of the creature's paw swiping at my throat just as I duck. I let loose a barrage of fire into the beast's chest, forcing it to fully appear. Blood oozes from the bear, and I finally get a good look at it.

It's three times my size; orange spikes protrude from the back of its arms and neck. An orange chaos ring in the middle of its chest indicates that it's an energy user, as if the glowing orange eyes weren't a dead giveaway. The massive black bear stampedes towards me and throws a chaos ring in my direction. I dodge to the left; the ring strikes a nearby tree, dissipating it.

I let off another barrage, this time aimed at the groin of the beast, and I hear a roar in the distance. The Dakar Bear turns invisible, and a blood trail tells me it slinks away.

I'll have to track it later. Something is coming.

The soil thunders as the trees sway back and forth. I inhale the scent of the nearby foliage deeply. I activate three flutter bombs to hover around my being. My vision locks onto an S-grade Forest Tiger as it emerges from the trees.

The thick green skin and spiked tail are a dead giveaway, while the massive, muscular front legs give me pause. The tiger curls into a ball with its thorns protruding. It barrels through the trees surrounding the clearing.

I let loose a flurry of shots, which bounce off the thickened skin of the creature. The flutter bombs fly towards their target, but the tiger maneuvers right and the then left, dodging the first two. The third explodes upon impact.

Now back in its normal stance, it roars at me again. I watch in horror as the gaping hole from my flutter bomb heals.

"It's a good day to die." I whisper.

My psionic blades are drawn as I move to tangle with the tiger. It lashes at me with its giant claws, but I duck. My blade slices the underbelly of the beast. Its guts ooze onto my armor, covering me in a foul stench. The forest tiger retreats a short distance, bleeding.

It roars, healing the wound.

"Allison to Vex."

"What?"

"A Forest Tiger has been defeated once before. You have to cut off the tail; that's the source of its healing."

"Copy that."

On what little energy I have left, I stretch out my palm to engage my grappling spear at a nearby tree. It catapults me into the air just as the Forest Tiger pounces at my former position. I drop down with both blades aimed at the tail. Slicing through it takes little effort; I smirk as the Forest Tiger hisses at me.

My breath is heavy, and my wounds will take several days to recover. But I taste the fresh beast that I'm about to take down.

The moment between life and death, when the creature knows its demise is coming, is a thrill that I live for. The increased heartbeat followed by the sudden last-ditch attempt to survive.

I hold both blades to the side in death-blossom stance and charge them with as much energy as I can muster. The sizzling sound of the imbued blades cause the Forest Tiger to back into a nearby tree.

Its eyes... I'll never forget its eyes. I've killed countless beasts to date but have never seen eyes like this one. Almost as if it feared death.

Can a wild monster feel fear? If it can feel fear, what else can it feel? Dangerous thinking.

A massive bomb lands on the Forest Tiger, disintegrating its head. I'm thrown backwards. Only by digging my blades into the ground, do I manage to come to a screeching halt. My armor is in shambles, exposing much of my dark skin.

The bulky Tyrant walks past me and pats me on the head.

"Heh, better luck next time kid."

I check my damaged timer to see that the alarm went off ten minutes ago. I glare at Tyrant and my big mouth gets the better of me.

"What do you think you're doing?"

"What does it look like? Securing my kill." He looks me up and down; he scoffs. "It wouldn't be honorable to kill you in such a condition. But don't push your luck. I squish bugs like you for a hobby."

Just as I am about to respond, his scavenger approaches in a large hover truck. It's slow but well equipped to defend itself from the jump-man teams. I watch as my unrequited adversary and stolen prey zoom off into the distance.

"Scavenger."

No response.

"Scavenger."

No response.

I check the communication system on my helmet to see that it's severely damaged. I activate my sky board, only for it to overload. Adding insult to injury, I will have to walk back to home base.

CHAPTER 6
CLASSIFICATION: NAVIGATOR

"Curses!" I slam my headset against the table in front of me as the other navigators glare. As if they haven't sworn before. My connection with Vex has been broken for the first time since becoming his navigator, a streak that I was holding onto.

The navi in the makeshift cubicle next to me whispers something that makes me want to dump hot oil on him: "Losing a connection isn't that bad. I've lost connection with my striker a total of twenty times."

I shoot back, "I bet he has the permanent brain damage to match his ineptitude."

"Mean."

"Yes, that's me, the mean green chubby machine."

I wipe the grease off my fingers with my shirt and get up to use to the washroom. I see the supervisor's head poke out as soon as I start to move. After I give her the hand signal for the washroom, she sits back down.

As navigators, we're only allowed a washroom break once every twenty-four hours, and meals are brought to us from the dining camp when on duty. They feed us sugary deep-fried meals because they take longer to digest. They also like fattening us up to keep us lazy and timid. Like placating a walrus. I don't mind; the food tastes good and we navis find other ways to occupy our time. Mainly games of online volute in between missions, quickies in the bathroom, and fantasizing about what it would be like to be a striker.

Waddling over to the washroom, I see Jacob Beaver Mouth eyeing this piece of candy. I avoid contact, not in the mood.

I still can't believe I lost contact with Vex. I hope he's ok.

Between deep breaths, I pry open the hefty door to the mechanized outhouse. This time it smells of vanilla instead of lilac. A nice change. Three minutes in, as I'm about wrapped up, I hear a soft knocking on the door.

"Third snack is here. Do you want deep-fried lizard or deep-fried cinnamon sticks?"

I ponder the most crucial decision of my day. Something chewy or something sweet? Part of me actually wants to skip third snack, maybe go on a diet or something. But that part of me is small and weak. Constantly beat up by the other parts.

"I'll take both."

"Sounds good. I'll put them on your desk."

I'm not one to be judged. This isn't an indictment of me, but of Vex. If they were to put me on trial for all my crimes, the list would be as short as Jacob's...

Another knock on the door.

"Fourth drink is here; do you want a root beer float or a milkshake? Today we have caramel, vanilla, and chocolate."

"I'll take a vanilla."

My hands tremble at the thought of consuming my sixth meal of the day. They say if you want to lose weight you need to eat six meals a day, to boost metabolism and whatnot. I guess I'm well on my way.

I wash up and re-enter the makeshift navigators' facility to an assortment of scents and flavors. The scent of cinnamon and deep-fried lizard fills my lungs. I can almost taste the meal. With one hand on the top of my cubicle, I turn the corner to my desk.

To my dismay, I am met with half-eaten deep-fried lizard. My cinnamon stick is gone, my vanilla shake all but finished.

I feel heat rise from my feet all the way to my head as my temper reaches the boiling point.

"Who the fuck ate my food?" The entire room erupts into laughter.

"No, this isn't a joke. Who ate my food?" The laughter is a steady stream.

The supervisor, three times my size, rumbles over.

"You know the drill. No seconds, and you snooze you lose. Please sit down and get back to your screen."

In the navigator classification, we guard and hide our food like pirates hiding buried treasure. Food is as sacred to us as breathing; take another person's food means war. Punishable by any means necessary.

I'm going to find out who ate my food, and they're going to pay.

My stomach growls while I wait for Vex to return to the encampment. I'm one of the few navigators left over tonight. A common occurrence. Like any good navigator, I often watch the sleeping vitals of my striker. My night doesn't end until well after his does.

Ten cubes over, I can hear the sobbing of a fellow navi. A small group gathers to comfort her. I join in. We're a complicated group: although we're very competitive, whenever one loses a striker it's like we all lose a striker.

"What happened?"

"I don't know. My visual feed was jammed—then suddenly there was this horrible scream. I've never heard him bellow like that before. It was as if something was tearing him apart, limb from limb, flesh from flesh. I sent over the scav to check it out but by the time he arrived, all that was left was our striker's psionic spear."

She paused and looked me in the eyes, tears forming.

"What am I going to do without a striker? How can I bond with another after such a horrible experience?"

Placing one hand on her shoulder, I manage to formulate words. "We're going to get through this together. Show me where your striker was."

She points on her screen towards the south. Vex has been hunting in the north. He's not going to like switching hunting grounds, but I'll have to convince him. For better or worse when it comes to these mysterious monsters, I believe our troupe is the one for the job.

"Runnymede to Allison."

"Go ahead."

"Vex has arrived on foot. His armor is in pretty bad shape, and we're coming in empty-handed. Gonna have to dig into the reserves for this repair."

"Copy that."

I check the reserves to see that we still have a sizeable number of credits left over. Enough to cover the repairs and leave some for a rainy day. Vex spends a lot, just like any striker. It's up to us to make the finances work as long as he keeps bringing in the specimens. But Runnymede has been overdrawing his account lately: a sizable amount each quarter.

I should have been paying closer attention to the reserves.

"Allison to Runnymede."

"What's up navi?"

"We need to talk."

"The last time I heard those words, I found myself single and homeless."

Walking over to the blacksmith's tent, I take a deep breath. This will be the first time I've seen Vex up close and personal in over a year. As one can tell, our paths don't cross often.

I open the flap to Tash's blacksmith tent. She's working on his shoulder, a repeat injury. He has his helmet on as per usual—would that I could get a good look at him.

"H...he...hey, Vex."

"Greetings, navigator."

"Allison." I do a half bow.

Why'd I do a half bow? Lame.

There is an awkward string of silence as several moments pass by with a quiet edge. Finally, to my relief, he breaks the silence.

"Why you here?"

"Oh, well... just wanted to see what upgrades you were getting, if any."

I've got to manage his spending on this one, lest he find out he's now on a tight budget.

"I was thinking a full armor upgrade, with reinforced titanium and bella rockets. There is a notable jump in speed, strength, and tactics with the A-to S-grade monsters."

Horror crosses my mind as I calculate the fee for such upgrades. My poker face wins this evening.

"You could, but have you thought of a stealth cape?"

"A stealth cape? For what."

"Well, you could move quickly while invisible, plus they look really badass."

He grumbles. "I'm not interested in aesthetics. Though I don't like the idea of a reduction in speed due to the reinforced titanium. Good lookin' out."

There is another long silence.

"Was that all?"

"Yup, that's all."

I stand there, foolishly gawking at his defined muscles and silky chocolate skin.

"Dismissed."

"Pardon?"

"You're dismissed. You came with a purpose, and now that purpose has been fulfilled. There will not be idle time in my troupe."

If he only knew what Runnymede was up to, he wouldn't be saying that.

I do another half bow.

Idiot.

And I back away out the tent. The heat in there was unbearable. Or perhaps it was me getting all hot and bothered. How Tash keeps her cool, I'll never know.

"Allison to Runnymede."

"Go ahead."

"What's your twenty."

"Twenty is right behind ya."

I whip around to see Runnymede, with his light purple hair, mechanical boots, and assistant arm pieces. He has his spectacles on and he smells like fresh cucumbers. His uniform's bronze coloring suits his lightly tanned skin. For a man in his sixties, his face is always vibrant and youthful.

Say what you want about scavengers, but they live a pretty stress-free life. Must be good for the skin.

I pull Runnymede over to the back of a nearby tent as his ever-knowing grin turns into something analogous to concern.

"What ails ya?"

"Credits. What have you been doing with our reserves? I mean, how did you even get in without my passcode or Vex's?"

"Vex has a bad memory when it comes to anything not mission related, so he hides a disjoined version of his passcode in his tent. Every quarter I ransack his tent in search of the code and decipher it."

"You're a true scoundrel. I don't want to ask, but I have to know. What are you spending all these funds on?"

"You may take me for a scoundrel, but I have a soft spot for that young sprout. Been serving his family since he was a wee one. It's for a surprise from a former blacksmith colleague of mine. Something extra special. It will help us bring in S-grade monsters at an alarming rate."

"You're crazy. What do you know about taking down S-grade monsters? I'm reporting you."

"You most certainly will not." He takes one step closer, invading my personal space without warning.

"What's to stop me? We don't need a scav like you."

"While I was digging through the reserves for the good of the troupe, I noticed a stream of finances going into an off-planet account. We've been on this planet for over a year, so that shouldn't be the case."

I know where this is going, so I take a step back and gasp.

"Yes, that's right. A little someone has been funneling ten percent of our funds every moon cycle to Venusian under the guise of a *home tax*. At first I wondered why Venusian, but then I remembered something you told me. Although you were high-born of the light elf race, your parents went broke on some bad business deals. Then your mother became sick. Medicine on Venusian is rather expensive, as they'd rather the sick die off to keep the population healthy."

I drop to my knees, trembling. I clutch onto his bronze breeches and feel tears forming until I realize we're in the same boat. Just as I'm about to rise to my feet, he pushes my head back down.

"While you're down there, might as well bless my cinnamon stick."

I recoil back, repulsed and prepared to scream, when he giggles.

"Can't you take a joke?"

"How ill-proposed." I respond. Arms crossed and stance firm, I glare at this old decrepit man with as much vile as elvenly possible.

"I'm high-born. As if I would ever..."

"Save me the speech, dumpling. You're one of the more scandalous ones amongst the navigators. In any case, from now on, one hand will wash the other. I have one more transaction to make with the blacksmith, so that is all but taken care of. In the meantime, I need you to find the value of this."

He reaches into his pocket and pulls out a palm-sized translucent pyramid with an amethyst crystal near the top.

"We're in a similar position. Why should I add sweetener to your pot?"

"Because I'm old. I am ready to die—are you?"

He holds the pyramid near my face. The mechanical device looks valuable, but it is like nothing I have ever seen.

"And you'll keep the money going to my mother a secret?"

"Of course. Us scoundrels have to stick together." He winks.

CHAPTER 7
CLASSIFICATION: STRIKER

"Wake up, it's time."

I rise sluggishly to the vision of Chaos in her full crimson battlesuit. With her sniper rifle at her back and revolvers at her side, she seems as formidable as ever. Checking the clock on my right wrist, I realize we're four hours earlier than my normal time.

"Striker to navigator."

"Go ahead, Vex."

To my pleasant surprise, my navigator is up and functional.

"Oxygen levels?"

"Oxygen levels are at acceptable conditions. Point five higher than yesterday."

"That will suffice. Copy that."

Chaos places both her hands at her hips while tilting her head. Reminds me of that tea kettle song.

"What?" I grumble.

"Let's go. We have hunting to do."

Not wanting to seem like a slouch, I quickly get dressed under Chaos' scrutiny.

"It would be best if you bulked up a bit. I checked your profile again, and your strength is only at a B+. You should hit the weights after a long day of hunting. We're skipping breakfast today."

"Now, why would I do that?"

"Because today we're hunting something special, and I don't want you puking out your innards."

"That has never happened."

"Not yet."

"What are we hunting?"

"Check in with your navigator. You'll see."

"Striker to navigator."

"Yes…"

"Put a pause on the attitude. Mark the location of my hunting ground, and send me the profile of the expected monster."

"Today we're doing something a bit different. I'm not sure what Chaos has told you, since you always have your comm network on visual only, but today we're hunting an unknown monster in the southern region of Marda. Runnymede has already switched to a larger cargo unit and is on standby."

"Striker to Scavenger."

"Ye?"

"What container are you carrying?"

"The maximum level that the bike can carry. A cargo carrier fit for six quadrants."

"Alright, copy that."

"Navigator, what special equipment will I need?"

"It is recommended that you bring extra flutter bombs for support. Maybe evolve Tirade, as her next upgrade provides her with a taunt."

I bite my tongue to prevent myself from lashing out at my navigator. Up until now, she has known better then to suggest I upgrade Tirade. The fact that she is suggesting it now means that either she is taking advantage of Chaos' presence or the situation really is that dire."

"So, what you gonna do? A Taunt would be pretty useful."

"Quiet, I'm thinking."

As we head over to the blacksmith's quarters, I see my blacksmith opening her tent. It's good to see my team up and prepared so early. Or perhaps I'm the one who wakes up late?

The distinct smell of iron fills my lungs when we enter the tent. The gravel beneath my boots reminds me that the blacksmith's tent is on uneven ground.

Turning to Chaos, I say, "If you'll excuse us, we have business to discuss."

"Oh my, am I intruding?" She doesn't budge.

The blacksmith holds her palm open and touches it with three of her other hand's fingers. She has three extra flutter bombs ready for me.

"Umm, Vex?" asks my blacksmith.

"Yes?"

"Do you want to upgrade Tirade?"

Stifling my ire, I swallow the saliva that rushes into my mouth. This pressure to upgrade Tirade, to wake up earlier, to team up with Chaos. So much change, so fast.

"I suppose."

The blacksmith nods and pulls out a large black case. She opens it to the first page, revealing an assortment of cards, each in its own slot. All show pictures of Tirade in different poses with different titles. She plucks the one that says "Tirade – Level 2 – Taunt" and hands it to me.

I place the metal card to my temple instinctively and say the words to activate the upgrade. "There is solace found in the shadow, for in our darkest moments does the light shine brightest."

Whatever mumble jumble that is.

A sudden wave of sorrow hits me as my deepest, darkest emotions bubble to the top. Struggling to maintain my balance, I suck in my breath to keep from squealing as tears flow down my face uncontrollably. After a few moments of this, the wave passes through, and I am my normal stoic and dominant self.

"Let's go." I take my flutter bombs and, with a simple nod to the blacksmith, I make my exit.

On the way to the southern location, I find myself more contemplative than usual. My mind runs on thoughts of Father and the missing strikers. He disappeared—and over half the striker community disappeared—in the span of a month. They completely dropped off the face of the planet.

My wish is that this isn't the same occurrence.

I grip my rifle for comfort. Somehow solace can always be found in the comforts of a high-powered plasma rifle. I picture my bullets striking a target between the eyes, downing it every time. It's been a few days since I last hunted, and my body is fresh. Who knew what a toll hunting every day takes on a person?

"We're here, look sharp and aim to kill," says Chaos.

"Obviously."

Chaos gets off her red sky board and points to the higher ground to which she will relocate. The plan is simple. Whatever it is, we identify it, draw it out, and kill it. We share the spoils sixty-forty, in favor of her.

I scan the area with my visor on the highest sensitivity. Three pronged tracks with talons. Could be some sort of large raptor, or a small T-rex. The ground is sturdy, covered with sweet-smelling flowers. The scent of honey fills my being, and then my visual jams.

"Vex, visual is being interrupted. You'll have to describe what you see, and I'll enter the profile in manually."

"Copy..."

A blur of black and yellow careens across my vision, followed by the blacking-out of the sky. What I see is too horrible for words, too inconceivable for thoughts. I muster two words. Words that in my entire life I have never spoken.

"Protocol disengage." I'm breathing heavily. "I repeat protocol disengage."

Chaos has already raced past me, sprinting at an alarming speed, I join her in the sprint. Sharp stingers rain down from the sky, threatening to kill us instantly. I hear the thundering roar of a larger version of whatever is dropping those stingers. Its very presence troubles my bones in a way that only the mythical Bee Rex could. A hybrid abomination of a massive toxic bee, combined with a T-Rex. Something that came out of a cheesy horror flick.

Feeling the ground beneath us rumble, I put my palm out and grapple a nearby tree, swooping Chaos up in the process. We watch in awe as the massive Bee Rex jumps in front of us blocking our escape. Audio communication knocks out as well.

"I suppose we fight?"

"I suppose so," says Chaos.

I signal to Chaos my plan. Activating my invisibility cloak, I creep from around the maple tree, silently making my way to the creature's side. Its honey scent overwhelms my sensors, and I turn them down to bare minimum levels. All I'm left with is the buzzing of the giant Bee Rex and the blocked-out sun from the countless other smaller monsters.

Upon reaching the back of the creature, I contemplate running. But thoughts of my father deter me from such a dishonorable act. If I am to die, so be it.

"It's a good day to die," I whisper.

Just as the creature is about to turn around, I grapple-hook onto its back and place myself with pinpoint accuracy. It shivers and shakes in an attempt to dislodge me, but my spear is deeper than one would imagine.

It is at this point that Chaos comes out with her sniper rifle, blasting shot after shot into the face of the beast. Standing on its back, I release a flurry of bullets at the back of its head. Purple liquid spurts out as the Bee Rex shrieks in pain. It charges at Chaos, forcing her to drop to the floor. My aim becomes shaky while it's moving, but I manage to unleash another flurry, this time at the back of its neck. The monster uses its wing to swipe at me, but I dodge, climbing higher on its back.

Chaos' phenome comes charging towards us, nearly nicking my neck. It lands atop the beast then turns into pure shadow. Chaos signals for me to get off, so I jump rolling upon impact. More stingers rain down, impaling an intruding striker. The disengage protocol ensured that any striker willing to assist in the extermination could. It's the same distress signal that Chaos sent out a few days ago.

To my dismay, a rocket-launched projectile careens towards the now alarmingly bloody Bee Rex, just as another striker is impaled by a fallen stinger. The Bee Rex turns towards Tyrant and spits a glob of boiling honey. Seemingly unphased, Tyrant takes out his multi-socketed grenade launcher and shoots four cabbage balls into the air. The balls bounce on the ground and roll before exploding at the feet of the creature, causing it to tumble. It drops, and the ground shudders. Tyrant raises his hands prematurely as it swings its tail. It catches him in the chest, sending him flying and breaking several trees in the process.

The monstrosity rises to its feet and rampages towards Chaos, who is overwhelmed by the smaller Bee Rexes. As she is about to be killed, I send out Tirade, initiating her taunt. The phenome and the Bee Rex lock eyes, freezing the bee in place.

Pulling out my psionic blades, I energize them and sprint forward. Thrusting my grappling spear, I catapult myself at the head of the beast and jam my blades into its forehead. The beast drops to the ground for the second time. I slash like a wild animal, cutting off its antennae.

Visual and audio return just as I place my blades in an X-formation and slice off the head of the Bee Rex.

"Not today, fucker!"

I don't know why I said that. Maybe I thought it would be a cool thing to say. In any case, from that day on, it became my catchphrase.

CHAPTER 8
CLASSIFICATION: BLACKSMITH

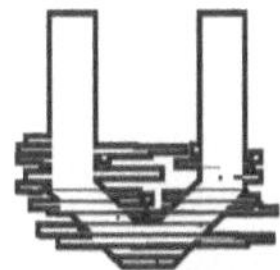

ex approaches me with an unusual swagger in his step. For once he seems almost cheerful when he speaks. A nice welcome compared to his usual bitter tone and gloomy posture.

They must have found something big over there in the south.

I see the large cargo carrier; but Chaos needs to be treated for major wounds. My curiosity will have to wait to be satisfied. First, I must heal the number-one-ranked striker. Most blacksmiths would consider it an honor. If she dies on my table, I will be disgraced. Even Vex might dismiss me. Abandoned by my striker—not something I'd like to think about.

Chaos stands up, bleeding from her arms and stomach. Fortunately for both of us, the wounds look worse than they really are. Her armor is exceptionally well-made. Why she didn't go to her own blacksmith, only she and the Most High knows.

"Tash, was it?"

I nod.

"Good. Please fix me up."

I nod again, as is my duty.

After an hour of surgical repair, I finish by wiping the sweat from my brow. Nerves and all, I did a great job. If I do say so myself.

"Not bad, not bad at all. Now let's see what you got for trade."

Vex pushes past her with his arms folded. "That's my line. If you want to boss a blacksmith around, go to your own."

Vex, my protector and savior. I smile to myself.

I take my scanner and scan the contents of the cargo hold. As it analyzes every single inch of the specimen, I raise my eyebrows. I scan it twice, but it still comes back as unidentifiable. It will have to be manually inspected with the files in the blacksmith's archives: parchment so sacred that it was not uploaded to the scanner.

I shoo Chaos and Vex out of my large blacksmith's tent and open up my nearby safe. The retina scanner identifies me and opens. I pull out the dusty parchments and carefully unravel them. One by one, I search for the document that discusses what I suspect it is—what I hope and pray it is.

Could my greatest prayers have been answered?

Finally, at the footnote of a larger article on the mixture of bees and T-rexes, I find the section that talks about grades of the species.

I exit the tent to see a large gathering of blacksmiths, strikers, and even a few scavengers who have taken interest in the specimen. A rare occurrence. With the official document in my hand, I read out loud the passage that applies to this specific kill verbatim. Although much of it was blacked out, there are parts still legible for this very moment.

"On rare occasion, there is a subspecies of T-rex that appears with a yellow coating and black-striped behind. This massive creature is often accompanied by a slew of C-grade of its kind. Although often mistaken for the mythical Bee Rex, this subspecies is considered to be at best a B-grade Bee Rex and not the mythical version, which has a titanium grade black torso and pure yellow abdomen."

I feign a sign of disappointment, though I am still giddy inside.

"In other words, this isn't the mythical Bee-Rex. This is the B-grade version, not the S-grade version that many have come to revere. But I assure you all this is a great sign. If the B-grade exists, there must be an S-grade—and it should be noted that this is an exceptional kill in its own right. A B-grade Bee Rex is the equivalent to some S-grade specimens. It is suspected that when one finds a B-grade Bee Rex, the S-grade can be found near the hive, if not at the hive itself. That is all."

"Hurrah, hurrah!" the group chants.

With the strikers all riled up, tomorrow will be an escapade for the ages. There will be many deaths, but I am confident that the team of Chaos and Vex can prevail against this S-grade Bee Rex.

I might be crazy, but I did lie about a hive. I hope I'm not sending them on a wild duck hunt. But one would presume such a thing exists.

The next morning, Vex returns without Chaos to collect his equipment. He spent all of his credits on upgraded psionic blades and bella rockets. The blades now cover twice the width, and six miniature rockets are ready to shoot out from his chest. A very destructive surprise attack. I see the smelly Runnymede running to Vex with what looks to be some kind of winged device in his hands. I head over to see what's going on. Here I thought I was Vex's only blacksmith.

Could he be double dealing me? I gasp. Have I not served him well throughout the years? Given him breaks when he was poor and out of credits?

"Uhh, what's this?" I keep my hands in my pocket lest I start a fistfight with my striker.

"This has nothing to do with you, Tash. It's between me and Vex," says Runnymede.

"Any augments to his armor need to be cleared with me. Vex, have you gone behind my back and gotten another blacksmith?"

"This is as big a surprise to me as it is to you. I don't even know what I'm looking at."

I scan the equipment briefly before touching the titanium-reinforced base.

"I can't believe what I'm looking at."

It's equipment far beyond my abilities. Something S+-level. With ease.

Runnymede and I speak at the same time.

"These are psionic wings."

I look at Runnymede with my death glare. If he sees it, he pays me no mind.

"These wings are S+-level and would provide you with exceptional maneuverability in the air, on land, and even underwater. Properly managed, you could fly long distances or maneuver for shorter destructive bursts. Coupled with your grappling hook, you could cover distances at an amazing speed."

Vex seems angrier than pleased. "Why isn't this on the list of procurable items? I'd have started saving up for something like this a long time ago."

"Because she can't make an item like this. She isn't good enough," says Runnymede.

I lower my head, feeling my fists clenching on their own. My face becomes red. The heat of my fury is unbearable. I turn and take off running in the opposite direction.

How embarrassing. As far as I know, no blacksmith on Marda could create an item that exceptional. He must have procured it from some other channel. Perhaps it's even dwarven-made.

How could a mere scav afford something so expensive? I suppose it matters not. Stolen, bought, or gifted. It's Vex's now.

I've grown complacent. I must get better. For the first time in a long time, I pull up the Marda blacksmith rankings. I search for my name and profile on the first page, where it was last time. But I see a slew of new names. Then I swipe to the next page, where I see some familiar faces. Finally, I swipe to the third page, where I am ranked twenty-seven out of seventy-five.

Collapsing to the ground, I slam my fists against the gravel. My hands are bloody and sore, but I care not. This is utterly pathetic. At one point I was the ninth ranked blacksmith. Everyone is rising in their rankings while I am falling.

What if he abandons me? I can't afford to be left alone and desolate. I'd rather die.

CHAPTER 9
CLASSIFICATION: STRIKER

Advancing deep into the southern forests of Marda, I am accompanied by Chaos and one of her allied strikers, known as Ivy. Her heavy battlesuit is even bulkier than Tyrant's. How they wear such hefty suits is a mystery to me. I'll take a light-weight maneuverable set any day. Ivy's face is clearly visible through the helmet she's wearing.

Not much to look at.

Although the three of us are the head of the pack, we are followed by about twenty other strikers. This will be a pack hunt where the goal is to eliminate all threats, then perhaps eliminate each other for the spoils. It isn't uncommon for strikers to kill each other during such times. For once I am relieved that I chose to run in a sub-pack. I look around me to see groups of two, three, and four. No soloists, not even myself. I suppose it's to be expected on such an uncertain mission. To think the Bee Rex, a mythical-level monster, is right at my fingertips! I have a strategy. With my enhanced bella rockets, flutter bombs, superior plasma rifle, and max-level psionic blades I am the terror of the town. I even pushed Tirade up a few levels, unlocking extended taunt, phase travel, and ride.

I may not see my troupe as family, but I have come to see Tirade as something more than a tool to be used. Every time I upgrade her, it is as though I am cleansing a part of me that was lost. Chaos is rubbing off on me, and I don't like it. I'm perfectly fine being miserable all the time.

Or perhaps that's just the story that I tell myself.

The deeper we go into the forest, the brighter it gets; eventually our visors must automatically adjust the brightness. It isn't until we reach a massive clearing with one gigantic tree that I see something that takes my breath away. A giant hive with what I presume to be A+ Bee Rexes fluttering about.

I look at Chaos and Ivy, who both nod. I guess we're going inside that hive. To wear the new wings, I had to remove my cape attachment. But I'm grateful. Climbing this tree would have wasted a lot of time.

I initiate the plasma wings at my back, which propel me into the air. I'm faster than I anticipated, nearly crashing into a nearby branch. I swerve.

"Striker to navigator."

No response.

Just like before, the visual and audio comms are jammed. I'll have to take down the S-grade Bee Rex without them. At this point, I look back to see Chaos with her rocket pack and Ivy with her rocket boots not far from me. The A+ grade Bee Rexes flying around the hive are paying me no mind.

It seems they don't see me as a threat, or perhaps they only get riled up when sent on missions—just like us.

Such dangerous thinking. Just like us? These are mindless beasts.

After waiting several moments for Chaos and Ivy to catch up, I land on the hive. The ground is flooded with honey to ankle level, and its scent overwhelms my sensors. Each step I take is sluggish, but I progress nonetheless. I catch sight of a sleeping Bee Rex in the distance. It is larger than the rest, its entire body is black titanium save for the yellow abdomen. Its wings are translucent, while its antennae glow bright yellow.

We surround the front of the creature in triangle formation. I aim for the antennae; Chaos and Ivy aim for the neck. Just when we're about to deal our initial attack, a rocket from Tyrant spirals towards the abdomen of the beast. It dissipates on impact, not even leaving a scratch. The Bee Rex stands up, causing the entire hive to shake. Seeing that it's cornered, it blasts a wave of searing honey at me. I use the wings thrusters to push myself to the side. It shoots out a stinger at Ivy, whose shield miraculously blocks the attack.

Tyrant and his five cronies rush in, guns ablaze. Their attacks do minimal damage, some shots bouncing off the titanium of the beast and firing back at us. Between dodging boiling honey waves and ricocheted bullets, I don't know which is worse—but the sound is horrendous. The Bee Rex stampedes into Tyrant's group, swinging one of his members in the air, then swallowing him whole.

I take this moment to regroup with Chaos and Ivy.

"We need to take out the antennae. Without visual and audio communication, we're at a severe disadvantage."

Chaos pauses her barrage of sniper rifle rounds to transform her weapon into a large war hammer.

"Ivy, lead the charge with your shield. Get us in close, and we will do the rest."

Ivy charges with her shield at maximum, covering all three of us. Although somewhat slow, it is effective. The ricocheted bullets bounce off of us, and the honey waves wash over us harmlessly. It isn't until the Bee Rex stomps on the fourth member of Tyrant's group that we are met with further reinforcements.

Ten other Strikers rush in, weapons on hot. Plasma fire erupts; bullets and explosions galore fill the room. The Bee Rex, seemingly unfazed, charges at the group of ten, wiggling its antennae. The projectiles pause in the air, then slowly turn around and are returned to their senders.

The cries of the ten strikers are something I will never forget. Their bodies collapse in a pile. By the time we reached the monstrosity, its antennae are leaking a little, and there are few dents on its abdomen. Otherwise, it seems more angry than hurt.

Tyrant unleashes his phenome. A giant fire-breathing ram scoops up the Bee Rex and slams it into the wall of the hive. The ram unleashes a wave of fire that melts away the titanium plating. I unleash my phenome, using taunt immediately. Dazed, the Bee Rex walks over to Tirade and locks eyes with her. Struggling to his feet, Tyrant fires twenty whistler rockets into the exposed side of the Bee Rex, causing it to stumble.

It is at this moment that Chaos and I make our way towards the antennae. With my psionic blades, I slash off one antenna with ease, while Chaos smashes the other into bits. The taunt ends, cause the Bee Rex to convulse rapidly. With video and audio returning, Chaos and I are about to deal the decisive blow when a splinter-sized stinger pierces Chaos' neck, causing her to drop to her knees. Another splinter-sized stinger nearly pierces my neck, but I dodge at the last second. I'm not S+-level speed for nothing.

While we scan the area for the culprit, Ivy covers Chaos, Tyrant, and myself with her shield. The orange protective layer serves us well as what was once one splinter becomes ten. I peer into the distance to see the last thing I ever expected to see.

My jaw drops and my eyes blur from the pungent scent of concentrated honey. I have to know. I must confirm that what I'm seeing is what I'm seeing.

"Navigator... are you seeing this?"

"Y... yes, Vex. She is walking on two feet and appears to be some elven-bee hybrid."

My audio comm goes out again.

Half her face is elfanoid, yet she has two antennae sticking out of her forehead below her black hair. She appears to be wearing yellow armor casing all around, with long, slender yellow wings. She walked atop the honey with ease, each step gliding towards us. In one claw she holds a concentrated ball of glowing honey; in the other, a yellow staff with a honeycomb at the end.

To my horror she speaks. The fucking wild monster speaks.

"Why have you elves been killing my children?"

She twirls her staff and slams the base end onto the floor of the hive. Globs of honey erupt from the ground, flipping all of us of into the air. In a flash of yellow light she teleports, jamming her staff into my chest. I feel my entire rib cage collapse and my heart nearly rupture. She follows this attack by elbowing me in the back of my head, knocking me unconscious.

I wake to a throbbing headache, another concussion. Perhaps even minor brain damage. But that's the least of my concerns. I survey my surroundings with my bare eyes, as I have been stripped of my armor and am left in my underclothes. With my bare chest and face exposed, I feel cold.

Beside me are Chaos, Tyrant, Ivy, and Tyrant's allied striker. We are all stripped down to our underclothes. As the moments pass, everyone awakens, save for Chaos, who has yet to stir. I glance at Tyrant, who can't stop staring at Chaos. Her curvaceous features and alluring skin tone, not to mention her face.

Struggling to breathe, I nudge him.

"Avert your eyes before I pluck them from your sockets."

"Whatever you say, lover boy."

The rest of us rise to our feet and eventually start roaming around to take stock of our surroundings. It's dark and cold, but something tells me we aren't going to be here long. One way or another.

The screams of Tyrant's ally fill the dark tube we have found ourselves in. Tyrant and I rush over while Ivy guards Chaos. We are met with a yellow maggot-like creature swallowing him whole. The stench is horrendous, as it spewed some type of green mucus all over the ally. Weaponless, I resort to my phenome.

Tirade is unleashed, dodging the mucus shot at her with ease, then lodges her teeth into the slimy yellow maggot. We hear a scream, followed by the voice of what I have now determined to be the queen bee. Her voice fills the entire room, though she is nowhere to be seen.

"I give you a noble death that assists in the circle of life, and you spit in my face?"

"I'd much prefer a non-death, if that's on the menu."

"It isn't. You elves are a pestilence. Swarming from planet to planet killing and hunting creatures that are minding their own business. Creatures that belong here."

"You're spewing nonsense. I liked your lot better when you couldn't talk."

"We the Arunkai are the most evolved of our kind, and we know much about you people. Yet your ignorance knows no end. The extinction of your people will come soon. Your leaders are well aware of our official declaration of war."

A wave of boiling honey emerges suddenly from the end of the tunnel. I jump atop Tirade and dash for the other side of the tube. From the corner of my eye I see Tyrant hopping atop his ram. Upon returning to Chaos and Ivy's location, I scoop Chaos up and hold her firmly in my arms. I phase travel through the wall and enter the previous room. At the dizzying effects of phase traveling, I am thankful that I didn't break my fast.

I see in the distance the scattered parts of our battlesuits and weapons. After assembling my own and activating Chaos' auto-assemble, I turn to see Tyrant breaking through the wall with the head of his ram. The majority of the Bee Rexes were eliminated by the remaining Strikers, many of which must have retreated after seeing us being mauled by the queen. But the few that remain come charging at us. Once again, I phase travel, this time past the seven charging A+ Bee Rexes, and out into the sky. As we tumble through the air, Tirade returns to the abyss where she belongs. I activate the wings at my back. Although severely damaged, they work well enough that I land, creating a massive crater upon impact.

I look up to see a glorious sight: Ivy riding a black unicorn with wings. Such an elegant phenome. Tyrant is hanging on for dear life, clutching her waist, as the unicorn dives towards my position.

Still in their underclothes, Ivy arrives, donning a concerned expression.

"I was hearing things, right?"

"No, there are more to these monsters then we are led to believe. Let's go. Chaos needs medical attention."

CHAPTER 10
CLASSIFICATION: NAVIGATOR

The navigators' office is buzzing after the news of the S+-grade monster. Pun intended. Can we even call them monsters if some of them can talk? Arunkai is what she called herself, and she implied that there are more of them. Does each monster have an Arunkai? Are they all as powerful as she is, can they all talk, and above all, are they all sentient?

These are the questions my people ask in the office. This is all anyone can talk about during breakfast, first snack, lunch, second snack, dinner, and third snack. But I have questions of my own. It's like everyone is focused on the wrong things, as if their minds are brainwashed to forget the last part of that queen bee's soliloquy.

She specifically said our leaders were aware of their official declaration of war. How melodic and eerie. Up until now, I have never thought of us at war. I thought of it as an extermination mission. But to be at war, that isn't something I signed up for. War leads to civilian casualties, and wars have counterattacks. She is right; up until now we have been invading their territory and killing them for what would appear to be sport. I mean, our entire organization is built on the collection and trading of these entities' dead bodies.

The moral ramifications are countless, but above all the danger. Oh, for elven sake, could I be in danger? Never in my life have I thought that I could be in danger. I'm a high-born light elf. We're all supposed to have clean, cushy classifications as navigators or blacksmiths. Yeah, there, I said it. There is some rigging of the

classification system. If you were in charge, you'd make sure the offspring of the rich and famous were safe and sound too. Got to have that steady stream of material and credits. The IGF runs on credits and specimens, but some of the planetary systems prefer the barter system.

You can buy most things with credits, even live C-D+-grade specimens as pets. On Venusian and the other rich planets, there are all kinds of exotic pets and foods, ranging from Sea Hounds to the ultra-rare Were Bat. We all have skeletons in our closest, some larger than most, so don't give me that pathetic look of judgment when you find out what I've been up to.

I check my system of record, or SOR as is usually called, to verify my clocked hours for the month. I scrutinize every minute, every decimal point, every numeral. Making sure all my credits will be there. I've been given a few extra hours and nod my approval. I don't play around with my money. What kind of navigator would I be if I did? Sloppy work is evidence of a sloppy person.

I think this just as I wipe fried bat grease off my hands and onto my clothes. I hear heavy breathing behind me. Turning around, I am met with the round plump face of Jacob Beaver Mouth.

"Hi, Jacob." I cringe as the words leave my lips.

"H... hey, Allison. How's it going? SOR okay?"

"Yes, Jacob. Thanks for everything." I manage a plastic smile and am about to take my leave when his hand lightly grabs my arm.

He might have stabbed me with one of Vex's psionic blades, the way I jolt. As I gently brush my hair with the hand of the arm he touched, there is a sudden awkward silence. I can't stand awkward silences, especially when they take up my break time.

"Something the matter, Jacob?"

"Just umm, I haven't seen you in the back lately. When are we going to fornicate again?"

There are few ways to dry up a woman faster than referring to a sexual interaction as fornicate. The very word makes it sound so mechanical and dull. Normally I'd entertain Beaver Mouth, for he enjoys licking the kitty, but I'm sick of having to deal with his poor equipment and ineptitude in the other areas of sexual pleasures. That, in conjunction with the stress of being in an arrangement with Runnymede, who is as reliable as a broken bridge, breaks my façade down momentarily.

"Listen here, Beaver Mouth… I hate to be the one to tell you this, but I suppose now is a good time. I can't intertwine with you anymore."

"But… why?"

"Many reasons, but the biggest is that you have a tiny pecker and don't even know how to use it. But you can kiss the beaver anytime you want."

"Kiss the beaver?"

I see tears forming in his eyes. He truly did like me—perhaps in his own world thought it was love. I'm not some heartbreaker, nor am I a major looker. But I know I can do better. Perhaps Vex will come around. If not him, then someone else. Anyone else.

"Yes… do you know what the ladies call you in this facility?"

"N… no… I don't."

"As I hope you know everyone has a nickname in this facility. Mine is Allison Stingy Pants and yours is… Jacob Beaver Mouth."

It's at this point that he turns to waddle away and bumps into Big Moss, spilling his homemade drink of moss and honey. The behemoth of a navigator pinches Jacob's nipples, picks him up over his shoulder, and throws him into a nearby cubicle.

That's one man who loves his moss. Kind of strong too. I wonder if…

"Allison, break's over. You too, Big Moss, get back to your cubicles this instant."

I waddle back to my cubicle to check on Vex, who rendezvoused with Runnymede on their way to the blacksmith's quarters. It seems Runnymede has identified the poison used by the Queen Bee, and the antidote is waiting for them at Chaos' blacksmith.

Part of me is relieved, because hunting with her is good for Vex and for me. It means more credits and better stats. But a slight part of me is jealous. If only I could go on a hunt with him.

I switch my computer screen from the visuals of their escapade to my volute match with an unknown person in Venusian. They still haven't made their move. I find myself pressing the keyboard in boredom. After a few moments of waiting, I check my private bank account on Venusian and track several large parchments that I am sending to my parents. Nodding my approval, I check the time on my wrist. It's getting late, and there is a special meeting for me to attend. I slink towards the exit of the facility, grabbing my coat on my way out.

I find myself in the nearby woods to the west of the Marda encampment. These woods aren't like the woods to the south or the marshlands to the north. This forest is covered in fruit trees galore. Star apples, bananas, grape vines, and so on. I'm wearing an old V2 battlesuit. Bulky and slow, but equipped with some hefty firepower. Before me stand three strikers dressed in black cloaks and hoods. They have no battlesuits, just cloaks. While two are equipped with daggers, their leader has a basic sword. They aren't very good as strikers, but as trappers they will have to do. Bottom of the barrel and desperate to make some extra credits. This is the life of a bottom-feeding striker. Too low on the totem pole to hang with the elite, and too unskilled to hunt the bigger and better game.

"Do you have them?" I inquire.

"Yeah of course."

"Cool. Introduce to me our new shipment."

The lead smoothly moves over to the back of the cargo truck, picks up a crate, and opens it. He reveals to me a Fruit Cat, C+-grade. As good as it gets for pets. The Fruit Cat certainly lives up to its name. Instead of fur, its skin grows grapes and strawberries. At C+-grade and below the fruits are edible, while at B-grade and higher, the fruits are a lethal weapon. Supposedly these cats provide some of the most delicious fruit in all the planetary systems.

"What's the rest of the stock like?"

"Ten Fruit Cats, three Turtle Scorpions, and fifteen Electric Serpents. Just as you ordered."

"Excellent. I'll transfer the credits, just hand over the key as usual."

The guy in the back is moving shakily.

"Why you moving like that?"

"Don't mind that, my hand is just acting up," says the one in the back.

"Yeah, Sugar Cane. Chill out," says the other.

My underground nickname. "Cool, pass me the key and we can move on with our transaction."

"Yeah… about that. We want to renegotiate."

I see the shaky striker grab the hilt of his dagger as if he thinks he can take on this suit and live. I press the two buttons beside my index fingers, letting loose the miniature rockets. They strike the two dagger wielders, downing them instantly. The sword wielder comes charging at me with his sword held high.

Panicking, I activate the drill arm, which connects with his sword. The power of the drill dislodges the sword from his hand, and it tumbles to the floor. He turns to run just as I unleash the six grappling spears on the legs of the battlesuit. They each meet their mark, piercing his body and pulling him into me.

I look down as the drill impales him, causing blood to spurt out.

"Sugar Cane doesn't renegotiate," I whisper.

Now, I'm no striker, but I'm not a push-over, either. I had to come prepared in case these low-level chumps decided to betray me—as they did. But if I had to pinpoint the beginning of all my problems this would probably be it. Killing a fellow elf is not like hunting a monster. Far from. This is something I wish I knew in the beginning.

Maybe I would have taken a different route.

CHAPTER 11
CLASSIFICATION: STRIKER

haos' blacksmith has a tent three times as large as my blacksmith's. The floor is made of blue marble tiles. To think that the scavengers took the time to lay out tiles on a temporary location is laughable. Yet, I'm kind of jealous. The tiles look nice.

"Put her down over here."

"Will she be ok?"

"Yeah, the poison is a grayanotoxin. In the dosage she was given, if accurately deduced by…your scav, it should be treatable. If the dosage was even a gram higher, she'd be dead instantly. Interestingly enough in lower dosages, it provides a nice high and other euphoric effects. Even poses for a peaceful death."

"I see. Good to hear she'll be ok. We came back empty-handed, but I managed to get this."

I pull out the antennae that I was able to slice off earlier. Handing it over, every fiber of my being is telling me to hang on to it. But I hand it over nonetheless.

"She deserves it, we agreed to a sixty-forty split."

"I remember the days when she was hunting alone… don't recall her ever coming back empty. Maybe you're bad luck. She should reconsider your presence. Goodbye, soloist."

The sharp words of her blacksmith strike harder than they should have. For once in my life, I feel vulnerable. I have never been dispatched by a monster like that.

It was quick and efficient. Calculated and graceful. But above all, it was filled with hatred. Could what it said be true? What she said? How can I doubt it though? She talked. Eloquently, might I add. It felt like I was speaking to a high-born light elf.

What has this world come to when I can't even trust what the IGF tells me? If we're at war, we should know. If there are entities we're hunting that can talk and think, then we need to rethink our strategy. The one-man team isn't gonna cut it. The entire economy would need to be rearranged. But above all, we would have to be trained to kill sentient beings, which is a whole lot different to hunting wild monsters. I need to know more.

I find myself traveling to my blacksmith's tent, where she ought to be waiting. Another day of coming home empty handed. What has this world come to? She will be disappointed. But since when do I care what Tash thinks?

Tash. Even thinking her name is unusual. This whole Queen Bee thing has my mind out of sorts. I forgo seeing the blacksmith to wander the base camp. I find myself in an area I've never been before. It smells like rotten fruits and dead rodents. There is a massive tent marked Scavenger's Quarters.

I'm compelled to enter. What the hell do the scavengers do all day? Their worktime, at about four hours a day, is the least among all the classifications. Approaching the tent, I am struck with another intense aroma: hard liquor and wine. Something I have yet to partake in. When one's life is dedicated to hunting monsters, their mind has to be sharp at all times. Or so I tell myself.

Upon entering the tent, I'm delighted to see an assortment of games and raffles. In addition to civilians of Marda, a slew of scavengers partake in the festivities. Drinking, hobnobbing, and simply enjoying themselves. Runnymede rushes up to me as fast as his old bones can carry him.

"Lookie here. A surprise to see you."

"Yeah."

"Lemme show you around."

Thankfully, Runnymede is one of the few who has showered in the past few days. He takes me to see his favorite game, called Wagner's Tale. One has to get their piece across the board faster than the other three opponents. It appears to be a story-based game that takes a lot of luck to win.

"Is there something a bit more skill-based?"

"Oh, I got the thing just for you."

He brings me over to a game called conqueror's pillage. It's a military strategy game—similar to volute, but instead of controlling a maximum of sixteen pieces, you control an army of a hundred. Each is represented by a piece on a massive board. The game is typically played by four people and the game tracker, who moves the pieces across the board and facilitates. The objective is to control the majority of the territory after the time ends. If your entire army is wiped out or you surrender, you lose.

I play blue team, which is my favorite color, and which is characterized by upgraded speed and acrobatics—resulting in frequent dodges for members of your army. Each team has an elite piece serving as the general as the army. If the general dies, you lose half your territory. This can be a major game changer. I choose an assassin-type general, skilled at attacking backlines and lower-armored generals. Wagers are placed as the game starts, but additional wagers can be placed during the final round before the time ends.

Across from me, playing as the red team, is a bulbous fellow draped in bright white cloth and decked out in platinum rings and chains. According to Runnymede, he is a very popular entertainer of some sort. I don't keep up with such things. Playing as the black team is a short fellow with a wide-brimmed hat and holes in his overcoat. Finally, Runnymede is playing as the white team. As I'm told is custom, white goes first.

After hours of playing, both black and white are eliminated, leaving myself and the entertainer. One of his consorts brings him another bottle of high-grade rum. He takes the bottle to his mouth and downs the entire thing. I don't know if it's curiosity or the depression, but I ache for a taste of the drink.

"Runnymede, get me one of those bottles, will you."

"Sure thing, Vex."

By the time Runnymede returns, I own thirty-five percent of the board's territory, while the entertainer owns the remaining sixty-five. Runnymede opens the bottle for me and pours out a glass. I take the bottle out of his hands and take the whole thing to my face.

I ain't no punk.

The bitter taste scorches my throat, while my face feels numb. My head starts throbbing as I feel the effects of the toxic drink.

"You like Beetle Bum Rum too? Haha, cheers," says the entertainer.

We both lift our respective bottles up to chug. I refuse to be the first to give way to breathe. As I'm downing the last of the rum, I notice a large group gathering around the table. Onlookers or thieves, I'm not sure. Not even sure if I care at this point. My mind is in such a daze that I just feel good.

Returning to the match I'm struck with a genius idea. I should all-in his army and take down his general with my own, considering his is a long-range spellcasting type. I would never have considered this before, since it's risky and borderline foolish to play in such a manner. But reservations aside, my counter-argument is:

Fuck it.

It's my turn, and there are five minutes left on the clock. I smile from behind my visor.

"Care to up the pot?" I ask.

"Sure, I got money to blow, baby."

"Don't call me baby," I grumble.

"Sure thing, boss. What do you propose? I mean, that rifle of yours looking real pretty. Could use that for my next show."

"Heh, my rifle for all those chains you got on. Plus, those rings. Gotta have me those. You can keep the vintage watch; it's ugly."

His face now turning a solid red, he takes off his chains and rings, placing them on the betting stage. I unhook my rifle from its strap and lay it on the opposite betting stage. The official analyzes everything to make sure it is in working order and of high value.

Runnymede tugs on my arm. "Are you sure this is a good idea? Maybe the alcohol is getting to you. The Vex I know would never wager his precious rifle."

"I got this."

The official nods that the chains and rings are of acceptable quality to match the rifle. I instantly make my move and go all in—to the shock of the entire crowd, including the entertainer.

The simulation begins; we all watch my army march forth in triangle formation. Just as we're about to be wiped out, my assassin general leaps across the field, decapitating his spellcaster in one swoop.

The timer goes off and the entire group around us claps. I raise my hands, only to tumble from intoxication. Runnymede helps me up as I gather my hazy senses. I manage to collect my rifle and my winnings. The entertainer storms off with his two consorts and security.

Runnymede escorts me back to my tent, the chains hanging around our necks. As I'm wobbling back and forth, I see what I think is the entertainer and his security blocking the border between the scavengers' area and the navigators'. I move to withdraw my rifle, though I am much slower than usual.

Before I know it, I'm lifted high into the air and slammed hard into the mud. Two behemoth guards start pounding on me with punches and kicks. As my battlesuit absorbs most of the physical damage, I withdraw my psionic blades and slice one of the guards in the ankle, dropping him immediately. Runnymede picks up my fallen rifle just as another bodyguard smashes me in the back of the head with something blunt. I stagger forward into a tent and get tangled up in it. I hear plasma rifle fire, then the distinct sound of bodies dropping. Runnymede grips me by the arm and helps me to my feet. I look back to see the bodies of all four bodyguards and the entertainer sprawled across the mud.

"Things might get rocky from here on out. But just know that you're like a son to me. I'll take care of this. You head back to your tent. Don't visit the blacksmith's quarters; she will only ask questions to which you have no answers. Don't worry, Vincent. It's gonna be fine."

Then he gives me his goofy smile.

The alarm goes off three times, and my navigator tries to contact me four times. By the time I wake up, it's late afternoon. The majority of strikers would have already made their way out for the day's hunt. My head is throbbing, and I still feel slightly intoxicated. My mouth is also dry, like sandpaper.

"Striker to navigator."

"Oh, thank goodness. I thought... I don't know what I thought."

"Looks like some after effect of the Queen Bee's attacks. I'm fine now."

"Perhaps you should take today off?"

"I'm not incapacitated. That's the only excuse for a striker taking a day off."

"Very well. But I'm not sending you on an S-grade mission today."

"Fine, fine. Just hurry up and have the profile ready."

I'm sure all the good territories have been marked. I may have to play invader today. Not a role I relish, but for some reason my credits are lower than I anticipated. The feeding tent is all but empty, and to my dismay the striker food is gone.

"What's left?"

"All we have left is scavenger food, sir."

"Sure, how bad can it be."

He gives me a sly smirk—the kind of smirk a poisoned rat would give before being eaten by a cat. After taking a big helping of the muck muck, as they call it, I head over to my usual spot.

The muck muck is a soup-like substance filled with an assortment of unknown creatures. In any case, it tastes the way it sounds. After one spoonful of muck muck, I push it aside.

"Striker to navigator."

"Go ahead, Vex."

"Where's that profile."

"I sent it to you already. Are you sure you're ok?"

I don't bother to respond. I bring up the profile.

Star Sprinter: A cross between a giant rodent and a cat. Purple in color, with a star on the side. Known for reaching high speeds. Although only reaching knee height, they move in swarms. Can be overwhelming if allowed to surround striker. Weakness: Headshots.

Making my way to the eastern section of the Marda encampment, I'm met with the carcass of the number-nine-ranked striker and his scavenger. It seems they were ambushed on their way back to base camp.

Those damn jump-man teams. A pox on their soul. Jump-man teams are vagabonds that work for the underground organizations. They trade in living and dead monsters for pets or for the consumption of their patrons. Unlike strikers who trade the specimens for scientific research and religious purposes. Not to mention that we are exterminating the threats to the civilians of each planet, as they appear. The most honorable of pursuits.

Simply put, we're the good guys, and they're the bad guys. Hunting down a striker and a scavenger when they are the most vulnerable? Pathetic.

Upon arriving at the hotspot of my territory, I notice the land is scattered with many holes. The soil is colored an eerie purple, and an odd scent fills my nostrils.

These must be the dens of the star sprinters.

I hear a squealing sound and see a purple blur, then I'm struck in the chest by a star apple. Another star sprinter pokes his head out from a den to throw another star apple at me, only to catch a bullet right between the temples. I unleash Tirade, who has been upgraded to mass taunt. She howls at the moon, causing twenty Star Sprinters to lift their heads in a daze. With pinpoint accuracy, my plasma rifle takes down all twenty B+-grade Star Sprinters.

"Striker to scavenger."

"I'm on my way, Vex! Good shooting out there."

"Yeah."

As I wait for Runnymede to arrive, I get the sensation that I'm being watched. Whether it's a monster or jump man, it matters not. Whatever it is will show itself when it's ready to die. About ten minutes pass before Runnymede zooms in on his hovercycle with a cargo attachment sized for these specimens. Say what you want about Runnymede, but he's one hell of a scavenger. Knows how to balance speed, cargo, protection, and having the right collection tool for the job. Even one of the better medics out there. In his old age, he is ranked number one. Been ranked number one for a while. The last sane thing my father said to me was.

"Keep Runnymede."

And I did.

"Let's go, I'm hungry. Can't afford to miss dinner."

"I gotchu, young snapper. We will be out of here in no time."

He takes out this green device and throws it in the middle of the field. It buzzes, then sucks together all the bodies. The device floats up, hanging each body like a carousel. It whizzes then stacks them inside the cargo carrier. The whole thing takes about five minutes, and we're off.

Zooming on the motorbike is always fun. I just attach my sky board to the side and I'm good to go. He takes care of everything else. Now that I think about it, Runnymede is the only person in this world that I've ever trusted a hundred percent. He's been with me since I was a child. Used to fix me up when the larger kids would bully me. That was back when he was a blacksmith though. I wonder why he chose to become a scavenger. Such a lowly life.

"Hey, Runnymede."

"Yeah, Vex?"

"Why'd you become a scavenger anyways?"

"Well, that's one of those questions where if I tell you I have to kill you. And we don't want that. Just when we've been getting along well lately."

I flash back to last night. Making sure my comm unit is still on private, I inquire about the bodies.

"Everything taken care of?"

"Not the first body I had to dispose of. Though some were definitely the heaviest." He pauses to glance at me.

"Did you know that entertainer was holding out on you?" He hands me a special ring. Something only a high-born light elf could ever dream of wearing. A dark elf striker is a nobody compared to such a high-status person. I press the button in the middle to activate three blue protective shields that hover around me.

"Had he been wearing this...not sure we'd be here right about now."

There is an explosion in front of us, causing Runnymede to slam the breaks. The ground ahead is destroyed. I hear the distinct sound of a sniper rifle shot. I cover Runnymede with my body just as the projectile hits one of the hovering shields. Two left.

"Get in the cargo carrier."

"Ain't gotta tell me twice. Don't die."

I keep low, waiting for the advanced squadron to poke their slimy heads out from the grass. With snipers and explosives, I presume them to be one of the more experienced jump man teams. I wonder if they know who they're dealing with?

Two chodes dressed in red and black rush to cover position; I pick the third one off just before he reaches cover. Their sniper rifle connects with another of my shields. That would have instantly killed me. Pinned down due to rifle fire, I roll out three flutter bombs. They swirl and buzz before speeding towards the two hunkered-down jump men. They try to shoot the bombs down, but only manage to hit one. The remaining two bombs land on one man, exploding him into parts. When the other man pokes his head up to fire at me, I pick him off. Plasma bullet right in the neck. I hear the gurgling sound as he takes his last breath.

The sniper is the only one I have left. I summon Tirade, who is immediately shot in the head, but a normal bullet has no effect on a wind shadow. I climb atop the phenome and stay hugged against the shadow as we race towards the location of the sniper. After we dodge bullet after bullet, another explosion goes off, dissolving Tirade instantly. I'm sent flying into the air, but I activate the thrusters on my wings. Rifle aimed directly in front of me, I see a slight gleam off the lens of the sniper.

My finger graces the trigger, letting loose a barrage of bullets. Blood pours out of the camouflaged sniper as I land a few meters in front of him.

"Striker to scavenger. Let's roll out."

CHAPTER 12
CLASSIFICATION: BLACKSMITH

run the Star Sprinters through the skinning machine. The machine does most of the work when it comes to the skinning and deboning of medium-sized creatures. All I have to do is know how the machine works. It's a pretty simple process, but time consuming when you have twenty-plus to skin and debone. A good blacksmith doesn't waste a single part of the specimen. The blood and organs will be sent back to HQ for scientific research, while the bones and skin will be used for a special ritual.

Tonight is the first full moon on Marda since we've arrived. All the blacksmiths will be dressed in their best collections. An assortment of fur, bones, teeth, and what have you. I have something special planned for this night. Although it wasn't a S+-grade Bee Rex, having confirmation that I wasn't crazy for believing in the myth is good enough for me. One has to make do with what they can.

Evening sun gives away to night.

For the first time in over a year I put makeup on, just a tad to accentuate my features and highlight my cheekbones. My attire is a tight yellow skirt and top made from the skin of the Bee Rex and a purple fur scarf from the newly-acquired Star Sprinter. I finish this off with a black belt made from the Bee Rex and a cup of concentrated honey. Although in large dosages the graynotoxin is deadly, in smaller amounts it provides a mild and euphoric high.

For my feet, I have something extra special. Although I'm relatively tall for a female elf, I enjoy wearing boots with heels. I find them rather empowering. They

make me feel more confident. After getting dressed, I spray a little diluted honey on my neck and wrists. Just to give me that sweet scent. It's such a rush to get dolled up. Feels good to look good, my grandmother always said. I wonder if she's doing alright. I should really get in contact with her.

As I set off for the sacred blacksmith grounds, I nearly forget to bring my new prized possession. The stinger of a Bee Rex. After latching it onto my belt, I head out to the hidden location in the eastern woods.

I see the sacred grounds in the distance, and I smile. I'm met by a few of my blacksmith colleagues, as well as the strikers chosen to secure the area while we carry out our ritual and celebrate. One of the guards is Vex, who I can tell would rather be sleeping, as he's more vexed than usual.

I feel myself blushing. After my actions last time we spoke, I'm shocked he even acknowledges me. When he didn't show up the other day after a hunt, I thought he had really abandoned me. I was absolutely beside myself. Chaos sidles up beside us, interrupting us before the conversation gets a chance to start.

She whistles.

"I knew you were beautiful but damn, you clean up nicely. If I didn't already have my sights on a certain someone, I'd wife you up. What do you think, Vex?"

Vex stares at me for a while

"I think I'm thirsty."

I'd be lying if I didn't say I felt slightly deflated after his obvious bail out. But I know better than to let that get to me. He has had trouble expressing his feelings ever since the situation with his parents. Besides, I'm not here for him. I'm here for—

The apple of my eye is walking toward me now. I adjust my skirt and bite my lip slightly.

"Welcome, Tash. You look absolutely divine."

"Roshane Sinclair... good to see you."

Someone else arrives to the festivities and, as any good host would, he greets them with a smile and welcomes them.

I barely managed to say his name. Roshane Sinclair is the highest-ranking blacksmith in the entire IGF. Not just our division. There are three divisions of IGF. The Frontier Division, the Planetary Division, and the Eclectic Division. Each division serves a specific purpose and is in charge of exterminating the monsters in a specific way. The Frontier Division is charged with planetary defense in addition to defending members of HQ; they maintain the borders between planets and defend them against incoming threats. The Planetary division is the meat and potatoes of IGF. They serve as the ground police force for the five wealthiest planets. Venusian, Saturna, Jupitra, Plutos, and Mercurius. And finally, we have our division, the Eclectic division. We're charged with moving from planet to planet via the Traveler's Cube. As dangerous as it gets, and as important as it sounds. We are a mixed group of classifications, each with a specific role. But our sole duty is to eliminate the monsters that appear from the rift—from a separate dimension. We currently don't know how they keep showing up, but we do know why.

Their dimension is unstable and could tear apart at any moment. However, that isn't our problem. They can't stay here. As we populate and spread across our planets, we will not coexist with these... monsters. They recently officially declared war on us, after decades of being hunted.

Chaos is snapping her gloved fingers in my face in an attempt to gain my attention.

I shrug.

"Oh, you like him, don't you?"

I shrug again, not seeing her point. As far as I know, every female blacksmith likes him. He's dashing, handsome, and above all married. Something about him being able to commit to another makes me want him even more.

"They have something called Blacksmith Ale. Not sure if it's anything like Beetle Bum Rum but here." Vex returns with a tray of liquor for the three of us.

I offer them a spoonful of the concentrated honey to add a nice buzz.

With the honey mixed in, the ale is exceptional—even better than its usual high quality. The instrumentals of the Most High fill my ears, making me move my body rhythmically. The instruments are made from the bones of a Vinyl Beast and the skin of a Were Cat. Like I said, we blacksmiths don't waste a single part of the specimens.

The night wanes on to the point where we must do our sacred blood sacrifice. Our god is not a war god, but he is not a pacifist either. He demands blood once a year from a special blacksmith. Out of the seventy-five blacksmiths, one of us will be used to keep the connection from the Most High strong and our skills sharp. Ever twisting and improving, we must have a constant link to our deity, similar to the relationship between a striker and their navigator, albeit more sacred.

The chanting continues, matched by the dancing. The seventy-fifth blacksmith approaches the middle of the fire pit, pulls out his knife, and slices the palm of his hand. Blood drips onto the fire pit, turning it briefly green to indicate that he is not the one. Usually this process will continue until we reach around the middle of the pack, when someone is chosen, but tonight is not a usual night.

Blacksmith after blacksmith slits their palm, dripping blood onto the fire pit, and we're well past the halfway mark. The top ten are getting nervous. It's my turn. I take a deep breath followed by another sip of my ale.

Turning to Vex, I'm met with Chaos. She squeezes my hand firmly.

"It's going to be ok."

I nod.

Vex turns to me, and for the first time in all his years guarding this ritual, he gives me words of encouragement. In typical Vex logic he says, "If your god wanted you, he would have taken you a long time ago."

I smile. Despite knowing that's not how it works, some reason it does make me feel better. Although it's a great honor and whatnot. At the end of the day, no one wants to die.

As I approach the fire pit, I unsheathe my stinger. Although awkwardly, I manage to slice my palm. I look around one last time to see the faces of my associates. Some are dancing violently, while others are in an absolutely euphoric state—and then there are the few grim faces of those left to give offering.

I inhale deeply, fully embracing the moment of sincerity. When I place my palm over the fire, the blood falls as if in slow motion. The fire intensifies for a moment, then turns green. I release my breath and wobble a few steps back as if I'm about to pass out. Vex is there to catch me.

We continue the process until we are down to two. The number-two blacksmith and the number-one blacksmith. The number-two blacksmith is a terror by the name of Conquest. A former striker turned blacksmith, with exceptional capabilities. He is ninety-eight, with the personality of a brute. Two years away from retirement, being a sacrifice would serve him well.

"Oh, you cunts been hoping it was me?" He raises both his hands in the air to the booing of the crowd. "Just because I'm better than you is no reason to wish my demise. Your time would be better spent improving your skills."

He steps up to the fire pit and withdraws his bone sabre. After slitting both his palms, he puts the sabre away and places both hands over the fire.

I hold my breath, praying that he is the one. The alternative is too unbearable to think of.

His blood oozes over the fire, and it flutters momentarily. I think I see a hint of blue, but it is overshadowed by green. My eyes tear up. I know what's coming next. Roshane Sinclair stares at the fire before turning to run. The other blacksmiths apprehend him with ease. They pull him over to the fire while he struggles immensely.

"You can't do this to me! I'm Roshane!"

The crowd's envy and hate become apparent in their eyes. Some of his closest friends are now his biggest adversaries.

"Throw him in the pit!" cries one woman.

"Yes, the pit," screams another blacksmith.

Surprisingly, it's Conquest who speaks with the utmost reason.

"First, we must confirm."

The brute of a man walks over to Sinclair, held near the fire, and punches him in the face repeatedly. Blood drips from his lips and oozes down onto the burning fire. It turns green for a moment, raising my hopes, then becomes a solid blue. The blue flames flicker, mirroring my heartbeat.

Rapid, chaotic, and painful.

They throw him in the fire, which increases in intensity. The blue flames begin to consume his body rapidly. I'll never forget the smell of his searing flesh. It somehow smelled different than the others—almost more enticing. I lick my lips in anticipation of the meat from his bones. I become beastlike, similar to my peers, I was once one of his devoted supporters, now I see him as child who could not accept his fate.

Just when Sinclair is about to meet his end by the sacred flames of the Most High, a large arrow flies across my vision and impales his neck, killing him. The strikers encircle us while the more beastlike blacksmiths rush towards his body to rip into his flesh. It's said to strengthen our connection to the divine and help us ascend closer to the god of smithing.

I search for Vex and crouch behind him. I can't connect to the Most High if I'm dead.

CHAPTER 13
CLASSIFICATION: STRIKER

etween the cries of some blacksmiths and the flesh-ripping from others, my sensors are overwhelmed. Dimming them down slightly, I manage to focus on where the arrow came from, and spot another flying my way. I catch it and try to break it. It's larger than an average arrow and made of some reinforced type of wood. Unbreakable by my hands.

Chaos is beside me with her sniper rifle out, crouched low and ready to eliminate any who show themselves. My instincts tell me we are undermanned, surrounded, and pinned down. There is nowhere to run in a situation like this. We will need to break through their lines.

Tyrant fires several large rockets into the forest, causing a massive explosion. We hear the whiney of a horse. Suddenly my visor seems to be broken, because what appears before me is a parade of elfanoid-horse hybrid creatures. The top half of each being is a shirtless muscular elf covered in green tattoos, while the bottom half is that of a green-moss-covered horse. The creatures are galloping our way with spears, bows and arrows, and dual axes in hand.

A monster that can wield a weapon? Carrying a staff is one thing... but to wield a bow and arrow? Sharpened dual axes and spears?

Sensing the mutual hesitation in the air, I yell out.

"Fire at will. They are beasts just like any other."

The creatures charge forward into a massive barrage of gunfire, plasma fire, rockets, bombs, plasma arrows, and every projectile we can throw at them. But

the majority keep stampeding towards us. I watch in horror as they target the blacksmiths, trampling them with their hooves, killing many upon impact.

I send out Tirade to use her mass taunt, which covers the entire area surrounding the pit. The creatures pause their actions for a brief moment, giving my comrades and I enough time to pull out our melee weapons. I charge to one of the towering beasts and cleave its head off with my psionic blades, downing the monster. A puff of poisonous gas erupts from the gaping neck. Fortunately, my visor is reinforced and immune to such things.

I shout, "Be careful, their insides are filled with poison. Blacksmiths, use this time to retreat back to base. Tell any striker you see to reinforce us."

The blacksmiths run away, including Tash, who gives me a brief hug. By the time the taunt has waned, we have reduced their numbers to something a bit more manageable. Although we are still the fewer in numbers we will not be defeated without putting up a good fight. The towering beast before me turns to me and smiles, revealing mossy teeth. He puts his fingers to his lips and whistles, causing a group of female horse-elfanoids to come out wielding magical staves. They all raise their arms and vines emerge from the ground to wrap around our bodies. The vines tighten around me, threatening to cut off my oxygen supply.

"What are you?" I manage to choke out to the one nearby.

"We are Forest Centaurs, and you are our prisoners of war."

I awake still wrapped in the vines, being carried over a Forest Centaur's shoulder. My rifle is out of reach, strapped to his back next to his green halberd. I squirm and wiggle to try to get loose, only to receive a karate chop to my back.

"Elf will stop wiggling."

"Fuck you."

Another karate chop, this time right on the spine. I shudder violently as pain surges down my back.

Now helpless with a sore back, I try a different tactic.

"Where are you taking us?"

"Elf will stop talking."

"You look quite elf-like yourself. You sure we aren't cousins or something?"

The Forest Centaur carrying me spits on the mossy ground several times. I must have offended him greatly.

"Elf, you are despicable. You will not live through the night. I challenge you to a gauntlet."

Now we're speaking my language.

The Forest Centaur rips the vines from my body with ease and removes his halberd from his back. I activate my psionic blades.

I glance around to see the other Forest Centaurs tying vines into the mouths of my comrades. It seems this is a tactic that will only be used once.

I charge with both blades raised high, but my attack is deflected with ease, sending me flying into a nearby tree. The centaurs erupts into a fit of laughter. I get up, dusting myself off. This time I charge my energy, so a blue surge surrounds me as I speed towards my opponent. After unleashing the ball of psionic energy at the centaur, I leap over it, aiming for his head.

Forced to choose between the ball or me, he makes the right choice. The centaur blocks my psionic blades one more time, sending me flying into another tree, but this time I land on my feet and catapult myself towards him with the blasters on my wings. The ball of psionic energy strikes him in the stomach causing severe psionic damage. Twirling towards him, I lower myself at the last second, dodging his blow to slash at his chest. The blades get stuck against his bones, giving him enough time to grab me and slam me against the ground.

He raises his hooves high in the air and is about to stomp on me when I roll to the side. He activates a green energy, imbuing his halberd with it, and slashes at the ground where I lie. I manage to dodge by activating my thrusters again, pushing me towards the beast.

Exhausted, I unleash all six of my bella rockets, which sputter out and twirl towards the creature, striking him six times and building into a large explosion. I rise just as he falls.

A worthy opponent.

My psionic blades are destroyed along, with my rifle. I glance at Chaos who in a muffled voice says, "Run, fool!"

I hesitate slightly, only to take an arrow in the chest. Fortunately for me it isn't too deep a piercing. I turn and run in an unknown direction. I'm followed by several of the Forest Centaurs, the sound of their hooves reaching me even with my thrusters on full blast. In the distance I see a ridge.

It's either I jump off or I let them catch me.

I shoot an obscene gesture just as I dive off the cliff. I'm fully expecting to zip through the air with my wings, but I run out of my energy which fueled the wings, causing me to tumble to the rocky seas below.

Oddly enough, as I fall to my death, my thoughts come back to my father. No flashback, no fond memories, just pure hatred. Come to think about it, I remember another sane thing he said.

"You're gonna die a dishonorable death, boy."

I see a giant rock that I'm about to hit, and I activate the ring Runnymede gave me—knowing full well that a fall from this distance will still surely kill me.

But a two percent chance is better than nothing. Or so I tell myself.

Here I thought I looked forward to my death? Yet I do everything in my power to survive.

The first thing I notice on opening my eyes is the sight of blood. Blood and more blood, everywhere. My blood. I try to rise to my feet, but several broken bones prevent me from doing such a thing. How I survived is what the blacksmiths would call a miracle, what the navigators would call a scientific probability, and what the scavengers would call luck. As a striker I simply say: another day, another monster to hunt.

"Anyone there?"

"Temperance, perhaps."

"Who's Temperance?"

"Me. Sometimes."

"Great. I've been saved by a mad man."

"Temperance not mad, Temperance glad to be in good company. Perhaps it is you that is mad? Why go cliff diving? Such an odd sport."

"I wasn't cliff diving for sport." *Is that even a thing?* "Anyways, Temperance...how bad are my injuries?"

"Bad, very bad. At least one moon cycle out of commission. Even with Temperance healing."

"By then everyone will be dead... the division can't take such a loss."

"Well, perhaps if you had a stronger phenome, you wouldn't have had to cliff dive."

"What do you know about my phenome?"

"Temperance knows much about many and some about a little. But about yours? Temperance knows that your phenome manifested at the last second to cushion blow along with shield, causing mighty splash. Temperance rush out of cave to see what was going on."

I look at him: a tall man dressed in yellow cloth, half-covering his chest and revealing a pacifist tattoo. That tattoo represents his oath to his saint, an elf that did many great deeds in life and ascended to godhood in death. Or so the stories say. In any case, the saint is worshipped by about five percent of the population. These pacifists take an oath never to do harm to any living creature but to heal all those they encounter. Or so the stories go.

Behind Temperance is large scroll, likely contains some unknown type of magic. Magic, although very powerful, is a rarity in the galaxy. Most of it has waned for some unknown reason. What we are left with is our own energy and the advanced technology that the dwarves created. Not too shabby a trade, if you ask me.

Temperance pokes me in the forehead.

"You narrate too loud. I can hear every word." He points to his forehead which reveals a yellow eye in the middle of his forehead.

"Sleep time." He waves his hands to the side.

"I'm not tired... I have to go..."

My eyes droop down heavy as sandbags.

CHAPTER 14
CLASSIFICATION: SCAVENGER

The capital city of Marda is a nice change from the mud and stench of the Scavengers' Quarters. The buildings are short and brown, but all have their own unique version of a floating cube design. Marda isn't a rich planet by any means, but it is far from poor. If I had to describe the capital, I would describe it as quaint. I must hide my face and badge lest anyone know that I'm a scavenger. Unlike the lofty blacksmiths, the other three classifications are banned from entering the cities of the planets we save.

Can you believe that? We save these planets from the threats from the rift and we're not even allowed to take part in their hospitality. What backwards rules we live under. Lucky for me, I'm on official scavenger business. And by official, I mean sneaky and downright dirty.

I approach an underground fence nicknamed Pinky Finger, or Pinky for short. I've had dealings with him before and thus this should be a quick in-and-out. My alliance with Allison has borne a little fruit, as she provided me with the name of the object that I hold in my possession. It's called a Crypto Pyramid. But she was unable to find out what it's used for or its precise value. These are things I like to know before any deal with Pinky Finger.

"How'd the wings turn out?"

"Premo, thanks for asking."

"I knew I had to do you a solid after that meteor mine you procured for me. That got the Red Rogue Alliance off my back."

"Red Rogue Alliance? You deal with those villains?"

"They ain't that bad, they pay well. Better than members of the IGF." He gives me an eerie look. "Show me, what wares you got to sell or trade?" He pauses. "I know your cowardly self wouldn't have made the journey here if it wasn't for something good."

I pull out two of the chains that Vex won from the entertainer and hand them to Pinky. He analyzes them for a few minutes using his electronic magnifying glass. After rubbing the chains together, he places them in his pocket.

"What you want for em?"

I walk around his shop of gadgets and wares, but I already know what I'll be leaving with. I run my hand across a battlesuit, then eye an auric shield. Finally, my gaze lands on the mechanical dragonfly, gold with red eyes, that serves as a flying visual and audio recorder. You'd think with such high-tech gadgets as ours that something as simple as a visual and audio recorder would be easily accessible. However, that is far from the case. Across all planets in the galaxy, there are few ways to record audio or video. All of them on the black-market scene.

"I'll take the dragonfly."

"The dragonfly…"

"Yes, the dragonfly."

"What could a scavenger like you possible want with the dragonfly?"

"That isn't your concern. Is it a deal or not?"

"Fine, fine."

He plucks the golden dragonfly from its glass case and hands it to me with a little hesitation. He puts his hands on his hips.

"There, you've damn near cleaned me out of my most prized possession. Anything else?"

I withdraw the Crypto Pyramid from my cloak pocket and place it on the metal workstation.

His eyes widen to the size of saucers. "Get that out of my shop now, and you with it!"

"What is it, and what does it do?"

His voice lowers to a whisper. "You're asking for a death sentence carrying that around. Where'd you get it?"

"It fell from the sky."

He squints. "Yeah, I'm sure. The Red Rogue Alliance has been looking for this for a while now. Supposedly it can crash the economy of a planet."

"What can you tell me about the Red Rogue Alliance?"

"They don't play around when it comes to their products, they pay on time, and they are serious about this revolution thing. Everything's in the name of animal revolution. Freedom to have these beasts as pets and for food consumption and whatnot. They want their rights and they want them bad. That's all I know, now get out of here with that thing. And if they come a knockin' asking around for that again, I'll tell em what I know."

"Thanks. I'll be in touch after I've gotten rid of this thing. Not tryna hold onto something this dangerous."

I take my leave but as I do, I can't help the nagging feeling that I'm being watched. I shake the feeling while scurrying back to home base.

Home sweet home. It's not much but I relish in the idea of being in the safe confines of my bed. Scavengers ranked ten and below must share a tent, but fortunately for me, I'm the best scavenger that ever lived. Even in my advanced age I dust these young snappers. I take a shot of Beetle Bum Rum then attempt to fall asleep.

My nerves are acting up.

It's not often that this happens. I must really be shaken up by this Red Rogue thing. It's one thing to have some random citizen on your back, but when it's the Red Rogue you've officially graduated to dire consequences. I hear they flay their enemies alive, cut off their peckers, and feed them to their rift tigers. Not the way that I want to go.

I stand and head on over to the back of my small tent. I decide now is as good a time as any to confess all my sins. Many of which have to do with Vex.

"Hey, Vex, how you doing? Knowing you, you'd answer with a 'yeah.'" I pause and start the recording over.

"Vex, if you're watching this, it means I have died prior to my *retirement*—the moment in some scavengers' lives where they meet their death by poisoning. Kind of a raw deal, don't you think? After all those years of service, we're the one classification that's deemed too useless to live on after we've served our purpose. But I digress. Hah, bet you didn't know I knew that word. In any case, Vex. There is no easy way to say this. So, I'll just come out and say it." I give him my best smile.

"I'm your grandfather."

CHAPTER 15
CLASSIFICATION: STRIKER

I wake up in a cold sweat. More barking from Tirade, though this time I am able to make out the words.

"The rift is key."

The rest of the barking mainly served to give me a headache, though each time I upgrade Tirade I feel our bond become stronger. I make a vow to myself that if I ever find myself back in base, I will be sure to train her to the max. Besides, I am starting to get curious as to what she is trying to tell me.

It has been gruesome waiting these past few weeks to heal, but I have learned much from the pacifist Temperance. He has taught me how to harness my energy for more than just offensive purposes, and I have even learned how to recharge my energy quicker.

The day I am meant to head back to the Forest Centaur encampment, he hands me a white rectangular box half the length of my body.

"Temperance thinks you should open it."

"Temperance is an oddball. But I appreciate everything you've done for me. If there is ever anything you need from me, let me know."

I open the white box to reveal the most glorious weapons I have ever seen: not one, but two psionic scimitars. They have the distinct markings of magic and thus will be unpredictable to use, but very powerful.

"Temperance calls these the Wind Blades of the Lotus. Draw these in honor, and sheath them in glory. I give you this because I have seen your destiny in my visions. You will accomplish great things."

The hilt is that of a lotus flower. My hand moves to touch one of the hilts, only for a sharp gust of wind to blow into the cave where we reside.

"Temperance sees this as a sign. It's time for you to go."

I tie the box containing the swords around my back and then begin the steep climb up the cliffside. It's a grueling climb, especially since my wounds aren't fully healed, but I manage to make it with only a few slips here and here. Once I reach the top, I immediately try to get in contact with my navigator. For two weeks I have been working on fixing the comm unit.

"Striker to navigator."

No response.

"Striker to navigator."

"Where have you been!"

"Never mind that. I'll fill you in when we have more time. What's the status update on the others?"

"We tried to make a deal with the Forest Centaurs, but IGF headquarters nixed it. They said we don't negotiate with animals, we exterminate them. At the appointed meeting time, we showed up with all the remaining strikers..."

"And?"

"It was brutal. It was a massacre. The Forest Centaurs trampled our strike force. They picked apart our units and impaled our strikers like they were nothing. Afterwards their leader, a female Forest Centaur, said we had one week to provide them with their demanded resources and sent back the remaining living strikers from the strike force."

"What have you gathered about the Forest Centaurs so far?"

"They are... how best to put it..." she whispers, "almost honorable creatures. Unless provoked or disrespected."

My breathing increases as my heart pounds against my chest. It's worse than I anticipated. As I slink towards their last known location, now in daylight, I think of all the possible scenarios.

There is only one that doesn't end in the deaths of myself and my entire division of strikers.

I track the Forest Centaurs to their encampment. To my amazement, they have built little huts out of tree bark and mud. Primitive but effective. They almost seem civilized, which is what I am banking on. I walk as straight as I can, poised to unleash my weapons at a moment's notice.

"Where is your leader?!" I bellow. "I call out your leader!"

A few of the Forest Centaurs poke their head out from their mud huts. Within a minute I'm surrounded by these horse-elf creatures. All are wielding well-made weapons from the rift. They place their weapons to my throat simultaneously.

"What business elf have with our leader?"

"I challenge your leader to gauntlet. Or is she too scared to face me honorably?"

"What elf know about honor? Elves the most dishonorable of all the races. Kill, steal, submission."

"Yeah, yeah. Save me the philosophical debate and send her out."

One of the Forest Centaurs whistles three times, and the most elegant of all the Forest Centaurs graces my vision. She is larger than the males of her species, with a distinct green tint to her upper torso, covered in more moss. Blue butterflies surround her body as if she truly is a creature of nature. She wields a green staff with a hook. Her energy is so peaceful, it almost sings me to sleep.

"Striker to navigator."

"Go ahead. We're all watching you, by the way."

"Cool, tell me something useful about their leader."

"Ummm." I hear a voice in the background. "If you get hit by a blast from her staff, you instantly die."

"Navigator... confirm that."

"That's been... confirmed."

"Sounds like fun. Striker out."

They bring out the strikers that were taken captive. All nine are still alive, including Chaos. They seem to be in good condition, though they have clearly been starved for the past two weeks. Chaos looks like she's in the best condition out of all of them, as though she refuses to let a little starvation diminish her excellence.

I turn my attention to the task at hand. I remove the box at my back, and the entire group of Forest Centaurs peers to see what I am doing. I know I still have three flutter bombs, and the ring has recharged. But will it be enough to take down an S+-grade Forest Centaur?

"Begin," says one of the Forest Centaurs.

I withdraw my swords, triggering a crisp gust of wind. The vibration of the psionic scimitars is so strong that I drop them upon clasping them. The Forest Centaur directly beside me chuckles. If things look too grim, I'll be sure to take his life before I lose my own.

"We still need to discuss terms."

"You're in no position to be discussing anything. I only fight you to prove that we Forest Centaurs are better than you elves ever could be."

"Let's discuss them anyway."

"If you somehow manage to defeat me, I will guarantee passage back to your home base for you and your strikers. If you fail, then your strikers will be our slaves of war. I assure you; our slaves are not treated nearly as well as our prisoners."

She twirls her staff in the air, creating an arena of poisonous vines around us. When she slams the base of her staff against the ground, inward-facing spikes grow on the vines, ready to pierce anyone who comes too close.

I twirl my psionic scimitars in the air, causing a massive gust of wind. Confirming that I caused the previous one makes me feel a bit better.

I sprint at blistering speeds but am stopped in my tracks by a blast from her staff. The deadly weapon leaves a hole the size of my body right where I once stood. She fires again, making me dodge left. I cross my blades together, creating a small tornado that shreds everything in its wake. The tornado strikes her on the arm, removing it.

I watch in dismay as sharp vines replace her arm. As I make my approach, she sends down a barrage of spikes from a rift in the sky.

No time to be impressed.

I tumble forward to avoid spikes protruding from the earth, but she follows that attack with more spikes raining down. When I'm about to be impaled, I activate the entertainer's ring. Three blue shields pop up, taking the bulk of the physical damage, and leaving me with one shield left. I summon Tirade, who is now in range to taunt.

Tirade howls menacingly. The leader of the Forest Centaurs becomes dazed, giving Tirade enough time to swipe her staff. I engage faster than before due to my lotus scimitars. The speed created by reversing the blades is astronomical. I catapult myself towards their leader. I'm about to decapitate her when she smiles and blocks me with her vine arm. She follows this defense with a fist to my helmet, but the shield absorbs the physical damage.

She grabs me by the neck and slams me against the ground, then stomps on my stomach. As her hooves dig into me, I cough up blood. Tirade drops the staff and focuses her attention on our foe, biting at one of her legs—granting me enough time to slash at her other leg.

I unleash the three flutter bombs which surround the leader. I quickly slash off all four of her hooves, ensuring that she will take the full blast of the flutter bombs. Knowing full well I won't have enough time to make it out of the bombs' radius, I close my eyes in preparation to meet my end.

Just as the bombs go off, I see Tirade wash over me, covering me in wind shadow. I'm overwhelmed with grief, sadness, and pain. My eyes well up, and my hand trembles, but the fox-like phenome saves my life once again. I collapse to the ground from my wounds. The wind shadow phenome kept me alive but I still took severe physical damage. As my blood leaks onto the soil, I manage to take my two fingers and place them on my forehead, where the third eye is supposed to be.

I whisper the words. "Health in all things, balance in most."

A wave of yellow energy washes over me, closing my wounds and granting me minor vitality. I rise to my feet, ready to meet what's next. Will they honor their former leader's words, or will her conditions go out the window?

A bulky Forest Centaur approaches me with his double axes glowing.

"This isn't over, dark elf. Take your strikers and go. We will be upon you like the plague that you are soon enough."

I rush to release my comrades, Chaos my first priority . She seems rather irritated. Something tells me she isn't used to being placed in a vulnerable position.

"About time, Vex. I would have freed you sooner."

CHAPTER 16
CLASSIFICATION: NAVIGATOR

"Hurrah!" We all cheer and salute to the successful rescue of our most elite strikers. Still, the fact that they were captured is not something that we can overlook. As navigators, it is up to us to decide when to move to drastic measures. Our supervisor sent out a poll after Vex saved the group.

The title was simple yet powerful. *Should we call in for reinforcements?*

It may not seem like a big deal, but this is a protocol that has never been activated. Our division has an excellent track record of cleansing the planets allied to the IGF. There are a total of a hundred-and-twenty populated planets within our galaxy, eighty of them under the protection of the IGF. To date our division has traveled to and cleansed over fifty of those planets, all without assistance from the other divisions. Such a thing would demonstrate weakness amongst our strikers and create a heavy disconnect between the strikers and the navigators, whose relationship is built on mutual trust and communication.

Taking all this into consideration, we are down to twenty-five remaining strikers out of the fifty we started with. We have never been in a situation this critical. Then there are the other circumstances. I mean these entities are clearly sentient, intelligent, and above all a greater threat than we could have ever imagined.

"Allison, mark your vote on the computer. You're the last one!"

I look around to see everyone staring at me, and I check the poll. Of the sixty navigators, there are thirty in favor of calling in reinforcements, while the other

twenty-nine wish to wait and see what happens. The shame is likely too much for them to bear.

I know Vex would never forgive me, but I press the screen where it says "YES" without hesitating, voting for them to call in reinforcements from the Frontier Division. That's the division that protects the space between each planet. In times like this, one must think about what she wants and not what others want. It does often pay to be selfish.

Nearly half the room grumbles on seeing my vote, as a stalemate would have been a vote for the status quo. I shrug off the disparaging words of the non-reinforcers and the cheers of the reinforcers. I feel numb. I know I made the right decision with the information that I have. Still, a part of me wishes it didn't have to come to this.

I chomp down on my grilled cheese sandwich and hope that none of this will be held against me when all is said and done.

Runnymede isn't looking too good these days. In fact, he looks worse than he ever has. Must have taken some heavy losses in the gambling tent. I wonder why he asked to meet with me, and why so late. I'm wearing my battlesuit with replenished rockets. I had to convince one of the lower-level blacksmiths to sell them to me. My hope is that his desperation for future business and the large lump sum I paid will both keep him quiet.

"What do you want, Runnymede?"

"I... I need your help." He looks down at the ground.

"More help? I thought it was you who owed me one now."

"Yeah I do, but there is nowhere for me to turn."

"What is it? And maybe I'll consider it." I relish in this position of power. Seeing him squirm in my vice grip. The desperate look on his face is priceless. He really does need a favor.

"I need you to find a way to contact the Red Rogue Alliance."

"How preposterous! You want to get me executed? Even having knowledge of them is considered treason."

"Listen here, Allison, this is life or death."

"For you." I place my hands on my hips. "I have nothing to do with this."

"What if I tell Vex about your sick mother?"

"Then I cry my eyes out and hope his heart melts. If not, I'll figure something out. But anything is better than being indebted to you." I'm turning to leave when a peculiar smile comes across his face.

"Help me figure something out... how'd you get the nickname Sugar Cane if the only thing sweet about you is what you put between your plump lips?"

"I don't know what you're talking about." Beads of sweat drip down my sides. Now with a drenched shirt and a new rage, I gaze at Runnymede through this helmet that I'm wearing.

"Listen here Runnymede. I don't know what you think you know but..."

"No, you listen. I've put two and two together. I knew there was something my fence wasn't telling me, but I never knew it would be this. By the time I got back to base, it dawned on me that someone or a group of someones in our division must be in cahoots with the Red Rogue Alliance. Then I thought about it some more after a few rounds of Beetle Bum Rum."

I watch as he leans back on the tent pole behind him. He must be feeling rather superior right about now.

"Making four wasn't too difficult. What group of lazy fat bastards with no sense of a code would be willing to work with such a group? Certainly, some bottom-feeding strikers, a blacksmith or two, maybe, but they would need a great navigator. Someone who could locate the monsters, and hide their traces, while also keeping up with their duties."

He beamed his goofy grin. "So I started from the top and worked my way to the bottom. Bribing for and vetting information on the top navigators. And lo and behold, look who I found sitting comfortably in the top ten with frequent tardies."

"You have no evidence," I say, my finger hovering over a button to blow him to smithereens.

"That would be true... except for the fact that I have this."

He pulls out a mechanical golden dragonfly with red eyes. After he presses a button, the eyes start blinking, indicating that it's recording.

"I have a recording of you leaving the encampment grounds to rendezvous with the group of strikers who died mysteriously. Is that evidence enough for you?"

"Fine, what do you want?" It's too public an area to eliminate him here. I'll have to comply for now.

"I already told you what I want. I want you to set up a meeting with the RRA. Tell them your colleague has something they have been looking for, and that I'll part with it for two hundred thousand credits."

"I don't even know how to contact them; they contact me."

"Well, I'm sure one as intelligent as you can figure that out. It needs to be done ASAP."

"Fine. I'll get it done. You scumbag."

"I love you too," he says, blowing me a kiss.

I make my return to the navigators' encampment to see Jacob in my seat.

"H... hey, Allison. I covered for you. I saw that you were running late. Everything ok?"

"Everything is fine. Thanks for covering."

"No problem. You know I'd do anything for you, right?"

"Sure... can you remove yourself from my seat? You're getting popcorn butter all over the arm rests."

He stands up sluggishly, causing him to breathe heavily. After much effort, he turns to me and says something that catches me off guard.

"I love you. You know that, right?"

The only response I can muster is something my ex used to tell me when I would say I love him. It was a response that was all of cold, sarcastic, but somewhat true.

"I'd love me too." And I throw in a childlike giggle for added effect.

Defeated once again, he shrugs and waddles his way back to his grey cubicle. *I have bigger fish to fry and better bread to bake. No one and nothing is going to stop me from making credits to feed my family, especially not Runnymede. A scoundrel like him will keep asking for favors until he asks for a piece of my pie.*

I sit down at my desk, too irritated to eat a full course meal. So I only eat three quarters. I know things are bad when they're messing with my appetite. I devise a plan so simple that it will work, yet complicated enough that it won't get back to me. I reach underneath my desk for the intricate password they gave me. A password that I have nearly memorized.

Diligently I type in the password, making sure to enter every character correctly. My screen goes white for a few moments, then the Red Rogue Alliance site pops up. An underground site so secure that it must have been created by an elite navigator, it runs on a separate server to the official IGF server, but somehow manages to piggyback off it. I fantasize sometimes about who could have built it. A tall, dark, and handsome man, with muscles. He's dashing and charming, with nimble fingers. Able to maneuver a woman just as well as he is able to maneuver the keyboard.

Anyone would be better than this lot.

My fingers move at lightning speeds as I go through the many loops and hurdles that they require each time I log on. You have to answer a ten-part questionnaire, beat some kind of weird jumping game, and then allow them access to your computer logs for the past week. The purpose of all this is to ensure you are as skilled a navigator as possible. Based off what Runnymede said, I presume I'm the only top-ten navigator that they have contact with in this division. That means it's time for me to play my hand. Return the Crypto Pyramid and get a raise.

"Sugar Cane to Rogue twenty-five."

"Rogue twenty-five available."

"I have eyes on Crypto."

"Turn eyes into manifestation and be rewarded greatly."

"Sugar Cane acknowledges, delivery boy = disposable."

"Copy that. Rogue twenty-five unavailable."

CHAPTER 17
CLASSIFICATION: STRIKER

y mouth is dry from all the talking I've been doing lately. It's like everyone in camp wants to hear the full story from my lips. I pause as I see Chaos passing by the crowd of onlookers.

"Chaos!"

I get up and push past the onlookers to walk beside her. She looks at me briefly, then speeds up her pace.

"What's your problem?" I ask.

"You're bad luck."

That stops me dead in my tracks. I'm not the type to beg for attention, so I let her go on her merry way.

But me, bad luck? Any idiot can see that we're facing more difficult monsters, and that my S+ cunning is causing me to make some gains. I suppose I should explain how the difference in stats comes into play. I've been mulling it over for a while now: how the difference between intelligence, cunning, and wisdom play out. Intelligence describes the knowledge one gains in abundance and excels when one has all or the majority of information at hand. Wisdom is the application of said knowledge in an accurate and effective manner; it excels when one needs to make a decision that will best benefit themselves and their team. Meanwhile cunning is the artful use of minor to medium amounts of information and excels when one is at a disadvantage.

Essentially, I'm not the smartest or the wisest, but one thing Runnymede taught me as a youth during his extracurricular training was that cunning in the right circumstances will trump both.

Come to think of it, my transition from scavenger classification to striker wouldn't have been possible if not for Runnymede's unusual training when I was a youth. I have a sudden urge to speak to him, maybe have another drink. That Beetle Bum Rum was good, though I could do without the aftereffects.

But business before pleasure. I decide it's best to pay my blacksmith a visit and see if the new list of upgrades is available. Plus, I suppose I should check on her status. Ever since I upgraded Tirade to level three, I've been more in tune with the emotions of others. How or why that will be useful to me, I don't know. But I do know that each upgrade removes a piece of the emotional block that stains my soul. I suppose that's why they're called our shadows. The higher they climb, the more enlightened we become.

I find myself standing outside my blacksmith's tent. I hear sobbing. A large part of me wants to turn around and not deal with the tears. I mean, what am I to say? I'm no counselor. I poke my head in through the tent, hoping she will berate me and tell me to go away. But she simply glances up and wipes her tears.

"Is... is there something I can help you with, Vex?"

"Just umm... as odd as it may sound, I'm here to check up on you." And see about that list.

"Wow... you really are experiencing changes. The regular Vex would have just barged in here, demanding to see the new list."

"Well, I've grown a tad bit, I suppose. I recognize that you're more than just a tool. You're an elf and have your own thoughts and feelings."

"That's basic elf decency. But I suppose it's a start. I'll take it."

The smile she manages is weak, but still warm and kind. I enter the tent to see things scattered all over the place. Tools on the ground, rifle parts out of their boxes.

"As you can see, things are in a bit of a disarray."

"What's wrong?" I inquire.

"Nothing."

"Nothing doesn't turn into tears and disarray."

"I suppose not…"

"Does this have to do with the ceremony?"

"Yes. The ceremony was interrupted before Roshane could perish by the sacred fire. He essentially died in vain. Our connection to the Most High has weakened. I can't create most of the stuff on the list—it's almost as though I've forgotten how to. Some of the other blacksmiths have it worse. But we've all been affected, in case you're thinking of dashing me away."

"Why would you think I'd dash you away?"

"Why not? When a tool is broken and cannot be fixed, you throw it away."

"I'm not good at these heart-to-heart things. All I can say is that I'm not going to dash you away. You and Runnymede have been with me since day one. Even our navigator has been with us for a while. We make a great team. We just need to pull together and get past this obstacle. What can be done to please this god of yours?"

"I've been wrapping my brain around it, and the only thing I can think of is to wipe out all the Forest Centaurs. As long as their species draw breath on this planet, the Most High will not be pleased."

"Oh, is that all?" I pause. "Here I thought you were gonna mention the Queen Bee. I'm not looking forward to seeing her again."

She beams me one of the most captivating smiles I've ever seen. Who would have thought my shy and timid blacksmith could ever be so alluring? But I shake such thoughts out my head. Frolicking with one's troupe is one of the ultimate taboos.

We embrace for a brief moment. This intuition thing seems to be quite the hassle. Has me acting out of character. Though it seems to make the people around me feel better. How that helps me, I don't know.

"Before I go… mind if I see the list, and what you can make off it?"

"Sure."

She transfers the list to my wrist link. I open it up and my jaw drops. Ninety percent of the things on the list are new upgrades and weapons. Things that would drastically improve my hunting. Unfortunately, there are no assault rifles available. The only things currently available are upgrades for Tirade and dual submachine guns called pain and suffocation: lightweight weapons that excel in mid to close range.

Pain deals more damage the longer it hits, while suffocation has a five percent chance of suffocating the target. They sound useful.

The next upgrade for Tirade, which will give her a fourth tail, is sly fox: the ability to copy myself or herself for a short duration. I'm thinking that combined with dual SMGs, two of me could really get my spray-and-pray going on.

"I'll take the dual SMGs and an upgrade on Tirade."

"Are you sure? This will damn near bankrupt you."

"That's fine, I'll just have to come back with a full stock of specimens. What else can you tell me about those SMGs? Honestly, I haven't touched one since advanced training."

"SMGs in general are light and efficient in hunting low-armored monsters. These ones in particular have armor-piercing rounds that give you extended range and damage against high armored targets. You should melt through them like butter. The downside is that they take up a lot of your energy and thus can be depleted in no time. Basically, they will go through your personal energy bar like water if misused. So energy management is the utmost priority when wielding them."

She places a finger on her lips. "This is between you and me, but I heard that pain and suffocation, if used properly, can easily surpass any assault rifle. But that's just a rumor, and you know how I dislike spreading rumors."

"Really?" My eyebrows raise. "Now, that's interesting. I'll take them."

"Sounds good. They will take about an hour for me to make, and you can get the Tirade upgrade when you come back. I'll be sure to add a little something extra just for you."

I'm shocked. She has never added anything extra for me in all these years. I suppose this sensitive guy stuff has some benefits. Or, as my blacksmith, says basic elf decency.

With an hour to kill before I set out on my hunt, I have to devise a plan on how to take down the remaining Forest Centaurs. I counted about sixty all A+ and above. I'm in dire need of allies. It seems the soloist can't do everything on his own.

While looking over the leaderboards in search of a top-ten striker whose hunting style would fit mine, I come up to a saddening conclusion. The strikers that would best fit my current style are ones with long range or explosive pressure. That leaves me with Chaos, who currently isn't speaking to me, and Tyrant, who is a dick. There are a few others in the top ten, but they won't budge without Tyrant, who usually hunts in a pack.

I curse my luck and head over to the second rank's tent, a massive orange tent marked with a Y. I knock on the pole and poke my head inside. To my shock, I see Tyrant and Ivy frolicking in the bed. Tyrant turns to me with a scowl and presses a button on his wrist console that makes his battlesuit quickly assemble itself against his person.

"I didn't come here to..."

His large fist connects with my stomach, and I spew out saliva. He follows this up by throwing me out the tent. He pounces on me like the hulking lumberjack that he is, pummeling my chest with his tree-trunk-like fists.

I'm able to activate my grappling spear between punches, catching him in the chest. He tears it out with ease and tries to use the spear end to impale me. I block with my forearm. I then reach for one of my psionic scimitars. Gripping the hilt summons a massive gust of wind that pushes him off me, slamming him into a tentpole. I rise to my feet and activate the other scimitar. As I stalk my prey, I twirl the blades, creating wind to swirl around his wrists and tie him to the pole.

It's at this point that Ivy comes out, dressed in her heavy battlesuit with her shield up.

"Why'd you poke your head inside? What are you, some kind of pervert?"

"I did knock. I'm not here to fight."

"Then what are you here for?"

Tyrant breaks the pole of his tent, managing to free himself.

How strong is this guy?

"Knock it off with the wind stuff," he says.

Sheathing my blades, I disengage the wind cuffs. We head over to Ivy's tent to talk privately. Tyrant turns to me and grips my shoulder. "Now, don't be getting any bright ideas, pervert."

I grumble, "You're not my type."

We enter the tent to see it has been redecorated from its standard issue. There are plants all over the place, including poison ivy.

I can see how she got her name. Wonder what she uses them for.

"I wouldn't have come here if things weren't dire. Are you aware of what's going on with the blacksmiths?"

"Yeah, what of it? That's between them and their god. We have no orders to intervene," says Tyrant

"Tyrant."

"It's 'number two' to you."

"I'm not calling you 'number two.'"

"That is my rank, and as I recall, you're barely number three."

"And as I recall, I was about to wipe the ground with your guts."

"Oh, so you wanna go all out? I'll mop you up and down to Venusian."

"Let's do this."

Ivy looks at both of us and sighs.

"You two will calm down and speak to each other like adults. I agree with Vex. We need to assist the blacksmiths in their time of need. What do you have in mind?"

"It is believed that if we can defeat all the Forest Centaurs, the blacksmith god will be pleased and restore their connection to the divine."

"A chance to kill off the horse-elves?" asks Tyrant.

"Yeah."

"How many strikers do you have on board?" Tyrant asks.

"Just you two. I don't have much of a relationship with the other strikers."

Tyrant cackles. "What you mean is you've been solo for so long that none of the other strikers will even talk to you. Isolation has its drawbacks."

"Cool story. Now are you in or are you out?"

"On the condition that we settle our duel after this horse-elf thing is taken care of. My troupe and my allies will lead the charge. You get ten percent of the kills. Non-negotiable."

I clench my jaw and my fist to prevent myself from biting off more than I can chew. But the cunning in me can't accept such unfavorable terms. Especially when I'm broke as a scavenger.

"Deal. With one caveat. If I kill more Forest Centaurs than you, I get bumped up to twenty-five percent, from your share of the pie."

"Pfft, and when I kill more than you, you get nothing."

"Fine."

"Fine."

CHAPTER 18
CLASSIFICATION: SCAVENGER

lean against my hovercycle, deep in the western forest of Marda: a place marked by its fruit bears and fruit cats. Lucky for me, they are some of the more docile creatures on the planet. Frankly, I'm shocked that Allison fell for my bluff. It seems all those years of Wagner's Tale came into use. While waiting I send my dragonfly recording device into a nearby apple tree. She has specific instructions to return to Vex if I don't turn off the recording after two hours. She will also follow me, recording, in a significant radius within those two hours. I may be a fool but I'm as sly as they come.

A part of me doesn't expect to come away from this meeting alive. There was something Allison said to me when she was giving me the information for the meeting—some mumbo jumbo on karma. I wasn't really listening. But the fact that she felt the need to lecture me on something seemed out of place.

In any case, here I am. A lone scavenger in the woods, waiting to meet up with the infamous Red Rogue Alliance. I peer into the distance to see three red hovercycles pulling up to me. S-class vehicles. Now, although my hover bike is A-class, it's suited for this kind of terrain, while those hovercycles' builds scream capital city.

I eye each of them, making sure the visual device connected to the dragonfly gets a good look at them to send the feedback to the dragonfly. The first is an athletic-built male dressed in a red cloak, with a deck of lava cards hitched to his side. The second is a female athletic-built in a red cloak, with a lava bow and quill of arrows at her back. The third is the most intimidating. A muscular man in red, with a lava cutlass in one hand and a lava grappling hook in the other. He is the first to speak.

"You have the Crypto?"

"Yes. You have the credits?"

"No. No need for those where you're going."

Swift as lightning, the woman pulls out her bow and shoots an arrow into my stomach. The arrow melts into my skin and spreads, leaving a fist sized hole. I manage to cover the burning hole with my hand as I hop on my hovercycle and speed away.

Another arrow careens in my direction; this time, it nicks the side of my head, causing what little hair I have left to burn away. The dastardly rogue with the cards catches up to my back bumper and tries to fish tail me. I press the red button on the front of my vehicle to unleash extra-slippery oil, which makes him spin out of control and crash.

I press the other red button to unleash my M.E.G.A rocket: my mechanically-extra giant-ass rocket. It spews out, but to my dismay, the archer shoots two lava arrows into the rocket, causing it to detonate prematurely. The blast threatens to throw me off my bike—something I cannot let happen.

Tightening my grip upon my handlebar, I unleash my final trick. I press the button in the middle where a horn would usually be. From a tertiary exhaust pipe drop a slew of multi-faced land spikes. As soon as the archer rogue hovers over them, a chain explosion throws her bike flipping backwards into the air. I watch in awe as she lands gracefully upon her feet and manages to let loose another lava arrow, this time striking my back engine.

I see the light of base camp. I'm so close that I can feel it. Suddenly, the grip of the lava grappling hook latches onto me. The rogue yanks me off the bike and sends me flying to the ground, where he takes the cutlass and stabs me in the chest, inches from my heart.

"The Crypto Pyramid. Now."

I take my grubby hands and reach into my now-soiled pants. Taking out the Crypto Pyramid, I hand it to him. I gaze into the rogue's mask.

Just as I draw my last breath, he speaks one more time.

"Sugar Cane says goodbye."

CHAPTER 19
CLASSIFICATION: STRIKER

"Striker to scavenger."

There is no response.

"Striker to scavenger."

My navigator chimes in.

"Status shows he is unavailable. He must have overslept or something. I'll arrange for a suitable replacement."

"Make sure you get me Runnymede. He needs to come in with a large cargo carrier; we're gonna be coming in heavy."

"Umm... copy that."

I double-check my P90s, making sure they are ready for action. Tash even painted them with a death wind design. Pretty fly. I triple-check my psionic scimitars, ensuring they are prepared to decapitate. I'm stocked full of bella rockets and flutter bombs. Tirade is upgraded to her fourth tail. Sly fox will do me well. I feel a stronger bond than ever with Tirade, something akin to a friendship, if I were to put it into words. At least I think this is what a friendship feels like.

In the distance, my eye catches Chaos with her new sniper rifle. I believe it's called the Devil's Advocate. A S+-level sniper rifle that disorients enemies in a radius while dealing explosive damage to the one hit. Not to mention its advanced reload time and lower-energy cost. Truly a unique addition to her arsenal.

Ivy must have convinced her to come along. Hopefully she finds success.

Our group consists of the strikers numbered one, two, three, ten, eleven, thirteen, twenty-three, twenty-nine, forty, and Ivy who is now fourteenth-ranked. We set off like thieves in the night to summon thunder and lightning upon our enemies. For the first time, I feel a twinge of hatred for these monsters. Before it was all business, simply putting an animal down to its rightful place. Now it's personal. These beasts will pay for making a mockery of the strikers.

We arrive at the home of the Forest Centaurs. As I move into position, I see that the majority of them are in a large circle watching a one-sided duel. A massive Forest Centaur is picking apart a smaller one. Their moves are swift and efficient. The wooden halberds that they wield are light and effective. This will be no easy task. But we are prepared.

Tyrant gives the signal for everyone to summon their phenomes. I call Tirade and prepare to send her forth with sly fox and mass taunt: a ruthless combination that will allow us to take down a large part of their army instantly. I check atop one of the huts to see Chaos in position, sniper rifle aimed at the biggest and baddest of the Forest Centaurs, the one who has now been crowned their leader.

Tyrant gives me the signal and I send double Tirade out. The white-and-blue wind fox appears on opposite sides of their army simultaneously. She howls into the moon, pulling the attention of over fifty Forest Centaurs that turn to face her. With their minds momentarily dazed, we unleash a hell that's never been seen before: rockets, bombs, plasma rays, lightning, thunder and everything else within our upgraded arsenal. I rush in to gain better accuracy. The armor-piercing plasma rounds spray out alarmingly fast. I struggle to maintain accuracy due to the recoil, but I take down the five Forest Centaurs closest to me with ease.

Suddenly I hear a loud popping sound, which is followed by a quick bright light from Chaos' location, and then a loud boom as the body of the largest Forest Centaur drops instantly. A deadly headshot. The wider-range disorientation hits, causing centaurs in Chaos' range to drop to their knees. Using this opportunity, I engage, slicing my psionic scimitars through every Forest Centaur I see like a crazed beast. I'm covered in blood. I sheathe one scimitar and pull out one P90 for maximum versatility. My eyes lock onto another Forest Centaur. I activate the thrusters, and once in range, I shoot out the grappling spear, which pierces one of his legs. I lock myself into place and aim my P90 at his back.

"Mercy, please! I have children."

For a second, I hesitate. Children? It never occurred to me that these things would have offspring. But I suppose it makes sense. The Forest Centaur within my grip drops to the ground at another echo of disorientation. Chaos isn't playing around.

In the distance, I hear words that make me think I'm hallucinating.

"Release the dragon! Release the dragon!"

I see two Forest Centaurs rushing towards a large cave. Whatever a dragon is, it can't be good. I activate my thrusters, combined with the wind force from my scimitars, in a vain attempt to catch up, but they are too far away. I yell to Chaos.

"Kill the ones heading to the cave!"

She nods and directs her attention to the two heading to the cave. I see that three Forest Centaurs are heading in her direction to take her down. I divert my attention to them. I run up behind them, my P90s aimed at the first two to release pain and suffocation on them. They drop like flies. Now within close range, I switch to my scimitars and enter close-quarters combat with the third.

He uses his shield to block my first attack, but my second catches him in the neck. Blood spurts out drenching me further. I twist backwards to knock away an incoming spear from behind, redirecting it to slice the other side of the third centaur's neck. The fourth Forest Centaur charges at me and pulls out his bow and arrow. I pull out suffocation and shoot a bullet. I watch in awe as white energy surrounds his head, removing the oxygen. He grasps his throat helplessly and dies from suffocation. A poor man's way to go.

By the time I look back at the cave, I see about nine bodies in front of its entrance. But there are two others galloping closer. On reaching the entrance, they unlatch the massive wooden gate. They stand there, dancing an awkward horse-elf dance. It's almost humorous.

"What are they doing?" asks Chaos.

"I think... they're celebrating."

"Such foolish..."

The terrifying roar of what must be the dragon echoes out from the cavern. A blast of fire emerges from the cave, sweeping both striker and Forest Centaur alike. The field is littered with the charred corpses of my comrades. The only ones left alive are me, Chaos, Tyrant, and Ivy. The dragon emerges from the cave, and to this day, I've never seen something so graceful and destructive at once.

A giant red lizard-like creature with large black wings and yellow horns crawls out of the cavern. It flaps its wings, and a huge gust of wind moves across the land, sweeping up huts and trees alike. We all watch in amazement as the creature takes flight with ease and disappears into the distance.

I get a really bad feeling in my gut. But I shake it off. I must attend to the duty at hand.

"Striker to navigator."

"Yes, Vex?"

"Send in the scavs."

"Copy that."

The surviving strikers meet in the middle of the battleground with a newfound sense of comradery. As the only ones to survive the Battle of Centaur Forest, as it will be called, we each give each other a nod.

Tyrant looks at me with his arms crossed. "I doubt you were keeping track, but that's your fourteen to my thirteen. I suppose you get to feast on this eve, boy."

"I suppose so, old man."

"Young enough to kick your ass."

"Now isn't the time. Let's head back to base." Ivy caresses Tyrant's shoulder. Their two bulky suits are a match made in hell.

I look into the distance to see a group of scavengers make their way to us. Keeping an eye out for Runnymede, I find myself anxious to see him.

"Striker to navigator."

"Go ahead, Vex."

"What's the twenty on Runnymede?"

"Couldn't get ahold of him. I found a suitable replacement."

"How in the planetary systems can there be a suitable replacement when Runnymede is the top-ranked scavenger in the division?!" My breath is heavy now. "What rank is this scav?" I ask.

There is a long pause.

"Rank...forty five out of a hundred."

"And you call that suitable?"

"Frankly, it's hard to get a scav on short notice."

"Where the hell is Runnymede?"

"I don't know. He's MIA."

I turn off comms and punch the air. When I get my hands on that grubby old man, I'm gonna strangle him.

I watch as each striker, even the dead ones, get their kills transported by their respective scavs. Chaos approaches me with her sniper at her back.

"Hey, you..."

"Oh, so now you're talking to me?"

"Yeah, about that. I shouldn't have called you bad luck. What my blacksmith said kinda got to me."

"I see."

"Let's just say, it was good to see you do some amazing work out there today. I'm having a private party in my quarters tonight. You should come."

"I'll think about it."

"Sounds good."

I watch as she and her two scavs zoom off in a red hover car with advanced phasing technology.

"Heh... must be nice."

As I ponder all the ways Runnymede is going to be punished, I see a clunky yellow car phase in front of me. The vehicle is puke yellow, with tinted windows and a large antenna coming out of the top. Its design is somewhat sleek, yet clunky and old. A miraculous feat that it's able to function.

Must be my ride.

I see a gloved hand poke its way out of the car and wave. Out steps this short, dark-skinned kid, can't be past the age of fifteen. She's wearing what looks to be heavy battle boots, a mech arm, and puke-yellow goggles. She's donning a blue bandana on her head and another on her left shoulder. Her hair is pulled back into two black puffs.

"You're late," I gripe.

"I arrived on time by my calculations."

I squint at this kid already talking back to me. I refrain from kicking her teeth in—something my father used to do, whenever I tested his patience. Which I admit was often. That's both before and after he went mad, mind you.

"Just hurry up and collect the important parts of the Forest Centaurs."

"Shesh, fourteen huh? Looks like you cleaned up."

"Save the talking for your friends. Just get it done. I'll be waiting in the car."

"Sure thing, boss."

I squeeze into the front of the car. The seat is pushed all the way to the front, with a bunch of junk in the back. I see gears, rifle parts, and ancient malfunctioned robots, among other miscellaneous things. My nostrils are filled with the scent of cat pee. I hate cats. They're somehow uppity.

After forty long minutes of waiting for her to extract the right parts of the Forest Centaurs, we're finally on our way. One thing I'll say about the yellow clunk is that it drives pretty smooth. No sputtering or stuttering, albeit kind of slow compared to Runnymede's hovercycle.

"What level is this vehicle?"

"If you must know, it's C+ level. Though I managed to make some upgrades to it, so it performs like a B+."

"Whatever helps you sleep at night."

"Are you doubting my abilities?"

"Yes. That's exactly what I'm doing."

"Oh, yeah? Watch."

I watch as she pushes on the gas pedal and we zoom off at an increased speed. Then she presses a large red button, and we phase travel a 500 meters into the distance, slightly above average. Finally, we're outside the woods.

"Not bad. Might not be a completely useless piece of junk."

I get out of the car, a little dizzy, and the first thing I notice is the repulsive scent of burning elf flesh. Then I meet the most horrific sight I have ever seen. The entire base camp has been decimated. Remnants of fire remain. The first thing that comes to my mind is: *That dragon will pay ten times over.*

CHAPTER 20
CLASSIFICATION: BLACKSMITH

I wake up to the shrill screams of my fellow blacksmiths, the distinct smell of cooked elf flesh fills my lungs. There is a giant red lizard-like creature completely wreaking havoc. Shivers run down my spine; I'm not built for such an abysmal morning.

Protocol is to hold down the fort with the strikers we have here until the remaining ones come back. Hopefully, we can save what's left of base camp. I rush inside my tent to get my AADU, or Anti Aerial Defense Unit: an automatic missile launcher that, once it locks on to a target, will fire three homing missiles to follow that target until it explodes. I put the pieces together swiftly and rush out the tent to see the other surviving blacksmiths doing the same.

The scaled lizard-like creature is swinging around for another barrage of fire on the encampment. I aim, lock on, and pull the trigger. I will always recall the sound of the homing missiles launching. As the missiles from the other blacksmiths join mine, it's as if we completely light up the nights sky. The creature takes the entire barrage to the face, chest, and wings. It tumbles down to the ground. Just as it's about to crash, it gathers its bearings and swoops low, landing on its feet. Its long red tail slashes out, swiping away another bunch of tents, and a bunch of blacksmiths with it.

How is it still standing with those wounds? What is it?

I rush back into my tent and look for my parchment records. After skimming through the many myths and legends, I come across the mythological creature

known as a dragon. Apparently, the red dragon is considered to be B+-grade. All it says here is *timid unless provoked, weakness unknown.*

"Tash to Allison."

"G… go ahead."

"I think what I'm looking at is a dragon B+-grade. Compile all the myths and legends on red dragons. We need more information for when our top strikers arrive."

"Copy that."

The dragon sends forth another wave of fire, this time taking out the scavenger's quarters. The musk in the air becomes unbearable.

Suddenly, in a flash of gold light, there appears a tall dread-headed dark elf with a golden battle axe in hand, dressed in gold-and-black medium armor. This dark elf is followed by another dark elf, this time female, dressed in gold-and-black light armor, wielding two curved daggers reverse; she also has dreadlocks. Finally, there is a really short light elf dressed in gold-and-red, with a red cloak, wielding a short sword and a round buckle shield.

I watch as the three approach the dragon, dodging and ducking the sweeping attacks. The tall dark elf male slashes once; a blinding golden light emerges from his battle axe to slice off the dragon's right arm and wing. Meanwhile the dark elf female rushes in and twirls, unleashing a flurry of strikes and blows that cut off the left arm and wing of the dragon. The beast is about to blow another wave of fire when the short light elf unleashes his phenome: a large, green bear with odd tattoos. The green bear charges and grips the head of the dragon. It squeezes, then rips off the head.

With a loud thud, the beast collapses to the ground. Everyone surviving and conscious sends forth their cheers and gratitude to the mysterious strikers. It seems the navigators called for reinforcements, and HQ sent these three.

"Tash to Allison…are you seeing this? Who are they?"

"They're the fabled executioners, a trio of strikers from the Frontier Division. Said to be a deadly and useful trio."

Such power, grace, and elegance. I know better than to think they will mesh well with the chaotic, brutish, and cunning natures of Chaos, Tyrant, and Vex. But who am I? I am merely a blacksmith ranked… I check the rankings, and to my surprise,

I have jumped up to the top ten. It seems surviving and taking charge have their benefits. Would that they didn't come at such a high price.

I look around at the devastation caused by one simple B+-grade dragon and shudder to imagine what an S or even an A would accomplish. We are severely outmatched and out-strategized. After a while, the other strikers trickle in; to their dismay, the camp is in shambles. Must be a real downer after securing such a victory on the Forest Centaurs. Finally Vex arrives.

"Striker to blacksmith."

"Go ahead, Vex."

"Seeing a lot of fire, you ok?"

"I'm fine Vex. Things are going to change, but it will be fine."

CHAPTER 21
CLASSIFICATION: STRIKER

The fire is intense, and the damage is massive. The casualties match. On sight of the dragon, the majority of scavengers ran away, so we still have plenty of those. Meanwhile, the navigators stayed bunkered down in their office. We lost about one third of them. The majority of damage came to the strikers and the blacksmiths who tried to fight the dragon off. To the strikers that stayed, defending the encampment with their lives. To the blacksmiths who tried to take it down: they lost half their numbers for their efforts. Then there are these illustrious executioners. A trio of strikers known for taking down S-class flight beasts in the space between planets. From the Frontier and whatnot. I don't like em already.

I'd assist in putting out the fires, but I'd rather spend my time making sure the members of my troupe are in good order.

"Striker to navigator."

"Go ahead, Vex?"

"How are you holding up?"

"I'm a bit shaken. Putting out the fires now."

"Alright. Need you to get me the last known location of Runnymede."

"The last known location is his tent."

"Copy that."

I head over to his tent in what's left of the scavengers' quarters. It's charred and nothing but rags, and no sight of Runnymede.

After spending the whole night searching for him, I head back to my own tent to rest. Hunting is called off while we regroup. Apparently there will be one hundred strikers from the Frontier Division being transferred to the Eclectic Division.

This means the rankings will be adjusted… does that mean I will drop?

I go back to my tent to see everything is in perfect order, save for the golden dragonfly on my bed.

Could it be a present from Chaos?

I shake thoughts of Chaos from my head to analyze the dragonfly. I pick it up; its eyes are a ruby red. I have never seen a device such as this before. Perhaps it's a new weapon. Perhaps a gift from my blacksmith. I press the first button on the back, and nothing happens. Just as I'm about to press the second button on the back of the dragonfly I realize it's time for the breaking-of-fast. Leaving the dragonfly on the bed, I step outside to the scent of charred flesh and burned cotton.

"Striker to navigator. You know the drill. What's for breaking-of-fast and what's the oxygen level?"

"Oxygen levels are severely depleted in the surrounding area, and breakfast is… muck."

"Come again?"

"Muck muck. The food that the scavengers usually eat. The dragon took out our food replicators. Those were the first thing it aimed for."

I walk towards the feeding tent dismayed, not looking forward to this bowl of muck. I arrive to see there is a long line—something I haven't seen since we first started going from planet to planet. Must be about seventy people in line. Fortunately for me, I'm number three. I don't line up.

I head to the front of the line. As I enter the tent, I notice the server is different this time.

The regular guy must have perished during the attack.

The rumors of how efficiently and effectively the executioners dispatched of the dragon have spread across the camp, and even I'm impressed—albeit disappointed that I didn't get a chance to dispose of it myself.

"What do you think you're doing?"

"Getting me a bowl of that muck muck. What does it look like?"

I look at the server like he's daft, not that he could tell through my visor.

"That's not a problem. Head to the back of the line and line up like everyone else. Then you'll be served. We don't do cuts over here. Not anymore."

"You must have me mistaken for some scrub. I'm number three. I don't do… lines."

"Frankly, I couldn't care less what rank you are. But you must not have gotten the memo, because your electronic badge says rank nine. Back of the line, buddy!"

A bunch of the guys in front start chanting, "Back of the line! Back of the line!"

Up until now, I had never felt that thing the average person called embarrassment. I don't care what other people think of me. But I do know disrespect when I see it.

Me? Rank nine? Pathetic.

It's noon by the time I'm back at the front of the line. The server gives me a knowing grin and serves me a quarter of a bowl of muck muck.

"What is this?"

"Rations."

"Son of a bitch. Give me more."

"Nah, next in line!"

My mother once taught me never to mess with the people who handle your food. They can make your life a living hell. So, like a scolded child, I take my muck muck and head over to my favorite spot.

When I get there, I see a short guy wearing a red cloak and black-and-gold armor sitting in my very seat. This doesn't bode well for him. No one, and I mean no one, sits in my spot.

"Hey, half pint. You're in my spot."

"I've been called worse. It's not your spot if you're not sitting in it."

"I always sit there."

"I can see why. It's a lovely spot."

My jaw drops as he loudly passes gas. The scent creeps into my nostrils like a jackhammer. I'm forced to turn my sensors down.

I take my bowl of muck muck and throw it in the face of this new light elf. I feel the eyes of the entire room on me immediately. Their glare is fear-inducing. The light elf stands up, wipes off the muck muck, and smiles.

"What are you, daft?"

"Not as daft as you are." He stretches his arms and continues. "Do you know who I am?"

"Nope. Not sure I care, either," I respond.

"I'm the guy who saved your pitiful encampment's behind. Not to mention…" He brushes some muck muck from his chest to reveal his electronic badge: number one.

"What, am I supposed to be impressed?"

Not gonna lie, I'm a little impressed that this little shit managed to surpass Chaos. But Vex doesn't back down. Call me stubborn or stupid, but that's just who I am.

"What's your name…" he squints and leans forward. "Number nine."

Just hearing the rank stings more than any blade could.

I respond, "My name is Vex. What's it to you?"

"My name is Tiddly, and I like to know the names of the people I'm about to kill."

Now at this point, your average person would have shivers down their spines and quake in their boots. But the way my mind is set up, that's far from the case. I fear no elf, not Tiddly or anyone else.

Can't break me. I refuse.

I unleash my P90s on him, but he's as nimble as he looks. It's all a blur, but I think what happens is that he dodges my barrage of P90s, then shadow steps towards my back, and slamming his shield into the back of my head and breaking my helmet in the process. Just as I'm falling towards the ground, I see the most beautiful of maidens: a dark elf with long, flowing dreadlocks wearing gold-and-black armor, with eyes that could sing me to sleep. My eyes close.

Another concussion… or perhaps death this time?

I awake with a massive migraine. My first instinct, after squinting at the bright light shining down on me, is to puke. My body is strapped to a table; I'm surrounded by Allison, Tash, Chaos, Ivy, and even Tyrant.

I raise my neck only to have to lower it back down. I manage to say, "Who died?"

"You did, silly. At least twice. Luckily, they were able to bring you back to life," says Chaos.

"What? Ridiculous. How badly did I get beat?"

Tyrant chuckles. "It was a monumental ass-kicking. The half pint slammed you in the back of the head with his shield, then systematically pummeled you with it, making sure to break damn near every bone in your body. When they wrapped you up to move you to the healing center, you looked like a mummy!"

Ivy punches Tyrant on the shoulder. "You're supposed to be here for support, not to make things worse," she whispers.

"Not like I wanna be here," he mumbles. She punches him again.

Chaos caresses my shoulder. "How are you feeling?"

"Apart from my throbbing migraine, I'm ready to get back into action. Ninth rank is no place for me."

Tyrant laughs, cocking his head backwards. "You think you're still ranked nine after two weeks of being out cold? Think again. Chaos is ranked five, I'm ranked ten and you're ranked twenty-one."

"Two weeks... unacceptable. Where is Runnymede? We need to have a chat before we get going."

Allison steps forward with her head low. "Vex, Runnymede is... dead. He was found killed in the western forest. Looks like some monsters got to him."

"What was he doing in the western forest? I was nowhere near there. This doesn't make any sense."

"We don't know. Maybe he was drunk and wandered off."

Now one thing I know about Runnymede is he never put himself in any danger unless he had to. And some low-level monsters taking him out doesn't sit well with me. He isn't... wasn't the top scavenger for no reason. That hovercycle of his had some serious diverting power. And I damn well know for sure that he didn't get drunk and wander off like some scrub.

I simply nod as I know no one here has the answers I seek, and I change the subject.

"What about my battlesuit?"

Chaos, still caressing my shoulder, speaks. "Those wings of yours are absolutely trashed beyond repair, along with the rest of your suit. It's completely decimated." She pauses, then looks at Tash, who steps forward with a brand-new high-grade titanium reinforced S-class battlesuit. "We all pooled together and dipped heavily in your reserves to buy you a new one. The price wasn't as steep as you'd think. With the Frontier guys flooding the economy and helping the rebuild, prices have dropped momentarily."

I clench my fists through the bandages. "A pity suit... you guys got me a pity suit!"

Tyrant cackles. "That's why I did it."

Chaos taps me on the head. "Why must you be so stubborn? Such a ding bat. Wear the suit or go in naked, for all I care." She storms off.

Tyrant and Ivy say their goodbyes and leave, and I am left with my troupe. Plus the young girl, who had been sitting in the corner tinkering with some machine. I glance over and point to her.

"Why is she here?"

Allison beams a wide grin. "She's our new scavenger. I hope you two got along well."

"Couldn't do any better than forty-five?"

The kid storms over and puts both her hands at her hips. "If I wanted to, I could be number one! But half my time is focused on training to becoming a striker. The greatest striker to ever walk the planets."

I laugh so hard that I nearly tear the lasered stitches. I glance at the brown eyes of this dark elf. Somehow she reminds me of a bootleg version of myself at that age.

"Listen here, kid. It's extremely rare to move up a classification after being designated. Only a handful of people have ever done it."

"Yeah, like you. You can show me a thing or two. It's why I requested to be your scavenger."

"I don't have time to teach you."

"You'll make time in due time. Sansa has spoken!" And with that, Sansa storms off.

I roll to my side and contemplate my situation. Demoted many ranks and relegated to a pity suit. I glare at the suit with mild contempt.

At the very least, they could have gotten it in my colors. Primary black with secondary blue is so villain-like. But other than that, I suppose it is a miraculous piece of equipment. It even has a beautiful blue stealth cape.

But my stubbornness gets the best of me, and as I close my eyes, I tell myself I won't be wearing it.

CHAPTER 22
CLASSIFICATION: POLITICIAN

My vision is going, and there is nothing the doctors can do. Soon my liver and kidney will follow. What's the point of being rich and influential if good health doesn't follow? As I look out into the crowd of civilians, I find myself irritated.

Putrid commoners with their grubby hands always asking for more this and more that. Why can't they run through the maze like a good civilian.

You see, in life, people are separated by the class that they find themselves. And commoners are the bottom of the barrel. They're the scum that will lick the feces off the cement for a couple hundred credits. I know because I've tested the theory out. It's rather disheartening to see so many gathered here this evening. I feel their commoner germs migrating from one cesspool to another, only to land in my precious air space.

Nonetheless, I carry out my duties as the most reputable and fourth-highest-ranked politician in the Galactic Federacy. I suppose as a recently unfrozen judge, you wouldn't know much about the Galactic Federacy. The Galactic Federacy is a recent corporation created with the sole purpose of managing the finances of a planet's economy. Essentially, we manage the money, regulating the maximum amount of credits a planet can manifest. Prior to the Galactic Federacy, it was a free market and things flowed at a free pace.

Somewhere along all that freedom, the higher-ups of the IGF realized it's one thing to control the military forces, but it's a whole other ball game to control the

finances as well. And thus, Galactic Federacy was born. A not-so-secret subsection of the IGF. The ability to crash or lift the economy of an entire planet by inputting a few numbers made the position of Inquisitor quite alluring. I didn't realize it would result in countless hours staring at numbers and boring investigations into money laundering operations.

But I suppose I shouldn't bewail. I am rich, I am influential, and I do have plans to leverage my position here to find a more active position in the IGF. I just need to gain some more clout, both physical and telekinetically. The one thing the IGF is built on is power, and I am a frail man in his early forties. With energy levels as low as mine, I can barely lift a pebble. But soon that will all change.

I wait offstage for my name to be announced so I can give my fortieth speech. The commoners on Marda are so foolish, they don't notice I'm saying the same thing every time in different words. I suppose that is the beauty in being common. Ignorance is bliss, as they say.

"And finally, the moment you have all been waiting for. I give you Inquisitor Morange."

My anti-gravity boots push me forward as I enter the stage. The buzzing of the crowd erupts into full-on cheers and hurrahs. It feels as though most of the capital city is here. Approximately 85,000 people are gathered in the Capital Square: the largest number to date. Members of the common class traveled from all over the planet to hear me speak. I suppose this is to be expected; we all watched the battle feed to see the Eclectic Division practically decimated by various monsters. We all know that members of the Frontier Division have been called in to assist—more embarrassing than it sounds.

People are scared and thus have a fear-based mentality. This is good. It means they will go along with virtually anything I say, with little hassle or complaint. The recent disaster with the Eclectic Division is icing on the cake: better reason to lower the credit distribution number. I pull up my screen from my wrist chip and tap into the feed of the commoner mind chip. Once everyone can hear me, I speak.

"Greetings, citizens of Marda. It is my pleasure to stand before you as your inquisitor. It is my hope that in these trying times, all are functioning well and advancing towards prosperity." I pause for effect. "As many of you know, the fiscal numbers are adverse in comparison to previous quarters. Thus, we will have to see another depletion in the quarterly credit numbers in certain areas." I add some fancy words to confuse the dumber ones. "The areas that will see minor depletion are food distribution by ten percent, care for the elderly by fifteen percent, and public education by twenty-five percent. These cuts are to ensure that we can satisfy the costs of planetary defense and land defense. I'll be taking questions from the media representatives."

Immediately a bunch of virtual hands raise. As always, I have plants in the audience. I pick one of them.

"You there, in the red cloak. Speak your mind and let it be heard by many."

The man who walks up to the stage wears a red cloak with black light armor underneath. He is unusually dressed for a plant.

Perhaps my advisor changed the plant at the last minute. He better not have changed the question.

"Mr. Inquisitor! I have a question for you." He raises his hands in the air. "Is it true that you're funneling credits from much-needed sources into your pockets for devious reasons?"

Though taken aback by the accusation, I maintain my composure.

"Devious reasons? Such vague tendencies will get you nowhere, my son. We are funneling credits from one avenue to another, but it is far from secret, and far from devious. The fact of the matter is that we have a monster infestation problem."

"A monster infestation problem? You mean the monsters that live deep in the woods where no elf reside? The same monsters that are passive unless their habitat is intruded upon?"

"They may reside there now, but these beasts are growing increasingly aggressive. The attack on the Eclectic Division encampment is proof of that. Next will be the capital city itself."

"Very well said. As I expected from a poly-rat like yourself."

"No need for name calling. It seems you are out of questions. Please excuse yourself from the stage."

"I do have one more."

"Go on then."

"How does it feel to die at my hand?"

The plant pulls out two lava revolvers and fires both, aiming one at my chest and another at my forehead.

One would think these guys had done their homework on me, but it seems not. I never travel these lands without my defensive bots, V1 and V2. Two top-of-the-line defensive units. Even in bed, they sleep next to me. Elves can be bought out, persuaded, even coerced, but defensive units V1 and V2 will always be loyal. The V1 bot activates an impenetrable shield that dissipates the lava blasts as the V2 bot activates an anti-gravitational wave that rips the attacker apart.

Hmmm, would have liked him alive. I'll be sure to tune V2 down a bit.

The V2 bot searches in the crowd for similarly dressed culprits that match the ID chip of the assailant. It marks them before activating another anti-gravitational wave and eliminating them in similar fashion.

I suppose I should address the crowd on what just happened.

I'll spin this as anti-defense protestors, but I know full well that the Red Rogue Alliance has struck again. Although they failed miserably to kill me, they have succeeded with several other high-level politicians in the past. I suppose my bots are just that powerful.

You'd think forty-eight hours without sleep would draw on me, but the case is the opposite. I am fully energized and full-well eager for the meeting to come, though it seems I have one more vetting appointment. I head over to the mirror of my private villa and wait.

Like clockwork, the mirror becomes distorted to the point that it resembles static on ancient televisions. Finally, the image of a cyber elf appears. I've been in contact with him for quite some time now. He isn't wearing his usual dreary cloak. It seems like he is celebrating; he has a wine glass filled with sparkly blue liquid. His skin is a dark blue, with blue lights streaking down his arms and face in a special pattern. His eyes are a constantly glowing blue, which slightly unnerves me.

"Greetings, Morange. It's been some time. I trust you're well, after the incident?"

Word travels fast to the cyber realm, the realm of information. The cyber elves are essentially a mixture of the elven species and AI. The cyber realm is a separate dimension from ours and from the rift. Not much is known about it, especially compared to the monsters' rift. What I do know is that once an elf, usually dark, becomes a cyber elf, they reach untold power, intelligence, and knowledge. They are immortal beings forever destined to travel through the cybernetic fields of life. It's a goal I must obtain, for my clock is running short. The one major drawback is that they cannot return to this world, their home world.

"I am fine, thank you for asking. To what do I owe the pleasure of your company?"

"It seems there are some questions amongst my peers…. in regard to your competency."

"Have I not done everything in my power to make sure things are expedited?"

"Perhaps. However, there still are concerns."

"What will you have me do?"

"Ahh, straight to the point. That's what I like about you, Morange."

The image in the mirror is getting fuzzy. It seems his magic is running out. Once, we could talk for hours on end without any distortion.

"I certainly hope you'll keep that same energy when you hear the task. We need you to spearhead it personally."

"My ears are welcoming."

"We need you to snuff out this Red Rogue Alliance before we execute the next phase of our plan."

"They aren't a threat at all."

"Your dismissive attitude is exactly why they have grown bold. They are loud and a nuisance. Obtain their Crypto Pyramid, and eliminate them before we move on to the next stage."

"As you wish." I know better than to ask about this Crypto Pyramid; if it were something I could know, he would have told me. Thus I humble myself, knowing that this half-brother of mine holds the key to my improved health.

He throws a bottle of purple liquid into a vial with a skull stopper on his side of the mirror. It flows through into this realm. I manage to catch it.

"Drink this. It will begin the transformation into divinity, as well as buy you more time. We will also be sending an agent to assist you."

A smile creeps onto my face. "Thanks."

"Don't mention it." There is a pause, and then he speaks again. "You ought to open the door." With that, Strider disconnects.

I hover over to the door and open it to see my estranged wife, crouching with her head bent low. I look down at her with disgust. I barely attempt to hide the disdain in my voice. "What do you think you're doing?"

"I thought I heard you talking to someone in there."

"I was practicing my next speech, but that's none of your concern. Now is it? Why are you here, Charlotte?"

She stands up straight and adjusts her mask: a mask that she hasn't taken off in over five years. Some stupid vow of celibacy to the goddess of virtue. She needs to be more virtuous to these testes.

"I came to see if you'd like to drink tea, like we used to. It's a wonderful day."

"If I wanted to drink tea with you, I would have summoned you." I close the door halfway before speaking once more. "Don't show up here uninvited again."

CHAPTER 23
CLASSIFICATION: STRIKER

finish my double rehab for the day. My body has nearly healed back to a hundred percent. It's been three weeks since my altercation with number one, and I am looking forward to meeting him once again, this time in a full-on duel. I have developed several strategies to avoid embarrassment—but that will have to wait. I need to get in tip-top shape, as well as secure my funds and ranking.

I check my credits, and despite the cost of the suit, it still looks rather low. But more pressing is the fact that I've now dropped to rank thirty. Then there is Runnymede's mysterious death, which I will have to investigate. Could it have been retribution for the entertainer?

There is no choice; I'll wear the damn pity suit. Pressing the blue button on my pull-up screen makes the suit automatically assemble on my person. The cape shimmers with a blue gleam under the light, while the armor fits like a glove. It's made from flexible material and will always adapt to my size, which will be useful in the coming months as I bulk up.

I assess the suit's new gadgets and tricks, and I must say I am impressed. Although it lacks winged thrusters, the cape acts as a fast advanced camouflage, which should serve me better. There's also a wind wall to temporarily deflect all projectiles, amongst other modifications. I know exactly what I need to hunt to regain my reputation and jump up quite a few rankings. There is only one hunting spot that calls my name on this eve, and I'm going solo.

To the Queen Bee.

"Striker to navigator."

"Good to see you back in action, Vex. I marked a few A+ hunting grounds for you to take on. Test out the new suit and whatnot."

"Scratch that. We're going for the hive. It's time I pay that Queen Bee a visit."

"I'm not sure that's…"

"I don't recall asking you."

"Copy that."

Before I leave, I make sure to upgrade Tirade to rank five, giving her the fifth tail and wind barrage, a deadly attack that causes a focused windstorm. She also gains a special, secret move that has a one percent chance of activating.

As I'm climbing the giant tree in stealth mode, I gaze at the vast number of Bee Rexes moving in and out of the hive. They almost look peaceful, buzzing about their business. A part of me wonders why I bother to hunt these entities. If they can somehow evolve into thinking, speaking, breathing beings, who am I to cut their life short?

Then the rest of me takes back over and says who the hell cares about all that philosophical nonsense. It's time to rise up the rankings and regain my top-three position. Besides, what would I be if I wasn't a striker? This is what we do.

I reach the inside of the hive, taking shallow breaths. It seems the suit adjusts for air pressure and exhaustion. I walk past the bodies of two S-grade Bee Rexes. While I head over to what I can only assume is the Queen's lair, it becomes clear that another group of strikers is here. I'm not going back empty-handed, so the Queen Bee is coming with me, or those strikers are going in body bags. While passing by the larvae, I notice they seem rather sickly, as if they aren't getting the nutrients they need.

Upon entering a large honeycomb, I see a tall dark elf with dreadlocks surrounded by five S-grade Bee Rexes. He's bloody and beaten, breathing very heavily. There are another five Bee Rex carcasses on the floor, but it seems his energy has run low. I see the queen clapping heavily as she watches the fight.

The closer I get to the Queen Bee, the more I'm reminded how outmatched we really are. This visor shows me some of the stats navigators can see, and I almost shit myself. The only option is a stealth kill. Otherwise, we're both dead.

Beads of sweat drip down my forehead as I inch closer to the queen. She is too distracted to see my footprints in the honey as I slink up beside her throne. Once in optimal range, I aim both my P90s at her chest. My fingers caress the triggers of both pain and suffocation. While applying pressure, my aim is steady and my focus intense.

As I completely unload my P90s into her chest, their sound is like music to my ears. Her body is thrown backwards, pinned against her throne. I smile at the sight of yellow blood. My energy levels are depleted to nearly nothing as my P90s run out of ammo. Instantly, the queen staggers forward with a blade in her hand. I unleash Tirade, who immediately taunts. The taunt lasts a brief second, but it's enough time for me to switch to my wind scimitars.

She pounces on me in a blur. Fortunately, I had my back against the wall, thus limiting her angles for attack. I block the strike on my left with one scimitar and slice off her head with the other. I watch as the body drops to the floor, twitching rapidly, her eyes still glowing yellow. The last words she says will haunt me.

"My children…"

Exhausted, I turn to the tall dark elf. He's grimacing, using his gold halberd for leverage.

"You saved me from a dishonorable death. Now I am indebted to you."

I glance at his badge to see that he is the current number-three-ranked striker.

I say the first thing that comes to mind. "Train me to take your spot and kill the number-one executioner."

Now that I look back, it was a pretty stupid thing to say to the number-three executioner, but hey, I wasn't the brightest back then.

In a flash of blinding light, he appears directly in front of me, halberd aimed at my throat; I manage to block and aim my other scimitar at his throat.

"Not bad… not bad at all. I'll train you. But first, let's divvy the spoils."

"I agree. What did you have in mind?"

"Fifty-fifty, of course. But you can keep the queen. Should boost you up at least ten ranks."

"Sounds like a deal."

"The name's Axis."

The fact that he manages to stand with his wounds and energy depletion is shocking, but that light flash was downright impressive. Axis sticks his hand out, and I shake it.

"My name is Vex."

"Oh, you're the guy Tiddly messed up, huh? Explains the rivalry. Just know that Tiddly is far superior to my sister and me. So you have a long road ahead of you, young buck."

"I have a plan."

"You know what they say... elves plan and the Most High laughs."

As we walk out to the edge of the hive, I notice that the air space is empty. I glance down to see about thirty A+ grade Bee Rexes on the ground in a heap.

It seems killing the queen kills the hive. Interesting.

"Striker to Scavenger."

"Yeah, yeah. On my way," says Sansa.

"Make sure to bring an extra-large carrier."

"When you going to start training me?"

"I told you, I'm not gonna train you. I don't have all day, hurry up."

Once again, my scavenger is late. I'd quip about it, but frankly I'm too tired to comment. I watch as she hops out of the raggedy car and pulls out a shiny green mechanism. My curiosity precedes my good sense.

"What's that?"

"What do you care? It's scav business."

"If it affects my hunting, I need to know."

"It will help your hunting. It's an antimatter disorienter."

"A what?"

"Don't you strikers know anything about the new tech out there? I study the new tech like it's a religion. Then I make my own version of it."

"So your gear isn't IGF approved? Sounds troutlike."

"It's not troutlike. It's perfectly allowed as long as I upload my schematics every once and awhile."

"And do you?"

"No... not really."

She throws the anti-thingie in the air, and to my amazement, the carcasses of the A+ Bee Rexes turn really small and float into the eye of the machine. Needless to say, I choose to put the Queen Bee's body in the trunk.

We zoom off back to base camp. Unfortunately, my new scavenger feels the need to engage me in conversation. I already miss the quiet rides with Runnymede.

"So..."

"So... what?" I respond.

"About that training."

"You mean the training that I'm not gonna give you? What about it?"

"If one were to go about getting a transfer to striker class, how would they?"

I sigh. "I suppose one would need to rank in the top five of their current class and then write a letter to IGF headquarters stating that there was a false analysis of your abilities. You would need to call the one who judged you into question, and then they would give you a difficult task to complete. If you failed, you'd be stripped of your rank and all your credits and would start from the bottom of the scavenger list."

She shudders. "Woah... scavenger hell."

"Yup, scavenger hell. The bottom ten percent of the scavenger list: where life is so dishonorable that suicide is often considered a better alternative. Still up for the challenge?"

"Of course. It's my destiny."

"I don't believe in destiny."

"What do you believe in? If anything."

"I believe we create our own world with our own hand."

"Yeah… I like that. Ok, it's my own created destiny." She looks up at me with this innocent smile, almost like Runnymede's wide-brimmed goofy one.

"Why do you want to be a striker so bad anyways?"

"That's a secret."

"Cool."

"You really want to know?"

"Nope, not really. Already lost interest."

"Well, I'll tell you. I'm the youngest of a family of seven strikers. All my brothers and sisters are strikers of notable rank. While me… I was designated a scavenger. The lowest of the low. Ever since my designation, it's like my family doesn't even see that I exist. They think I'm nothing. I aim to show them I am something, but above all, I aim to show myself."

She speeds up and prepares to phase travel.

"I see."

"Yeah, so why did you want to become a striker? Why did you try all of a sudden?"

"Who told you that?"

"If one were to be honest… I hacked the records."

I look at this teenager who has just casually admitted an interplanetary offense to me. Somehow she reminds me of my deceased sister. She was always up to no good, and silly me was always trying to follow her.

"I see. Well, to answer your question, I didn't want my legacy to be that of the scavenger son of a madman who got two troupes killed. I don't believe in others creating my path for me, nor will I allow others to define me."

"Nice!" she bellows.

"Yeah, I suppose so."

CHAPTER 24
CLASSIFICATION: NAVIGATOR

chomp down on my third double-decker cheeseburger. The onions mixed with the pickles and the secret sauce make a delightful meal for sure. It's as if I'm having an orgasm in my mouth. I think to myself how grateful I am to be eating such glorious meals every day. Those two weeks of muck muck made me damn near sick.

I make eye contact with one of the new navis. A handsome light elf with muscles to boot. My type of guy. In fact, most of the navis from Frontier Division seem to be in pretty good shape. I'd be a bit self-conscious about my weight if I didn't know I was pulling it off. I mean, I'm chunky, but that's just more cushion for the pushing—or so they say. And I like to go with what they say on this one.

Just as I'm about to send off my final report to the Red Rogue Alliance, I hear the tile creak next to me.

After making sure everything is accurate and up to date, I swiftly click send. Why they want the updated list of all strikers is strange to me. But what harm can it do?

"Hey, Allison." The heavy breath of Jacob Beaver Mouth caresses my neck. I cringe as I turn around. My voice comes out in its most disparaging tone.

"Hi, Jacob. What brings you over to my cubicle?"

"Just uh, just, uh, wondering. What's going on with that rendezvous?"

"I thought I told you what's what."

"Yes, but I figured, since I've been watching your back and adding more time to your SOR, that things would have changed."

It's true that he's been covering my behind due to my frequent meetings with the pet accruement unit. And I have been noticing an influx in credits—not to mention the fact that business has been picking up. But the thought of another two-minute rendezvous with Jacob is enough to make me gag.

Then again, his mouth does wonders.

The thing about being a woman is that no matter how you look, there will always be a guy willing to sex you up. The higher your sexual market value, the more men will flock to your insides. It's quite the phenomenon. The problem lays in desire. However, I have a certain criterion I'm not willing to forgo. I have morals and standards, and thus I'm not going to whore myself out for some extra credits and someone to watch my back. I have a loofah for that.

"You can stop doing those things. I'm not going to sleep with you again. I already told you why."

"Why aren't you being reasonable? I'm a nice guy!"

His voice thunders throughout the room, causing several people to look up from their screens.

"Nice guy or not, just leave me alone. Ok?"

"You'll regret this, you... you... bizatch!"

I couldn't help but erupt into laugher. The nice guy turned into a fiery kitten real fast, but he couldn't even call me the word he really wanted to call me. Such poor execution. Still, I'm not surprised. It fits his track record. The problem with "nice guys" is that first, they are very boring; second, they're usually only nice because they want one thing; and finally, they put you on a pedestal while being complete pushovers. Women often want a guy who keeps them on their toes. Someone more dominant and purpose-driven—not someone who worships the ground they walk on.

Ugh, disgusting.

I return to my computer while I finish my extra-large diet Goomba berry soda. The sweet berry flavor washes down the pickles with ease; it's heavenly. The volute match window pops up at the bottom right of my screen. My opponent finally made his move, and it's a very peculiar move. The chat window also pops up. It's first time we've communicated since starting the match. Out of sheer curiosity, I open it.

"Hi, beautiful. Trouble at work?"

"How do you know I'm beautiful? And who says I have trouble at work?"

"Look at the top of your touch pad."

I glance up to see the green light blinking, indicating that the touch pad is on a one-way feed.

"Are you recording me?" I hiss.

"No, of course not... not unless you want to get naked for me."

Now, usually I'm supposed to report such shenanigans to my supervisor. But I'm somewhat impressed. It would take some serious know-how well beyond mine to hack into a navigator's touch pad. Even the RRA needs permission. Not to mention that his rugged frankness kind of gets me hot and heavy. A stark contrast from the feeble attempts of Beaver Mouth.

"Why don't you show me a little something? Then I might think about it."

He turns his feed on, showing his muscles but hiding his face. Then he starts dancing to some odd cybernetic music. The vibe is so good that I lose track of time, and my entertainment is interrupted by Vex.

"Striker to navigator."

"Um, go ahead, Vex?"

"What's wrong with you? I been calling you for two minutes now. Tell the blacksmith we're coming in with a heavy load. She better have some serious upgrades on the table."

"Copy that, Vex."

I return to the screen to see the feed is off and the chat is offline. It's my move.

After breakfast with Tash and Sansa the next day, I walk over to the navigators' quarters, where I see everyone gathered outside.

I go straight to my supervisor.

"What happened?"

"It seems Jacob died last night while on the touch pad. His mind was fried."

"Wow, I was just speaking to him! This is so sudden."

"Yeah, about that. Apparently, they're sending in an inquisitor to investigate all the mysterious deaths. I must ask: Did you have anything to do with this?"

"No, of course not. How can you even ask me such a thing?"

"It's just that you were one of the last people to speak to him, and he seemed rather aggravated."

"Yes. He was upset that I wouldn't sleep with him. Said he was a nice guy and whatnot."

"Yeah... he was a sweetheart." We both stare at the body being carried out.

As soon as I return to my desk, I pull up all the strange deaths that have occurred since our arrival on Marda. One thing the IGF doesn't like is unexplained deaths and missing persons. They'd rather hear a striker snapped and took out their scavenger than that a scavenger died with a hidden blade in his gut.

I raise an eyebrow at the staggering number of deaths within the camp. Only some of it can be explained as normal.

In the scavenger classification, there have been twenty-three murders due to scavenger-on-scavenger violence. Even Runnymede's death is sorted within that category. I wipe my brow. Under the navigator classification are two deaths. The first one I vaguely remember from when we arrived, something to do with eye sockets burning. Then there is Jacob's, another touch-pad-related death. Could these new and improved touch pads be hazardous to our health?

Next we have the mysterious blacksmith deaths, of which there are three. Supposedly a murder-suicide due to a love triangle. A rarity indeed.

Then the strikers: also three deaths, but I'm connected to all three. It's listed as high priority.

I wipe the sweat from my forehead and air out the armpits of my t-shirt. Suddenly I feel the heat of Marda's summer.

Finally, the highest priority murder is that of an entertainer called G-Sleezy: a famous cyber rapper known for his sleazy lyrics and sexual innuendoes.

I sit back in my chair to search for the name of the inquisitor. I hope they're sending someone incompetent; I can't afford a murder charge. My entire underground empire will crumble. My parents will perish without me subsidizing them, and my luscious self will get molested in prison. Worse yet, they'll give me the death penalty.

My breathing quickens rapidly to the point where I'm exhaling more than I am inhaling. I start hyperventilating.

CHAPTER 25
CLASSIFICATION: STRIKER

With the haul I recovered from the beehive, I manage to stock away a tidy sum. I've begun to suspect that someone is dipping into my credit account. I'm going to monitor it like a hawk, in addition to my training, and the follow-up on Runnymede's murder. Although my plate is full these days, I know it will pay off.

The south and east forests have been cleared of all monsters and are thus considered Cleansed. All that is left is the north and west. With half the map closed off for hunting comes a rush to get the best hunting grounds.

It's four in the morning here, and I am ready and prepped to go into battle. Decked out in my new battlesuit, I feel all but invincible. Though drowsy, I'm in good spirits. The training I have endured up to this point has borne fruit. I am faster, smarter, and above all stronger. I am one with the battlesuit and the suit is one with me.

"Striker to navigator."

"Go ahead, Vex."

"We're deep into the western forest. I'm not seeing any monsters. Are you sure about this location?"

"Vex. Have I ever let you down?"

"Not yet."

"There will be something. It's supposed to be S-grade but we don't have a profile on it yet."

"Copy that. My favorite."

While hovering towards the hot spot, I spot Axis coming out of the woods. He ambushes me, kicking me off my sky board. I roll to my feet and prepare to engage him in battle.

"Heh, it's not that kind of party, Vex. I came to assist on this hunt."

"I can handle an S-grade anything."

"Not this...my navigator estimates that the S-grade has been eaten by the S+-grade."

"S+-grade? You mean something akin to the Queen Bee?"

"Something worse."

"I see. Fifty-fifty?"

"Sure, why not? I won't be getting rank two any time soon." He takes in a deep breath of the warm air. "I love the scent of the forest in the morning. It's somehow thrill-inducing."

While traveling towards the hot spot, I admire his golden sky board. It's flashy and very expensive, something I can't afford these days. I'm saving up for a sixth tail for Tirade. Apparently, there is a huge jump in price once the upgrades reach six and above. They cost nearly as much as an S-grade part. But then again, the benefits far outweigh the price.

Tirade and I have come to some kind of understanding in my dreams. She is actually starting to make sense. So far, I have deciphered three messages: "They are watching you," "They fear what you're capable of," and "They won't stop until they have flooded the planets."

What these messages mean is a mystery to me. Who is this *they* she keeps talking about? But it's much better than the whines and barks that used to ruin my sleep. While I'm contemplating past dreams, I notice Axis is engaged in deep conversation with his sister.

I have yet to speak with her, but apparently, she was the one that prevented Tiddly from ending my life. I'll have to thank her the moment I am strong enough to stand in her presence. Right now, I'm too weak even to stand near her without stuttering. Would this be what the average person calls nervous? How a beauty like her could be single is a miracle in itself.

A rhythmic hissing suddenly comes from the forest directly in front of me. The sound causes my spine to vibrate. I find my body swaying back and forth with it.

Out slithers the most grotesque creature I've ever seen. It's a massive three-headed blue serpent with legs. Its scaly tail goes as far as the eye can see, while the inside of its mouth is a putrid purple—it's toxic. It has yellow eyes and reinforced scales. I find myself captivated by its movements as the beast closes in to feast on me. The middle head coils back and spews a glob of poison in my direction. I break the trance and dodge.

Axis does the same. On landing, I'm face to face with the left head of the serpent. It screams in my face; every muscle in my body weakens to the point where I buckle to my knees. Tirade pounces, hoping she will buy me enough time to gather my senses. She uses mass taunt, which is ineffective. The middle head swallows her whole, causing her to dissolve.

Axis charges with his halberd held high and uses his phenome, a level-eight light butterfly. The phenome shines bright light at the serpent, blinding it. The serpent thrashes around wildly, sweeping Axis in the process and slamming him into a nearby tree. The tree snaps in half as Axis' body cracks and crunches.

I unleash a barrage from my P90s at the left head, riddling its face with energy holes. The serpent's left head goes down with a loud thud. The serpent recoils back from to whence it came. That gives me time to breathe and check up on Axis.

Miraculously, he's standing with only a broken rib. That flashy golden armor is sturdier than it looks.

He transforms the halberd into a sunbeam cannon that he uses this time to set up. We're both on guard waiting for the creature to return, feeling its deadly glare surround us.

The serpent comes barreling out of the forest curled into a ball, shaking the ground as it rolls across it. I unleash my six bella rockets and three advanced flutter bombs, which zoom in on the beast. The direct hits halt its barrel roll towards us.

The sunbeam cannon goes off, completely obliterating the serpent's right head—but to our dismay, the left head has now regrown and seems angrier than ever. The beast withdraws once again into the darkness of the forest.

The pure silence makes goosebumps rise on my skin as I await another onslaught.

"We have to eliminate all the three heads at the same time. Otherwise, it will just keep regenerating," says Axis.

"I'll take the left; you take the right, and we meet in the middle."

I twirl my scimitars in my hands from habit, impatiently waiting the reemergence of my serpentine opponent. With the warm air of the forest filling my lungs, I wonder whether this creature will be the end of me. Somehow, I doubt it. It doesn't strike the same amount of fear as the Queen Bee. I am poised, I am improved, and I am—

The ground beneath me cracks open to the depths of hell itself. The three-headed serpent comes at us in a flood of poisonous fluid. Axis and I are both catapulted into the air. While falling, I manage to release my grappling spears from the wrists of my battlesuit. They launch towards the target, piercing the face of the beast. Axis eliminates the right head with a light imbued attack.

Energy shocks flow down the wires, causing the head to lash out. Just as the tail comes careening towards me, I flick my wrists, and the grappling hook pulls me in. Landing on the beast, I slice off its head with both my scimitars. I make a hasty, wind-imbued jump onto the middle head just as Axis cleaves off the middle head with his halberd. The head drops to the floor with a loud thud.

Watching the body struggle without its head strains me. It's almost sad. The beast tries its hardest to stay alive, despite facing a superior foe—similar to how any elf would try their best to survive. My inner debate alights once again on the moral value that killing these creatures has.

"What do you know about these creatures' abilities to talk?"

"Not much more than you. I do know that IGF HQ moved land and sea to keep the intelligence of these creatures quiet. I hear the Queen Bee and the Forest Centaurs were sent straight to the disintegrator instead of being analyzed. You got the credits you deserved, but it didn't contribute to the betterment of society, like usual."

"Unacceptable."

"Allison to Vex. Distress call coming from a location near you. It's Rank 2, Afiya. I've marked the spot."

Axis and I look at each and nod. We make our way to the location on our maps. It's been six months since the Frontier Division has arrived, and there have been very few distress calls, much less than usual. They really have been showing out on us. The fact that Afiya has called for help means it must be something deadlier than her. Something S+. Although that serpent was dangerous, I'd mark it as A+ at best. Nothing like the Queen Bee.

"Striker to navigator. What was the profile you compiled on that serpent anyways?"

"We gathered that it's essentially a Land Hydra. The more heads it has, the more dangerous. The one you fought had three heads, meaning it was A+"

"I thought I told you to send me to S-grade and above only?"

"Frankly, I don't think you're ready to take on the more dangerous S-class beasts. The Forest Centaur was an anomaly. After studying Centaur culture, we realized the female leader was not battle-tested. She was their leader due to her vast amount of wisdom. And the Queen Bee was a stealth kill with assistance. I can go on."

"I didn't ask for your damn opinion. If I can't trust you to stay out of your feelings, then I will find another navigator."

"I just don't want you to get hurt... like before. We almost lost you."

I turn off communications.

Axis smirks. "That's the problem with navigators. They think they know what's best, sitting in their comfortable chairs all day, analyzing profiles and numbers, when we're the ones taking the real risk."

"Exactly."

"It's fine. We will dispose of this threat, then you can give her a good verbal thrashing."

"Just might have to do that. I'm here to rise in the ranks. That can't be done if I don't challenge myself and take on S-grade monsters."

"You're preaching to the congregation, brother."

The buzzer goes off, and the ring around the territory appears.

"It seems we've arrived."

And arrived we have. An eerie green fire burns around us, and it smells like death. I see no corpses. The ground is scorched, burned to a crisp. Afiya is sprawled across the ground behind a tree. Her chest is bloody, and her arm seems broken. The worst of it is the wound on her left foot. It oozes green pus, and maggots are already eating from it. How a wound turned that bad that fast is a mystery to me. One thing is for sure: It will need to be amputated.

Axis rushes over to her while I secure the perimeter. I set up the remaining three flutter bombs and prepare to do battle. My energy levels have recharged to half, giving me some P90 rounds. I still have another flurry of bella rockets, and Tirade will be ready for deployment soon.

I hear rustling in the tree above and immediately aim my P90s up.

"Don't shoot."

The familiar voice of Chaos sings down from the tree.

"What are you doing up there?"

"What does it look like? Getting ready for battle. We can talk later. The battlefield is no place for conversation."

I mutter something meaningless under my breath and go back to patrolling the area. Just when I'm about to call in my scavenger, I see a dark fog coming my way. The fog is pure green and black energy, and it has eyes, a mouth, and an arm.

It speaks, and the smell of putrid decay fills the area even more. My visor says it is the sickly-sweet odor of more than four-hundred organic compounds. A melting pot of death.

"Greetings Elves. It seems you have trespassed one too many times."

Another one with sentience. Not a good sign.

Axis is the first one of us to speak. "This isn't your forest; these forests belong to the citizens of Marda. Look what you did to my sister!"

"She was in poor order, attacking me from behind as I was planting a tree—a tree that your kind destroyed. She will get what she deserves." The thing before us pauses before looking up to the blue moon of Marda.

"You elves will never understand. All these creatures wish for is peace. They need a home, and your planets are scarcely populated. Why fight for land you do not use?"

The air suddenly feels lighter as each one us contemplates that very question. Axis is the first to break the spell of logic. He fires off his sunbeam cannon, striking the beast of decay with a large beam of concentrated sun energy.

The creature continues to swirl translucently, absorbing the attack; a puff of green vapor releases into the air causing an even worse stench. I let loose a barrage of my P90s while Chaos expends several rounds of her sniper. The beast just floats there and releases more vapor.

"Are elves finished?"

"Won't be finished until you're dead," says Axis.

The anger in his voice is evident. He lunges forward with his golden halberd and slashes at the creature, but he is forced to retreat due to the intense toxic vapor.

"Return from whence you came and promise to put down your weapons forever. Then I will spare your lives."

"We don't need your pity, you mongrel. You're nothing but a talking beast—no sense to you." I say this full well knowing this not to be true. As far as I can tell, its intelligence is higher than even the average elf.

"Very well, if you insist."

The creature shrinks to about the average height of an elf and turns into something near indescribable. It wears a raggedy, black-hooded cloak, but its body is a sickly translucent green distorted by the skulls of souls attempting to escape it. The head of this monstrosity is reptilian, with a plethora of sharp green translucent teeth. It essentially looks like green jello, taken elven form. The five souls contained within it wail to be released. A blue horned skull pin holds its cloak together.

This beast can only come from one place: the shadow bridge between the rift and the cyber realm. It is said to contain creatures that defy logic and to be the home of all the damned souls of murderers, rapists, and child molesters.

A storm surrounds it. Decay whirls in a tornado made of toxic vapor. Each step this monstrosity takes towards us causes the forest life beneath its feet to die.

Axis finishes tending to Afiya. He is about to do what I am hesitating to do. Just as he stands up to face his maker, I grab his wrist.

"Not today, Axis. It's my turn to play hero. I will hold this thing off. You guys retreat."

"Are you sure?"

"I'll figure something out. I always do."

"Very well. I'm counting on you." With that, he picked up Afiya and made his retreat.

"Chaos, you too. Get out of here. It isn't safe."

Her voice echoes from a tree nearby. "You must be a fool if you think I'm retreating. Let's take this thing down."

I'm not sure I know what love is, or what it's supposed to feel like. But I do know that at that moment, I feel something for Chaos. Something special. Something damn near unbreakable.

"Elf creatures, what are your tags?"

"Tags? You mean names?"

"If names are what identify you, then yes."

"What a peculiar thing to ask me." Then I remember Tiddly. It must have something to do with some kind of honor code.

"My tag, as you call it, is Vex."

"No, it thunders. Your real tag."

"Vincent... is my tag."

"And the lady in the trees?"

She must be using some kind of de-location device; as her voice echoes once again, sounding like it could come from anywhere. "My given name is Lynne."

"Well, Lynne and Vincent. Fortunate on this eve, you are. I have been summoned to a rather important meeting. But know this. Things are brewing, and you're on the losing side. The rift is here, and the cyber realm is coming. Not to mention the bridge."

"What is your tag?" I ask.

"My tag is too long for your primitive elf brain. But you may call me Drexel the Unsung." He dissipates in a flash of green vapor.

CHAPTER 26
CLASSIFICATION: POLITICIAN

After drinking the purple liquid, I had a heart attack. The defensive bot V1 had to revive me. But in the aftermath, I feel better than ever. I can breathe without my breathing apparatus, and I can move things from a greater distance, although not by much. I await the arrival of the agent that is to accompany me on the raid of the Red Rogue Alliance. Unlike my half-brother, they are one minute late. I impatiently contemplate going by myself. After another minute of waiting, I step outside into the heat of the capital. With my two defensive units beside me, I am near invincible.

The stench of death gently caresses my upper lip. I turn around to see the creature invading my personal space. How V2 didn't kill him instantly, I don't know.

I recognize this being as something from the shadow bridge—a mythological place that is supposed to connect the rift and the cyber realm.

This confirms my suspicions that the cyber elves are working with the most devious and despicable of entities to achieve their lofty goal. Now there are four factions at play. The Arunkai, the cyber elves, the IGF/GF, and the pitiful Red Rogue Alliance. It's important for me to keep track of which group is at the top of the food chain so I know where to keep my allegiances. The IGF is currently doing a splendid job of keeping the Arunkai and their legions of monsters at bay. The monsters' numbers dwindle by the day. However, my main concern is the increase in monsters coming out the rift. It's unprecedented, and their power is like nothing we have seen before. The fact that we had to draw forces from the Frontier Division is evidence of that.

"In deep thought?"

"Nothing that concerns you. What are you?"

"Something that doesn't concern you. In time all will be revealed."

'Very well."

"I am here to bear witness to how you dispatch your enemies."

The creature reaches inside himself and pulls out a green vial with a skull stopper on it. I consume the bubbling liquid without hesitation. My eyes roll to the back of my head; my heart beats rapidly. I drop to my knees as an intense pain shoots through my heart. Clutching my chest, I leak blood from my eyes until suddenly the pain stops.

I rise to my feet and wipe the blood from my face. The creature has already started walking towards our destination. I sidle up beside it, only to wish I hadn't. The distinct scent of death follows this being everywhere it goes.

We arrive at a red-and-black villa in an upscale neighborhood. Four guards outside are dressed in black suits, carrying plasma revolvers. Star apple trees decorate the front lawn, a bunch of kids climbing them to pick fruit. One of the guards has an illegal B-grade forest tiger as a guard pet.

"Are you sure this is the place?"

'Are you doubting our resources or doubting your own nerves?"

"It's just, I expected something less sophisticated. A run-down basement apartment or such."

"That's what ails you elves. You constantly underestimate your opponents until they grow like a festering wound. This excursion will reveal many things to you. We hope you are ready to comprehend."

I lower my head slightly at the chastising that I have received. I will not tolerate it when I have achieved good health and power.

I'm doing this for my health. I must endure.

"I'm only here to observe how you handle yourself against a formidable opponent. I won't be assisting."

"Not like I'll need your assistance. My defensive units will take care of it."

I walk over with V1 and V2. In the evening's glow, I get close by hugging the front of the bushes. The kids climbing the tree are the first to notice me. I blitz over with V1 leading the way and engage shield protocol, covering myself and the three kids. V2 unleashes two plasma beams, piercing two of the guards in the heart. It instantly kills them.

The other two guards return fire only to see it absorbed by the shield.

I whisper to the children, "Don't be scared. Stay inside the shield, and everything will be alright."

One boy gives me the finger and dashes to the edge of the shield. I hold out three fingers on my left hand; with my other hand, I place two fingers to my temples. My telekinesis slows the child down, but he forces his way out of my limited range.

The child gets shot down by a lava bullet. The projectile impales his neck, creating a burning hole.

My V2 takes down the remaining two security guards. I walk over to the fallen child with my head held low. The other two children have tears streaming down their faces.

No time to grieve.

I'm making my way towards the entrance of the villa when out pop up two red rogues with sniper rifles. They shoot their weapons on my shield, causing it to ripple for the first time since getting the V1. I continue walking to the front door as V2 returns fire to the snipers. It catches one of them in the forehead, and she tumbles out the window. I reach the front of the villa, pull out No Mercy, my shotgun, and blast open the door. I am met with four red rogues, each wielding a different lava weapon.

Quicker than usual, I use No Mercy on the one closest to me. I blast open his face, spattering blood everywhere.

My V1 shield endures a barrage of bullets, plasma, and lava fire to the point where it is about to overload and explode. The second gear of the liquid kicks in, and I am filled with energy. My eyes roll to the back of my head as I hover above the ground. With the flick of my fingers, I pick up a large desk and send it flying across the room, crushing one of the rogues. In my other hand, I pull No Mercy's trigger and unleash havoc into the chest of the female currently rushing me with a great sword. Needless to say, she is blown back.

Rushing down the stairs is a behemoth of a rogue with a lava-imbued rocket launcher. He fires off the explosive, striking my shield with such force that it dissipates. I fire back with my shotgun but miss horribly. The behemoth pounces on me ,but V2 downs him with ease.

With shields down for the first time in a long time, I feel vulnerable. But I will not be deterred. My legacy will not be one of perishing to some filthy red rogue. Reaching the top floor, I kick open each door, ready to blast apart anyone who stands in my way. Each room is empty until I reach a barricaded door. I move the object on the other side of the door with my mind, sending it flinging across the room. I use V1 to push open the door, and it explodes into several hundred pieces. The door was mined.

"Come out now and your death will be swift."

"Come in and your death will be painful."

I hear fast typing—either calling for backup or sending out an important message.

I risk sending in my V2 as well. Another explosion, this time farther inside the room. My mind is made up. Either I die by a third mine, or this rogue is going to feel the weight of my wrath.

I push inside the room. My vision lands on a young female in a red t-shirt and shorts, typing furiously on the computer.

"Stop typing."

She places her hands up.

"Turn around... slowly."

"Inquisitor Morange. What a surprise. You came here yourself. Here I thought you would have sent your goons."

"Where is the Crypto Pyramid?"

"I'm afraid you won't find it. It's well on its way to achieving its lofty goal."

"Have it your way."

I am not a man to ask twice.

With a flick of my wrist, I snap her neck. My powers are growing, and I like it.

I am fully energized for the third day in a row. I tried several times to sleep, but it seems sleep did not want me. I spend the entire night searching for a new defensive and offensive unit. Part of me is sad; I have had the V1 and V2 unit for seven years now. As far as the child dying, I equate that to losing your favorite touch pad. You are upset for a while, but then you get over it.

Finally, I settle on the V0-4 Bot: a multipurpose offensive and defensive unit that shoots out high-powered lasers and has a 17-mega-hulk-shield rating, anti-gravity dispersion, and a few other bells and whistles. I am quite pleased. I order two from the official IGF site, making sure to get it verified with the deluxe seal.

There is static coming from my bedroom mirror. I turn around to see my half-brother on the screen drinking that same blue substance.

"Greetings, brother."

"Hail." I give a half bow to my older half-brother.

"We have found the location of the Crypto Pyramid. It seems the RRA has a hidden base deep in the north forest. It's supposedly their training facility. There are more than thirty armed combatants and twenty trainees. For this excursion, you'll need extra fire power."

"I am authorized to take several teams of strikers with me. I need to investigate a few murders in their encampment anyways. I can kill two birds with one stone."

"Good. That's what I like to hear. You will snuff out the RRA on your planet, find the Crypto Pyramid, and return it to me."

"As you wish." I inquire unhesitatingly, "Do you have any more of that power liquid?"

"Feeling weak?"

"On the contrary, I'm feeling stronger than before. Curiosity seems to have overwhelmed me."

He gives me a knowing grin and tosses another vial, this time red.

With newly swift reflexes, I catch it and down it instantly. This time it's bitter, but I manage to stay standing as the liquid works its magic. The pain subsides soon; the energy in my bones rattle tremendously, as though I am top form.

I wasn't always so frail. It was only five years ago that I was a vitality-filled striker for the Planetary Division. The division that houses the strikers tasked with defense and offense for the richest planets. It was a splendid position, but I couldn't advance any further due to my superiors disliking my demeanor.

"Cocky, arrogant, and rude," they liked to say. Wish I could rendezvous with them now, raise their bloody taxes and eat out of their pockets. Though I have learned to hide my cockiness, arrogance, and vile tongue behind a pleasant politician's demeanor. Appear the rose, forever divine and sweet, but be the thorns underneath.

A motto that I absolutely live by. As I put on my older battlesuit with its green cloak, I smirk. Green energy oozes out of my pores when I lift up all my furniture with a simple thought. I am nearly at full power, like my old days. At this rate I will surpass even my prime, something I have been looking forward to for quite some time. Aging and sickness are scary things. One day you're fine, and then the next you're not.

I pull up the list of available strikers for this mission and mark the ones whose abilities will be best-suited for a stealth attack on the RRA. I can't afford to remove more than thirty for my excursion, lest they let up on the monster hunting.

Controlling the rift is of utmost priority.

CHAPTER 27
CLASSIFICATION: STRIKER

I make my way to the blacksmiths' emergency healing quarters where Afiya is. I hear a commotion. When I enter the large tent marked "EY," a surgical table comes flying at me. I pull out my scimitar and slice the table in half. In the distance, I see Axis throwing a massive tantrum while the surrounding blacksmiths are rushing to the exit. I'm met with the foul stench of decay.

"What's wrong?"

"She's going to die."

"What do you mean? Her wounds weren't that bad."

"The decay from her foot is spreading rapidly, killing every living cell in her body."

"Have they tried amputating the foot?"

"They already tried that."

He removes the cloth covering her leg to reveal that the foot is missing, but the decay has transferred over to the stump. I clench my teeth to keep from gagging.

"We need to take this thing out at the source. Eliminate the beast ,and hopefully the decay will stop," I say.

"Allison to Vex."

"Now is not a good time."

"I know that, Vex, but the inquisitor has called your name for the stealth task force."

"Curses, I have to go." I look Axis directly in the eyes. "Do not return to that area without me. We will finish this together."

He is too caught up in his sister's potential demise to respond. Or so I think.

As I make my way to the north section of the encampment, my mind wonders as to what this inquisitor will look like. He was supposedly once an elite striker; now he is an inquisitor, one of the more controversial politicians. Forever relegated to poking into other people's business and taking money out of their pockets.

I release my sky board and join the lineup of fourteen other strikers with elite stealth equipment.

"Striker Vex, ranked thirteen. You are late."

"Yeah."

"What do you have to say for yourself?"

"Better late than never to have shown up."

"We will see about that."

And with that, we are off to the northeastern section. Among the strikers I recognize are Chaos, Tiddly, and a few other notable heavy hitters based solely on rank from the Frontier Division. I sidle up to Chaos and engage her in conversation.

"So... how have you been?"

"Been good. Climbing up the ranks. Soon I'll have a top four spot. What about you?"

She flashes her waist badge to show she is at rank five and counting. It's almost otherworldly, the pace at which she eliminates her targets.

"I've been fine. Just been thinking... a lot lately."

"About what?"

"About the sentience of these monsters, and why we bother to kill them."

"Oh, is that all?"

"What do you mean?"

"I made my peace with that a long time ago. Listen here, Vex. We are strikers. We strike fear into the hearts and minds of these beasts. Sentient or not, they are a threat to the people on the planet that we secure. This is our life."

"Yes, I made it that far... but then it hit me. Apart from the dragon, not one monster to date—after a decade of hunting these things since I was twelve—has ever stepped foot into a base camp. It's almost as if they respect our boundaries, but we don't respect theirs."

"What you're talking is mad talk. Only renegade strikers talk like that. I expected better of you. What are you gonna do? Become a tree hugger like your father? Start hunting down strikers until they kill you? I, for one, will not take part in such shenanigans."

That stings more than it should have.

"No, it's just I..."

"My suggestion is you leave the thinking to the egghead navigators. That's what they are best at. We got monsters to kill and ranks to level up."

"I suppose you're right."

"What are you gonna do without me to knock some sense into you from time to time?"

I smile behind my visor, though I still have that nagging feeling.

"I don't even want to think about it."

"When are you going to come to one of my parties?"

"When's your next one?"

"Tomorrow night, after all this task force stuff is over and done with. Can you believe it? We are being used like the Planetary Division. Taking out the Red Rogue Alliance. It's all kind of exciting."

"Yeah."

We arrive at the location to see the Red Rogue Alliance training a couple dozen members in combat. There are an estimated fifty well-armed members of their alliance, each equipped with a deadly lava weapon. That's the go-to underground contraband, known for its high offense capabilities, but very volatile. In the distance, the highest ranked visible member is training the rookies.

Chaos has already marked him with her sniper and is just waiting for the rest of us to get into position. The stealth squad, led by Tiddly, is to infiltrate the building and get eyes on some kind of pyramid.

Tiddly issues the go-ahead, and we all enter our various means of stealth. I watch as Tiddly sinks into the ground and moves through the soil like water. Quite the dangerous sneak attack.

As I maneuver past the training rookies, I see some really young faces. They remind me of when I was a youth entered into the IGF—raised by it, even. It's a pity they will perish simply for joining the wrong military group.

Such dangerous thinking.

I tap my head in an attempt to knock out thoughts of pity and mercy. These are things that can get your comrades killed—or worse, yourself. Tiddly emerges from the ground and dispatches with the guards watching the back door.

He really is fast. Much faster than me. I'll need to find a way to counteract that speed.

We rush into the back door to see the entire facility is empty. The top stairs are clear, first floor clear, the basement clear, and the kitchen clear. The gunfire has already started outside, havoc brought down by our direct engagement team and snipers. I look at Tiddly, who looks back with mild amusement.

"Why you smiling?"

"Why you breathing?"

"Because you held back. What's your point?"

"Glad you recognize. Keep your mouth shut around me, and there won't be a repeat."

Call it fate or divine intervention, but just when I'm about to try my hand at Tiddly once again, the timer on the oven goes off. Guess who happens to be standing right beside it? In the millisecond between the timer and the explosion, I have the wherewithal to activate the ring that Runnymede gave me. The shields go up just as the lava hits my body. I'm sent flying several meters into the distance, along with the charred bones of Tiddly.

The explosion takes down the entire house, killing all fifteen members of the stealth team except for me. I rise to my feet, dazed, in the middle of a fire fight between the strikers and the RRA. Surrounded by the backs of the RRA, I pull out my P90s and unleash pain and suffocation on the closest RRA member. My aim is slightly off, and I thank whoever is up there for the spray and pray. The bullets connect with my opponent, whistling. I turn my sights to another, then another, taking them down with ease. It's at this point that some of the RRA members notice me—but it's too late. Muscle memory has already taken over.

I extend Tirade and she wind walls their attacks, sending their projectiles back to them. A lone rogue is about to cut my head off when he's blasted away by a sniper rifle. I give the nod to Chaos somewhere out there, always watching my back.

Eventually, the slaughter is so complete that the RRA members drop their weapons and surrender. Only a handful are left, two of them just teenagers. They can't be more than Sansa's age. I'm about to accept their surrender when Inquisitor Morange pops up from the ground with his two V0-4 bots and shotguns the bloody teenagers in the face.

He then turns to the three adults and speaks. "Where is the Crypto Pyramid?"

"Go f…"

Boom. His shotgun goes off, and brain matter splatters all over my battlesuit. He turns to the next one.

"I'm not going to repeat myself."

"It… it's off-planet already. On its way to Venusian Oasis. Nothing you can…"

Boom. His shotgun goes off again.

He turns to the final RRA member with a wide grin.

"I suppose there isn't anything you can tell me that's worthwhile, huh?"

"I suppose not. Take my life and be done with it."

"As you wish."

Inquisitor Morange snaps his fingers and breaks the neck of the RRA member. And with that, I know where the next Traveler's Cube is going to take us. They say it's random, but that's another lie they tell us to keep us on edge. The cube somehow always follows the agenda of the IGF. And there seems to be no bigger agenda right now than acquiring this mysterious cube.

But I do know one thing. There will be a lot of monster hunting on the way.

I arrive at Chaos' party with a melancholy feeling. Between Tirade's rambling and my own contemplation, there isn't much room for quiet in my head. The last thing I need is music blasting. But here I am. Dressed in my party suit. My favorite colors: an all-white suit, with a blue plasma tie and blue earrings. I'm not wearing my helmet, as I could already hear Chaos in my ear about it.

Chaos approaches me, wearing a tight red dress that accentuates her womanly curves and long earrings in the shape of Cs. Her smile is sun-like. I feel my heartrate increase and a portion of my blood rush to my genitals.

Calm down.

She brushes my shoulder slightly.

"So, that's what you look like underneath your visor. Couldn't tell much through those bandages. Quite handsome. I like the scar across the eye—makes you look sophisticated and battle-tested. It gives you a constant brooding expression. Very sexy."

I nearly jump out of my suit and run from the tent. How can she just casually mention my hideous scar like that? It's a parting gift from my father. I struggle to maintain my composure and resort to the only thing I can think of.

"Umm, thanks. I think. Do you have anything to drink?"

"Oh my, where are my manners? Of course, we have plenty of options. We have Beetle Bum Rum, as well as Vixen's Glare wine, Spiral Sentience liqueur…. The list goes on. What takes your fancy?"

"I'll have some Beetle Bum Rum"

She gives me a frown. "Let's start you off with some Spiral Sentience liqueur. I don't want to be responsible for you not being able to get up." She winks.

Does she mean up? Or up? I'm not the best when it comes to flirting, but I do recall Runnymede telling me that a wink usually means sexual innuendo.

Accepting the Spiral Sentience, I give her my best smile. It feels almost plastic, and I hope it doesn't appear forced. My hand trembles a bit as I grasp the wine glass and put it to my lips.

Spiral Sentience, huh. Not bad. Not bad at all.

CHAPTER 28
CLASSIFICATION: BLACKSMITH

I'm not sure why I was invited to Chaos' party. I never get invited to such things. Apart from the blacksmith events, I have never seen people in such glorious outfits. Of course, all of this is odd to me, as the other classifications typically stick to themselves. Blacksmith with blacksmith, navigator with navigator, and so on and so forth. I do notice that a striker party has a lot more alcohol and something called meteor sugar. They put it on the nail of their thumb and then suck it off. It looks funny, but seems to be rather exhilarating. Sometimes couples will suck it off each other's thumbs, which seems rather sensual. My mind wanders to Roshane, and how pitifully he died. My glorious image of him perished with that fire. I suppose I am just to continue with thoughts of my work and not concern myself with men.

Vex approaches me already drunk and in a daze. I can tell he's drunk because he is rambling on about the dreams he's having of Tirade and the warnings or prophecies she's supposedly giving him. I'm no expert on the shadow self, but I do know quite a bit, so I try my best to bring understanding.

"The shadow self at level one represents all the aspects of yourself you do not find appealing. The parts of you that you wish you didn't have, and the parts you are embarrassed about. Overall, it is the source of your unconscious denial. Your phenome is a manifestation of that."

"I see. And what of the emotions that I feel as I progress in levels? The dreams? Am I simply going mad?"

"One question at a time. Typically, childhood trauma resides in the shadow because this manifestation of ourselves is a safe place to hide our negative emotions; thus it builds to the point where it explodes. This is what results in the madness that many elves experience, especially dark elves, because you guys typically have harsher upbringings and whatnot due to your place in society."

I can read the usually poised and nuanced Vex like an open book. He is seriously sad and concerned about these dreams, but more than anything, his past is coming to haunt him. I think he has been sad for quite some time, but he's never let anyone in the way he's letting me in now. I won't let this moment go to waste.

I take a sip of my Vixen's Glare wine, a smooth red with a tiny kick at the end. Quite the experience.

"I think you're simply clearing out the mental trash you've been holding on to. It's common as you progress. You'll notice Tirade seems brighter in color and more vibrant as she is upgraded. Trust the process."

He gives me a smile that's almost plastic, but genuine, nonetheless. It would seem he has smiled on such few occasions that he has almost forgotten how.

"Would that Runnymede were here in these times. He could help me with the childhood trauma."

"How so?"

"Well, he was there for all of my trauma. Maybe he could make sense of it all. He knew my father very well."

"You don't speak much about your father... I just remember hearing the stories."

"There isn't much to speak on. He was a brute even before he went mad, or perhaps he was always a bit touched. When he came back from the ash mountains, bloody and defeated without my mother and sister, I knew things would change. But I didn't think he'd turn into a psychopath. His phenome slowly took over his brain to the point where he was all shadow and no consciousness. You'd look in his eyes and see this vacant glare. There was no soul. One thing my father always said, both before his failure and after, was that I'd never amount to anything worthwhile."

Vex downed a glass of his liqueur.

"Isn't it kind of cliché for you to turn into an alcoholic?" I say this as I firmly hold his hand.

He gives me a less plastic smile this time; it seems much more natural.

We're joined by Tyrant and Ivy, who seem to be joined at the hip these days. One can often see them galivanting on missions together. It seems even Tyrant has a soft spot.

Tyrant crosses his arms; he, too, is piss drunk.

"What are you doing here, Vex? And Vex's blacksmith."

"We were invited," shoots back Vex.

"You sure? I don't recall inviting you."

"It's not your party. You dingbat."

"What?" Tyrant raises his voice.

He turns to Ivy and whispers, "It's not my party?"

Ivy lowers her head. "It seems Tyrant here has had one too many. We'll be going. Good to see you guys."

I hear her cursing him out underneath her breath.

The illustrious Inquisitor Morange suddenly enters the large party tent—with his defensive units. The floating red-and-silver V0-4 is a sight to behold. It emanates red energy, and the head of the unit scans for potential threats and tags them instantly. It can neutralize an entire room in a few seconds. The V0-4 bot is the way of the future and may one day take over the striker position, something that some strikers fear to no end. The bot is so expensive it makes a striker S+-class suit look like peanuts.

The fact that the inquisitor is here means the rumors are true. He came here with a hidden second purpose: to investigate the unusually high number of unsolved murders in camp. I for one am all for it. I have nothing to hide. Allison has been rather shaky lately though, talking about the investigation at every moment. I suppose that's why she is a navigator. Not built for the pressure.

In any case, I take another sip of my wine and watch as the inquisitor single-handedly ruins the party. People leave in droves, which is clearly what he wanted.

Just as Vex and I are about to take our leave, he hovers over to Vex and blocks the way.

"Who might this lovely lady be?"

"She is my blacksmith, Tash."

"May she excuse us for a few moments?"

I do a half bow. "Not a problem, Inquisitor, sir. Vex, I'll retire for the night. Suppose I'll see you tomorrow after the final hunt."

He nods.

CHAPTER 29
CLASSIFICATION: STRIKER

The inquisitor leads me to his improvised sleeping quarters, a large hover truck fully decked out with the latest equipment. Some of it off-market, and some is grey-market. I suppose when one is a politician, they can get away with such contraband out in the open. He has an antique mirror, which strikes me as odd, and he sits quietly, going over his notes. The defensive bots give me an eerie feeling. I keep my hand tucked over the ring on my finger in case I need to activate my shields. Not to mention that I need to cover the fact that I even have this ring to begin with.

After watching him analyze his notes for over twenty minutes, I grow impatient. But I suppose that is what he wants. Thus, I sit and wait. Not willing to give in to his tactics.

"So."

"So." I repeat.

"You've come a long way from being a mere scavenger."

"Yes, that is correct."

"Tell me, what are your ambitions? Where do you see yourself in five years?"

"Well... by then I should be number one."

He erupts into laughter. "Such a noble, yet square-peg-in-a-round-hole thought."

I feel my fists clenching.

"What's so funny?"

"With your skill and talents, you can accomplish much more. I was once like you. All I thought about was the rankings. But then I realized that the rankings are a minor part of what we do in the IGF/GF. Surely you have concluded that the Eclectic Division is essentially closed into a loop. You go from planet to planet, killing monsters that show up from a rift we can't close. You cleanse one planet only to have another pop up immediately. It's a never-ending sick joke, if you ask me."

"With all due respect, sir, I don't recall asking you. I'm developing my own philosophy at this moment and not taking on someone else's."

I expected this to vex him, but he erupts into another fit of laughter, to the point of coughing.

"Your profile says you have a rash personality and a rude demeanor, as well as disdain for other opinions. I must say, your navigator was spot on with that one."

He leans in close.

"But are your repressed tendencies truly manipulative, narcissistic, and borderline psychopathic?"

"She... said that about me?"

"It's right here."

He shows me the data screen with my profile and lo and behold, under "Repressed Tendencies and Potentially Threatening Traits," it says that I am manipulative, narcissistic, borderline psychopath, and above all difficult to handle.

For some reason the last word pisses me off the most.

Handle.

As if I am some kind of pet that needs to be controlled. But on to more pressing matters.

"Why are you telling me this, and what do you want from me?"

"Now you're asking the appropriate questions. Simply speaking, I am creating another task force that will one day enter the rift. Not any time soon, mind you. We're in the testing stages currently. But I do need elite strikers on my side in the meantime. Strikers that know how to carry out instructions to the letter and how to use their own judgment when necessary."

"I see. Well I that case, I decline."

"I thought you would. That's why I brought this."

He pulls out the golden dragonfly with red eyes. I had half-forgotten about it.

"What of it? It's just a gift someone left on my bed. Doesn't even do anything."

"I had a feeling you didn't access its full capabilities. You're too one-track-minded for your own good. Allow me to widen your perspective."

He presses the tail end and a small, holographic Runnymede pops up.

Vex, if you're watching this, it means I have died prior to my retirement—the moment in some scavengers' lives where they meet their death via poisoning. Kind of a raw deal, don't you think? After all those years of service, we're the one classification deemed too useless to live on after we've served our purpose. But I digress. Hah, bet you didn't know I knew that word. In any case, Vex. There is no easy way to say this. So, I'll just come out and say it." He dons his patented goofy smile.

"I'm your grandfather. But most importantly, Vex, I have seen you grow into a man that your mother would be proud of, your sister would be jealous of, and your father would despise. I do feel that your growth has slowed down a bit. I remember the long nights we used to train, just to get you into the entry-level striker exams. In any case, I suppose now it's down to the gritty stuff. I'm meeting with some ruffians from the RRA to sell off this Crypto Pyramid that I procured from some vagabond in the scavengers' quarters. I don't know if I'll leave the meeting alive, but I want you to know that the person behind it is the underground trafficker known as Sugar Cane. I am one of the few people who knows her true identity. Her real name is..."

Then it cuts off.

At that moment, I feel myself stifling a mix of emotions. The one thing that surfaces to the top is fury. Unadulterated fury. That I understand; sadness, I don't. So I choose fury.

"What... what happened?!" I raise my voice above the acceptable threshold, and the stupid bots give a warning while locking high-powered lasers onto my forehead. Shifting in my seat, I manage to calm down a little.

"It seems on its way to your tent, someone remotely hacked the dragonfly and managed to delete the final part of the message. A very impressive feat, considering these things are damn near impossible to hack, especially remotely."

"Now what?"

"Now we discuss the contraband you had in your tent. This is a recording device I'm holding in my possession. That is punishable by death. The situation is rather sticky, Vex." He says it with a sly grin.

"Says the one with contraband laying in plain sight. What are your terms?"

"Now, we're talking." He hands me the dragonfly.

"Join my task force, and I will assist in taking down this Sugar Cane. She is a notable figure in the underground community: someone known for trafficking a large number of middle-grade monsters for use as pets and exotic food. The rich and famous are known for indulging in this."

"That's despicable. It's one thing to eradicate them from our world to keep them in their own, but to take them out of their habitats and force them into servitude is disgusting. Not to mention eating them. That is horrendous. Why don't you tackle it by dealing with the buyers?"

"Because they are rich and famous. In this world, they are near untouchable. The rules do not apply. Unless people like you and me step up."

Now, I know I need to take what he says with a grain of salt, as he is also rich and famous. But at this point, I'm not in the best position to negotiate. What he is offering is what I want. Still, I can't help but feel that I'm sleeping in a den of snakes. I'll have to rest with one eye open until I can cut off their heads.

I didn't sleep much that night. I spent it consuming meteor sugar, a substance popular amongst strikers, known for heightening senses and numbing pain. It served me well, as I am high as a kite in the morning when Chaos enters my tent to check up on me. She's wearing her full battlesuit while I sit in boxers, with no shirt and no helmet. Her comments the previous night got to me: hiding my face due to my heritage and scar is cowardly. Not to mention the fact that I need to know my troupe inside out. Not for the pursuit of family, but so I know what they are up to. How can I trust these people with my life when I barely know them? What kind of a fool works with people for over a decade and doesn't even know their last names? Doesn't know their likes and dislikes? Doesn't know what makes them truly tick?

But above all, Allison is right about one thing. I can be manipulative. And that will have to be my strongest trait, at least until I can find out who killed my grandfather. A tear threatens to rise, but I stifle it.

No tears left to cry.

"Hey. I was surprised when you entered my tent last night. I thought you wanted something else besides the meteor sugar."

"Like what?"

"I just wanted to let you know that if you did, you wouldn't have gotten it. I'm already seeing someone."

"What are you talking about?"

"It's just that, maybe once we could have been something, but not now."

"Who?"

"Axis and I are a thing. We intertwined."

My heart drops to my stomach. I try to recollect my thoughts, but all I feel is a cold wave wash over me.

"I see."

"That's all you have to say, huh?"

"It's your body, right? You do what you want."

"That's your fucking problem. You act so tough and cool. Like nothing bothers you. But that's far from the truth. How can I be with someone like that? Not to mention you take too long to make a move. What are we, children? Some slow burn approach? Miss me with that."

"First of all..."

"Don't wanna hear it."

And with that Chaos storms off. Probably to the warm embrace of her new lover. I take out the vial of meteor sugar and place some on my palm, then lick a handful. Euphoria and ecstasy flood my being as my pain dies away. I'm left with a cool, calm, collected, ultimately numb feeling—although a bit giddy.

No wonder some of the strikers hunt with this.

As I stagger outside to the breaking-of-fast tent, I nearly forget to put on my battlesuit. Lucky for me, it's now a push of a button away. I press the button and my suit assembles piece by piece. I give a wide-brimmed smile for no reason.

My feet seem to be moving on their own as I join the line. In the distance my eye catches Axis and Chaos embracing each other. Their public display of affection sickens me, and I lose my appetite. But I don't worry; I have other things to distract myself with. I head over the blacksmiths' tent to see Tash reading an ancient scroll.

"Hey Tash, how are you on this glorious morning?"

"Umm… fine. Are you ok?"

"Never better."

"Ok, what brings you to my tent so early?"

"I should have enough credits for an upgrade for Tirade."

She nods.

"Well then, please go on ahead and upgrade her for me."

Tash raises an eyebrow and hands me two cards; it seems this time I have a choice for upgrades: to turn Tirade into a fire element or to keep her with wind. I decide to keep her wind and unlock the next skill. It's something called meteor dash: an ability that allows me to step rapidly on air, allowing me to take on unique angles and higher-level evasive maneuvers even when she lays dormant.

"That party was something. Never been to something like that before," she says.

"Same. Did you have fun?"

"I did, until the inquisitor came. Kind of a buzz kill."

I start touching a few of her things. "Wow, did you always have these shiny things laying around? So beautiful."

"Are you high off that meteor sugar? You're rather giddy."

"Maybe."

"Vex! You can't go hunting while high off that stuff. It's not healthy."

"Other strikers do it."

"If other strikers stirred up a giant pot of puke and jumped in it, would you do that, too?'

"I didn't come here for this; you're ruining my high."

I stagger towards the exit and make my way to the northern forest where the final hunt is commencing. That's the grand event at the end of a planet's hunt cycle where we clear the final area. There are no teams and no territories. Essentially, it's one big free for all. A great way to rise on the rankings. My goal is to explore the deepest end of the northern forest, where we met that decay beast. My newfound intuition is telling me that it was guarding something.

"Striker to navigator."

"I'm not giving you directional points. You're high and you'll just embarrass yourself. Or worse yet, get yourself killed."

"Fine. I'll navigate myself. Striker out."

Not like I need her, with her condescending tone and trivial assessment of my personality. I can do it myself.

I point in the direction of what I presume is north and head that way. I'll have to go off memory.

As I make my way to the northern section, the effects of the meteor sugar start to turn to poison. My heart is beating too quickly, while my entire body is sweaty. It becomes difficult to breathe. My head starts to burn as if someone were jamming my skull with a hot red poker. Now I see why you're supposed to do quick hunts if you're on this junk. It's a mistake that I won't be making again—my only hope is that I'll have the opportunity.

Hovering on my board, my mind drifts towards Allison and Tash. They truly seem to want what's best for me. How can I suspect one of them for even a minute to be this underground queen pin? I'll need to repair the bridges I've strained all these years. Maybe dedicate a day or two to breaking my fast with them. That would be appropriate.

Slowly but surely, I am developing my own philosophy on life, and it feels good. Slowly but surely, I am climbing out of the muck that is my depression. I'm quickly finding out that intoxicants are not the answer. I mean, one night on this junk and I'm already regretting it. It's time I admit that I have a problem with boundaries and building healthy relationships. I don't let anyone in and that's my biggest problem.

Damn, this upgrade has me on to some heavy stuff.

Upon this epiphany, I feel my unconscious cleansed in ways that it has never been cleansed before. I realize that the journey between one's shadow self and their waking mind is a journey that climbs to the heavens. It rivals any drug, any alcohol, maybe even sex.

Maybe.

Eventually my mind drifts to Chaos, and my heart drops once again. How foolish I have been. Downright cowardly. Slow burn? What a foolish notion. I was simply scared of rejection. Scared that she could never love the real me. But do I even know the real me? I have this tough, cool guy demeanor, but on the inside, I'm just an angry child. Angry at the world, angry at everyone in it.

Heavy stuff...

While I'm thinking deep, the smell of decay reaches my sensors in the northern forest. I inhale and am filled with the scent of death. Littered on the ground are the carcasses of my striker comrades. I see a multitude of ranks scattered on the ground, each defiled in ways unknown to me. Their battlesuits are shredded to pieces; the skin oozes off their bones like prime ribs. I activate my stealth and withdraw pain and suffocation.

The deeper into the forest I go, the stronger the scent, and the more bodies that pile up. It's almost as if every striker was summoned to this location, only to perish miserably. I hear the distinct beating of a heart.

Thump, thump, thump.

It fills my ears, and my own heartbeat begins moving in synch with it. As I approach the source, I am amazed to see a massive round red heart connected to the branches of a multitude of trees.

The voice that appears behind me strikes fear into my thoughts.

"The heart of nature, the source of the powers of the Arunkai on this planet. Go ahead, try and destroy it. It's what you elves do."

Just as I'm about to turn and unleash pain and suffocation on the decay beast, he jams his slimy hand into my chest towards my heart. I feel his fingers wrapping around my beating heart. He tugs on it gently and chuckles.

"Feels uncomfortable, doesn't it?"

I manage to nod.

"This is what you have brought the Arunkai too. They have stooped to your level, destroying the innocent and the feeble. This planet is no longer their home, and thus they have no desire to see any living thing come to fruition on it."

"Who do you work for? What is your agenda?"

"Good questions, to which you'll have no answers. Now scurry along, little dark elf, and try to save this planet from desolation. What will destroy the planet first? The Arunkai and their legions, or the Traveler's Cube, should you fail to wipe them off the planet?"

My eyes widen and my heart skips a beat.

"Oh, they didn't tell you that part did you? All these years of success I suppose they figured what is the point. If each Arunkai that has not entered to your servitude is not eradicated by the time the Traveler's Cube arrives, there is a wipe, and the planet becomes completely desolate. Devoid of life."

He lets out a loud laugh.

"Up until now, if you ask me, they have been playing pretty fair. But now they are desperate, and you know what that means. Desperate times lead to desperate tactics."

My mind focuses on the citizens of Marda, the children, the innocents, the ones that we have been fighting for all this time. It's not even about rank, it's about them.

"Release me, this instant."

"As you wish."

Drexel the Unsung removes his hand from my heart and drops me to the ground. Sharp pain rushes through my body, but other than that I feel fine. I bolt towards the capital, which should be southeast from where I am.

"Striker to navigator."

"What?"

"This isn't the time. Have you been watching my feed?"

"Yes, but as usual, no audio without your permission. What grabbed you?"

"Drexel the Unsung, the decay creature, said there is going to be an attack on the capital city."

"Vex, can we really trust one of them?"

"I believe it's from the shadow bridge, a place that has no hard ties to any other plane."

"So how can we believe what it says?"

I pause for a few minutes, thinking as hard as I can to find a way to get her to call in the Striker's Emergency Call, or SEC: a call that will allow the Eclectic Division permission into a city for vital protection causes. If I'm wrong about this, the entire division will certainly be dis-badged and sentenced to ten years' imprisonment. She is right not to take this call lightly.

"Have any of the other strikers encountered any A+ monsters so far?"

"Let me check."

"Hurry up."

"Obviously."

A few minutes pass by in silence as I'm left to my own thoughts.

What if I'm wrong? A promising career down the toilet. What if I'm right? A promising career launched to the stars. It's not about that, it's about the children and the elderly. It's about the average citizen of Marda, who hired our military force for one reason. They were scared and needed protection. It's for the honor of the IGF. This is bigger than me.

"Allison to Vex."

"Go."

"Well... it seems they have only encountered C and below monsters, but an unusually high number of them. Almost as if it's..."

We speak at the same time.

"A distraction."

"Are you going to make the call?"

"I have to speak with my supervisor, I don't have authorization."

"Do it. I'll be at the capital. ETA ten minutes."

"Copy."

As I rush towards the capital, I see the large tracks of an unidentifiable beast.

"Striker to navigator."

"I'm working on it. Vex, she's being stubborn like you are. Telling me I need to fill in the proper requisition forms."

"Put her on the line."

"This is Allison's supervisor. I'm sorry but there isn't enough evidence to issue an impromptu SEC. We need more…"

As the words leave her mouth, I first see the backs of over fifty A+- and-above-class monsters. I'm confident that there are a few Arunkai sprinkled in for good measure.

By the time one turns around, I manage to activate my stealth. Turning my comm unit to the lowest volume, I stay within eyeshot of the legion.

"Now do you believe me? Send in all the Eclectic strikers and ask for further assistance from the Frontier Division. We cannot under any circumstances let Marda fall," I whisper.

"And Vex. We have another problem."

"What now?"

"We estimate a Traveler's Cube destined for Venusian is due to arrive any hour now. It's imperative that we finish off the legion before the cube leaves."

"Otherwise all elf life will be wiped out?"

"Where did you hear this?"

"So it's true."

"Vex…"

"Don't want to hear any more cover-ups. From fake random Traveler's Cubes to monsters that have sentience. You navigators keep too many secrets from us strikers. We are more than just grunts on the frontline. You don't have the answers. Vex out."

Once again, I'm filled with a mix of emotions, and fury bubbles up to the top: the near-uncontrollable rage that my father passed down to me. I know I need to slow down this horde of monsters. Otherwise we stand little to no chance.

I speed up my sky board, zooming past the horde and then turning to face them. I'm met with a catastrophic sight: a horde of A+-, S-, and S+-grade monsters. I see the elven Arunkai wielding weapons and marching towards me. I aim my P90s in front of me to act as a distraction, and then I freeze. Call me a coward, call me a failure, or call it good timing, but right now I can't breathe. My stomach pains me and I drop to my knees, still in stealth mode. The horde passes me by unknowing and makes their way to the capital.

My vision is blurry, but I recall Temperance's training. The healing of the mind, body, and spirit are all paramount to one's wellbeing. I place my index and middle finger on my third eye and close my eyes. I envision myself purging the toxic meteor sugar from my body.

A few minutes later the healing energy swarms me and causes me to purge all that lays in my stomach. With my mind, body and spirit clear, I rush towards the capital with a new plan.

I managed to sneak past the legion and make it into the capital thirty minutes before the legion will arrive. What I'm about to do is a major breech of protocol, but I know that we can't hold off such a mass force at once. We're not a military force that deals with such upfront tactics. We specialize in guerrilla warfare.

Vex dialing to Inquisitor Morange.

"Vex to Inquisitor Morange."

"It's four in the morning; why are you calling me so early? Matter of fact, why are you calling me, period?"

"It's an emergency. The capital is under attack."

"How preposterous. I haven't heard an SEC call. Is this not what we pay the IGF for? Protection from these beasts? Protect and serve. I expected..."

Rhythmic beeping was coming from both my own and Inquisitor Morange's mind implants.

"There is your SEC call."

"Okay, so protocol is to what. Bunker down with our defensive units while you guys eradicate the problem."

"The protocol is bullshit. It doesn't take into consideration the S+-grade monsters. They were supposed to be mythical beasts, rumors of rumors from ancient pasts. I have a better plan."

"What is it?"

"Take all the food you can carry and the warmest clothing you can wear, and head to the encampment. There will be a Venusian-destined Traveler's Cube. You're going to have to depart using the cube and migrate to the Venusian Oasis for now."

"What about the Frontier Division? Can't they swoop in and reinforce you, or at least…"

"You should know better than anyone that the Frontier Division will hesitate to assist and thus kill an enormous amount of precious time. You have twenty minutes to evacuate the city."

"That's not enough time."

"I know. Instruct everyone with a defensive unit to leave it on open source and send the unit to the west wall. It will buy us all precious time. Vex out."

Within a few moments, I am met with a plethora of defensive units and the tail end of civilians rushing towards the exit. Some idiot civilians are poised to watch the battle live. Must-watch T.V., I suppose. Fortunately, each city is built with mass evacuations in mind, and as such, has many exits for each wall. With the SEC call enforced, the remaining strikers will be here soon. I just need to buy us some time.

"Striker to navigator. Do you see the open-source defensive units on your idle screen?"

"Yes."

"I need you to hack into the units and set their defensive perimeters to maximum joint venture."

"That will take some time."

"You have five minutes. If you can't do it in five, get me someone who can."

"I can do it… I will."

I scan the massive group in front of me in order to pinpoint a leader when my eyes lock onto a S+-grade elven creature. She is elegant and graceful, like the previous S+-grade Arunkai. She has green skin, with long flowing green hair with pink flowers in it, and two wooden horns pointing out. She wears a blouse and knee-high wooden boots; her arms and torso are made of wood, as well.

I pull up her profile screen from the mythological creature files the blacksmiths updated. It reads:

Dryad: A mythological nature spirit that resides deep inside the woods, each Dryad is connected to a specific tree and only leaves the confines of the forest to wreak unknown havoc on those that disrespect nature. Dryads can be an elf's best friend or their worst enemy, as they have the power to seduce a male and make him turn on his allies. Additionally, they have the power of nature at their fingertips and are known to use it. Weakness: If a Dryad is away from their home tree for too long, they will perish, or if a Dryad loses their "heart," they will perish.

Beside the Dryad are two giant Earth Spirits, creatures made of stone imbued with the spirit of nature. Both carry large stone pillars that could be used as weapons or as rams.

I hear footsteps behind me. I turn to see Chaos, Tyrant, Axis, and Ivy among a group of about fifty-five strikers.

Just as I'm about to address the group, maybe give them a rousing speech, the first projectile is fired. A large boulder is thrown against the shields and deflected back. I breathe a sigh of relief that the shields came up in time. Otherwise, we would have been wiped out before the citizens got away to safety. Three giant Forest Elephants charge towards the walls, tumbling them down with ease. The shields hold up, managing to disintegrate the beasts. We unleash a barrage of fire on their legion and take down many. This sequence continues on for ten minutes: our shields reflecting back any projectiles coming our way while we tear apart their army. It comes to the point where we feel as if we can actually win against such odds. Then comes the Forest Wurm. A massive wormlike creature with a mouth full of wooden teeth emerges from the ground underneath us, dislodging us from position.

The Wurm rises from the ground, swallowing several members of my group. It wriggles in the air before slamming its body against the ground, killing several more. I dash forward, getting into close range, and shoot it in the eyes, causing it to flail. Tyrant flings his grenades into the mouth of the beast, downing it with ease. By the time the wurm is down, the shields are burned out. We watch in horror as the legion, led by the Dryad and her Earth Spirits, storm the capital city.

"Striker to navigator."

"Go... ahead."

"ETA until the Traveler's Cube?"

"Estimated time is ten minutes. If you're going to retreat now is the time."

The civilians are only about halfway through their evacuation. We have one trick left. I throw my flutter bombs in the air and put them on standby; every striker with a mine or flutter bomb does the same. There is a certain quote for times like this, but I never bothered to memorize it.

Chaos sidles up beside me with her head lowered.

"Desperate times call for desperate actions. A striker must live so that ten may survive. This is our oath."

"Allison... call for the retreat. Eclectic Division... is retreating from planet Marda," I say.

CHAPTER 30
CLASSIFICATION: POLITICIAN

While I wait for the Traveler's Cube to arrive, I gaze out the one-sided window. The masses are panicking. Some are fighting for a better position, knowing that the cube will only stay for a limited time while it loads. I am surrounded by my "peers," who are nothing more than sniveling puppets for the IGF. Do this, hop there, buy that. They huddle in my automatic AMT truck like flies. I hold them in higher contempt than the strikers, who have failed at their one task.

I suppose a part of me should be grateful that I had the inside scoop, allowing me to get ahead of the commoners. With the advance notice, I simply prepped my truck for the trials to come, used the chaos to eliminate a couple up-and-coming politicians in the rankings, and curried favor with some influential members of the GF by granting them safe passage in my truck.

I am used to moving from planet to planet, so losing Marda is of little consequence. The mass deaths sure to occur are meaningless in the grand scheme of things. What matters is that we head to Venusian and retrieve that Crypto Pyramid. If the cyber elves want it, then it must be powerful—and vital to the next phase of our plan. This means I need to take a more involved approach in the actions of the strikers.

It's as they say. If you want something done right you must do it yourself.

It's been a while since I've slept, and still I am as quick witted as ever. It seems the special liquid has added benefits for my sleep schedule. I look forward to another

dosage the moment I gain some privacy from these wretched politicians.

All they do is gabble on about how unfair this is and how the Eclectic Division are failures and should be eliminated immediately. But I know better. For ten years, one entire decade, we have relied on the same strategies to defeat the monsters from the rift. It was only a matter of time until the monsters adapted. Those influential enough to know are aware that the Arunkai have a council of six overlords. Six all-powerful entities with the intelligence, cunning, and wisdom ratings of the S+-class. If this is true, a collective force to be feared. But it begs the question: Why take so long to adapt? Why take so long to show that you have S+ creatures who can cross the rift? Or perhaps the rift has grown larger and it is only now that these entities can cross.

I speculate and ponder, but at the end of the day, I do not know.

One thing I do know is that I will not stay in the dark much longer. Once I acquire that Crypto Pyramid, I will have the leverage to make my ultimate ask. I will be turned into a cyber elf and gain immortality.

My mind shifts gears to my estranged wife and child. I supposed it would have been courteous to warn them. They lived deep in the capital, in an area troublesome to evacuate.

Good riddance to them both.

"Inquisitor Morange."

"Yes?"

"Might I say, these are lovely multipurpose units, but I thought we were under instructions from you to leave our bots in the capital?"

"Yes... our defensive units. As you said, these are multipurpose units. They also carry my breathing apparatus."

"I'm sure you could have used a servant for that. In fact, I notice you have a certain liking for the robots. Not as single living elf in sight."

"What's your point?"

"Just peculiar, that's all. Don't you think?"

"What I do think is that you're swimming in murky waters without a safety vest."

"How so? I mean I am the mayor."

"The mayor of what? Your city is now moot. You have no authority anywhere else. You're nothing but a buffoon who licked and sucked his way to his position."

"Oh my, well I never!"

The multipurpose bots turn their lasers on his forehead for sound violation. After the warning, we all watch as the former mayor pisses his pants.

"Matter of fact, get out of my truck. You've defiled my facility enough."

"But... wait. I am the bloody mayor."

"Look at me. I don't bloody care if you were the chief of operations of the IGF. You are nothing now. I want you out of my truck."

The plump man that was my superior for my time in Marda sneered.

"I see where this is going. You think you have power now that we're stock-piled in your damn truck. I can walk like the rest of the commoners. My feet work. That's fine. A pox on you and your selfish ways, Morange. A pox on you and the inner workings of your scheming mind!"

He makes an egregious mistake by raising his voice a second time. Just like me, my bots have little patience for those who do not follow instructions. I have placed them on the highest sensitivity level.

The lasers go off, sending two rays of concentrated light into the middle of his skull, and dropping him instantly.

"Anyone else have a problem the way I conduct myself in my own damn truck? You're free to leave and be subject to the angry and scared masses."

One of the more sniveling politicians raises his cup of custard.

"Might I say, this is wonderful custard. The texture is absolutely delightful."

CHAPTER 31
CLASSIFICATION: STRIKER

When this is all said and done, what will we be remembered for? As the group that lost Marda, or the group that prevented its people from complete and utter annihilation? My stomach grumbles as I look at the line for the rations. The cooks are at their best right now preparing ingredients, but the food replicators cannot keep up. It's unfortunate that the food replicators cannot prepare full meals themselves.

I leave the line for the good stuff and join the average-length line for the muck muck. Better muck muck than nothing. At this point, the food replicators will shut down for the day before I'm fed.

All the tents are secure and marked safe for travel except for the feeding tent, which is usually the last one to go. I head over to my usual spot, where I see Axis waiting for me.

"Vex," he nods.

"Axis. How is your sister?"

A bittersweet expression crosses his face; his lips curl in disgust.

"I have used all my influence and most of my credits to secure a Frontier Division medical ship. It should arrive before the cube does. They will treat her with advanced techniques, but she will need me by her side."

"I understand. What about... Chaos?"

"Chaos? She discarded me. Said I lower my guard before I parry and she couldn't be with anyone who does that. If you ask me, I think she was just looking for a reason to get rid of me."

"I see... she is quite unpredictable."

"Unpredictable is an understatement. I guess they don't call her Chaos for no reason. I'd watch out for her if I were you. She's a real heartbreaker."

"I'll keep that in mind," I say as my eyes drift to Chaos approaching our very table. Her physical features as always shine through her battlesuit.

"Hey boys." She places one hand on both of our shoulders.

"Hey Chaos."

"Hello," says Axis.

"What might you two be talking about? I hope it wasn't little old me."

She raises her visor momentarily to give the two of us a raised eyebrow.

"N... no. Not at all," I stutter.

"We..."

"We were talking about," I mumble.

"The cube!"

"Oh splendid, I love a good mystery story."

Axis leans in and begins to tell us everything he knows about the cube.

"Well, in the Frontier Division, we get a full-sized view. Not just one side like you guys. At the very top of the cube is a giant C carved in blue energy. We don't know what that C stands for, but it does imply that the cube was created by someone. I mean, eighty-five percent of the time it assists the Eclectic Division by instantly transferring the entire division to the next planet infested by the rift. The rest of the time, it takes five percent of the population and turns them into cyber elves. Or so we presume."

"Fascinating. Speaking of the Frontier Division, why didn't they send help? We could have saved twice as many civilians. My navigator said that when their supervisor finally got someone to connect, they laughed her off the channel," asks Chaos.

"I shouldn't be telling you this, but the Frontier Division is highly dedicated to the cause in space. But as far as the cause on the planets, as far as they are concerned, that's your job. But the biggest reason was that Marda couldn't afford the evacuation clause, nor could they afford the additional assistance package. Thus, no help was sent. No credits, no support. Simple as that."

"So what you're telling me is that we shouldn't expect any assistance on Venusian either? It's going to be our job to get the civilians to the Oasis safely."

"Pretty much. Unless IGF HQ intervenes and gives direct orders, there won't be any support. And knowing HQ, they will look at this crisis as a reason to raise prices. This will all be seen as a test of how competent you are in an emergency situation. Don't you see? We're just numbers to them."

I slam my fist against the table, cracking it.

"Anyways, I must tend to my sister. My ship will be here any minute. Until we meet again. Chaos, Vex... take care of yourselves."

And with that, Axis made his way to the emergency healing quarters.

"So, all we have to do is figure out a way to feed about forty thousand civilians when we're used to taking care of only a hundred troops. Sounds like fun."

I'm about to respond when the alarm for the cube goes off. The siren blares, and the cube drops in the estimated area just in front of the feeding quarters. We blitz in an orderly fashion in an attempt to make good use of every second.

First the strikers, then the blacksmiths, then the navigators, followed by the scavengers and the civilians.

I enter the cube and watch my particles be torn apart. The sensation is like a needle being under my skin: a sharp yet bearable pain. Then as my body fades away, my particles become an itch that I am unable to scratch. A voice calls out to me.

"Come to us... Vexation."

"Who are you?"

"We are the all-knowing, the all-seeing, the all-hearing, the all-hating, the all-taking, and the all-loving."

"I don't know any all. What do you want with me?"

There is only silence as my body is put together, and I emerge into the dark moon of the Venusian tundra and mountains. Slowly my bodysuit adjusts to the blistering cold. It's as I anticipated: we were dropped off on the tundra side of the Oasis instead of the desert. Either way, we must travel through a large portion of the planet to meet in the middle.

Venusian is expected to be one of the most challenging planets to cleanse due to the added effects of the climate. The blistering cold side and the scorching hot dry side are both filled with monsters of unparalleled grades. It's also a planet very rich in nutrients, minerals, and credits, where the light elves and dark elves are in constant competition. Regardless, the dwarves reign supreme with their advanced technology. They are robust and stocky creatures, with a love for ale and mechanical devices. All advanced technology is initially created by dwarves and then recreated by elven blacksmiths.

The fact that the cube took us to this planet when we are in search of the Crypto Pyramid means this isn't some random assignment. It's not even an act of God. There are overarching themes here, and the main one is that we strikers are constantly being lied to, or at the very least having vital information hidden from us. I will build a stronger relationship with my troupe. And I will learn more about what they know.

I am more than just a brute to be used for killing.

Then there are the voices that called out to me. Could this be the first step to becoming a cyber elf? It's fate worse than death: to be a mere code, stuck forever in the cyber realm.

My fellow strikers and I secure the perimeter. Where we landed isn't a good spot for such a large number of people to set up base camp, so we have to make preparations to move to higher ground, somewhere relatively safe. Now that the scavengers have arrived, we head out with them to find a suitable spot.

I hop in Sansa's raggedy car; she's blasting some track that has a lot of vulgar words. Something a teenager shouldn't be listening to.

"You mind turning that down?" I grumble.

"Yes, in fact I do. This my jam!"

I turn the dial down from max to halfway.

"We're in unknown territory with a crap ton of civilians. We need to be cautious and make sure we secure a base camp. Eliminate anything that might stir. But that also means the element of surprise is our best friend. I'd rather not announce our presence. You got it?"

"Yeah, yeah." She waves me off.

I grit my teeth, forced to hang on as we zoom past the rest of the scavengers boldly navigating the snowy terrain. I look outside to see we're surrounded by hilltops and mountains. This crisp breeze is damn near intoxicating, as is the sight: an abundance of snow and what the scanner says are called pine trees. Their scent is invigorating, which will make this a great place to hunt. As far as I can tell, the planet has two suns that shine down warmth simultaneously, one blue and one red. Quite the interesting feature. We can certainly redeem our names here.

So fresh, so clean.

"Striker to navigator."

"Yeah, Vex?"

"How many did we lose to the cyber realm?"

"Vex...it isn't good. We lost about fifteen percent of the civilians to the cube, while another five percent have gone mad. We have about thirty-two thousand left—still a hefty number to feed and house."

"Have we gotten in contact with the Planetary Division of the Venusian Oasis?"

"Yes, we have open communication with them."

"That's good. So what's the word?"

"Due to harsh conditions, they can't send any assistance until winter is over, when the ice defrosts, and the snow gives away. There are too many hidden threats to send out any rescue teams. But they wish us the best of luck and expect us to arrive by the time they can open the Oasis walls."

"Best of luck? Cowards."

"By the way, Vex."

"More bad news?"

"Well, the Frontier Division has met some resistance on their way to Venusian."

"What do you mean? Spit it out."

"Well, they have encountered S and S+-grade galactic monsters and are getting damn near wiped out. A medical ship was blown apart on its way to the mothership. Just thought you should know... Axis and Afiya, along with the pilot, are dead."

"Blast!" I slam my fist against the deck, then change it to something a bit more my flavor.

"Grow Rough" by Dexta Daps starts playing. A dancehall tune.

I start singing along to distract myself from the fear that I feel. Although Axis and I weren't two peas in a pod, while he trained me, I felt as though we shared a bond. More than anything else, we can't afford to lose capable strikers. Not at a critical time like this, when the monsters are adapting.

Sansa starts bumping along to the track as well in a moment of great synchronization. We continue driving, taking our minds off the loss and nearly catching up to the lead striker and scavenger pair. One thing I will say about Sansa's junk heap: It's fast when she pushes that pedal.

I look ahead to the hilltop as we scan the area, and I see something with pitch black eyes approaching. It's a white gorilla with four arms and fists the size of my head, and it flips the hover car in front of us. The car goes flying, doing three flips before crashing on the ground. The beast starts charging in our direction.

"Striker to navigator. What am I looking at?" I say as I calmly step out of the vehicle.

"You're looking at a Frost Yeti. Looks to be a B+"

A large gorilla- type monster commonly discovered defending sources of underground water found in caves and caverns. Frost Yetis have been seen of the grade A+ variety and below. The higher the rank, the tougher their skin. These beasts have a tremendous roar, which can cause horrific avalanches. Weakness – Has poor eyesight

The Frost Yeti leaps into the air and lands on another vehicle with a crunch. It rips the vehicle in two like paper. The striker fires off rounds of his rifle to no avail. I rush in with my P90s blitzing at the creature's face. The energetic damage is severe to the point where the beast is forced to back flip away. It rolls up a large ball of snow and launches it at me. I dash to the left, then use my two grappling spears to reel myself in closer to the beast. A massive surge of energy flows through the spears, now stuck inside the creature's neck. It drops to its knees.

Two giant laser beams blast from the front light of Sansa's car, drilling two large holes in the creature.

I walk over to the body to investigate. It's burnt to a crisp.

Those lasers really did a number on it.

I find myself speaking the last rites. Am I getting more religious or am I starting to empathize with these creatures? Perhaps it's both.

We drive into the cave that the Frost Yeti was guarding to find the end of a stream of clean, clear water. The cave is a massive series of empty tunnels, each leading to a different path. It will take some time to clear out the Frost Yetis that call this their home. But it's insulated, and thus a warm place for the civilians. Additionally, as disgusting as it sounds, the Yeti meat will serve as food.

"Striker to Navigator. I have found a suitable base camp. Send the strikers in hot. We're going to have to clear the area of these pesky Frost Yetis."

CHAPTER 32
CLASSIFICATION: NAVIGATOR

t's been two weeks since we established an encampment in the tunnels. There have been an abundance of Frost Yetis that we use as a food source for the civilians, while the Eclectic Division and the politicians use the replicators. It is not an ideal situation, but it will do for now.

Meanwhile my underground operations are flourishing. I have ten strikers and fifteen scavengers on payroll collecting, processing, and transferring C+ Grade Baby Frost Yetis through to the Venusian Oasis. That's a long strip of land acting as the central hub for the entire planet. The Oasis is filled with exotic monsters used as pets and food. Additionally, it's filled with some of the richest civilians and politicians under the IGF rule.

And where there are credits, there are the RRA, doing their best to protest the clearly one-sided regulations. I mean, it does not make much sense. You make it illegal to traffic and house the monsters, but don't crack down on the rich people buying them? Meanwhile, the ones that are providing the service are captured and flayed in public hangings. It's atrocious. Now I admit this is not the only issue on which the Red Rogue Alliance and the Interplanetary Galactic Force find themselves at odds. It's simply the easiest one to understand.

Essentially the RRA wants a free market—something akin to the ancient worlds' capitalism. The IGF, on the other hand, maintains a heavy-handed dictatorship. It's their way or the highway. One does not have to look too far for examples of what happens when a planet is not under IGF protection. Those planets have the lowest

standards of living and are often the source of brutal monster attacks, even more devastating than what happened on Marda. They are constant war zones. These are planets dominated by Orcs, green brutish creatures who cannot harness their own energy. It's a different ball game when you can simply pay the IGF to come in and handle your monster infestation problem while the GF *adjusts* your finances.

When one looks at it from an outside perspective, it's downright atrocious the way we're handled. As children, the best and the brightest are plucked from their parents' homes and assigned under the four classifications, groomed for a role that they can rarely escape. That's a practice that the RRA wants to dismantle.

As one can tell, I'm not simply some underground monster. I do believe in what the RRA is doing, and I do believe that we can find a better way to operate. So I do my part. And I'm damn good at it. As long as doing my part comes with a heap load of credits.

While adjusting my suit, I look forward to the arrival of my new battlesuit. Acquired through grey market means, of course. Can't afford to have any traces back to me via the IGF-sanctioned blacksmiths. In any case, some of the unsanctioned blacksmiths are just as good, if not better, than the IGF ones—probably because they are dwarves. This is a feat in itself, as dwarven-made technology rarely functions well with elf hands. It's very hit or miss.

Although I'm not expertly trained like Vex, I have always made sure to maintain the best battlesuits underground credits could buy. This allows me to strike fear in hearts of the ill-equipped peons. The vast majority believe me to be a rogue striker when in fact I'm far from. Simply a chunky, average-looking navigator. Who would have thought? The most feared underground trafficker, a navigator.

I look in the distance to see the RRA members arriving with my suit, while my jump-man team and I spread out, making sure the coast is clear. The RRA members in their typical red attire approach, albeit cautiously. This is my first time dealing with them face-to-face and I hope it will not be my last. But I can't put anything past anyone, and thus my finger hovers around the trigger of my explosives.

Oh, I failed to mention. Yes, I started a jump man team. I figured I'd capitalize on the snow by taking down up-and-coming strikers that would pose a threat to Vex's ascension. Not to mention the credits. Apparently there are a shit ton of credits involved in selling A to A+ specimens for consumption. How could I say no?

"So you're the infamous Sugar Cane."

"I suppose one could say that."

"I can see why you want to upgrade battlesuits."

"And I can see why you wanted me to deliver the shipment personally. I hear the Planetary Division are cracking down on your shipments."

"Now, how'd you hear about that? I only learned of this today."

"A little birdie told me. Let's see the goods."

Being a navigator has its perks.

"Very well."

The rogue alliance member heads to the back of the truck and wheels out a fully decked-out battle armor 4.5. One of the newest models. Fully equipped with high-powered shields, rocket blasters for movement, a high-tech mp5, whistler rockets, and a chainsaw. The helmet is a bit clunky, and skulls decorate the suit, which is a beast for close to mid-range. But above all, its defensive capabilities are top of the line. Could easily rival an A+ IGF battlesuit, maybe even S. I will have a fun time training in this. I've been studying Chaos and Ivy's movements in my spare time and look forward to putting study into practice.

"Sweet."

"Now show us what you got for us."

I clap my hands and my jump-man team hustles to get rid of the stinking baby Yetis. One of my goons pulls out a Yeti and manages to get his helmet removed. We all glance at the buffoon. He nearly drops the Yeti trying to put his helmet back on.

"You oaf. That Yeti is worth more than your life. Bring it over here," I say.

He rushes over with the Yeti. As he plops the cage onto the snowy ground, the rogue alliance members study its grade and fortitude.

"Excellent specimen," says the rogue alliance member.

I place my left hand on the shoulder of the fifty-seventh-ranked striker.

"Did you see his face?"

"Yup."

"Cool."

I pick up the chainsaw and cleave the neck of my team member. His blood squirts in every direction, covering my old suit in blood one last time.

"Can't be too careful. Good help is hard to find, but a face once seen can lead to complications. You understand?"

"Yup. You cherish privacy, we respect that. Besides, it's as they say: The only thing sweet about Sugar Cane is the name, or something of the like."

I smile behind my helmet as the RRA takes their leave and we take ours with the battlesuit and credits downloaded directly to our accounts.

"What about the body?" asks one of my members.

"Let the Yetis eat it."

This is something of a secret, but the first time you kill someone is the hardest. When it's done out of necessity, you only hope you get over it and you don't get caught. But what the average person doesn't understand is that a part of you feels good. Holding life and death in your hands, teetering on the brink of destruction. There is a certain high one gains from that—a certain euphoria.

Now the second time is much easier. I dare say I enjoy it. The fear of getting caught is still there, but somehow diminished. By the time I make it back to the navigators' quarters, my supervisor is breathing down my neck.

"Where have you been? Vex is already in the field. We had to put in a reserve navigator. You know how much he hates those."

"Had diarrhea from the crappy breakfast we had. Could be all those milkshakes, I don't know. Need I say more?"

"No, no. Keep those things to yourself next time."

"As you wish."

"Allison to Vex."

"What?" he grumbles. He is extra cute when he's mad.

"The area you're entering is an uncharted tunnel. Be careful out there."

"Copy that."

I look at my secondary screen to see that my volute opponent is back online. He has made his move, and it's a pretty damn good one. He placed my entire board on the defensive just by moving his king. A bold move.

The chat opens and the message sound goes off.

"How's it going?" he asks.

"Good. A little flustered, I must say. Didn't expect that move."

"I bet you look cute when you're flustered."

Not one to get distracted by compliments more than once, I get straight to the point.

"Did you have something to do with Beaver's death?"

"Perhaps. What if I did?"

"Why'd you do it?"

"I didn't like the way he was harassing you. It pissed me off."

"What if you get caught—or worse yet, they blame me?"

"Not going to happen. I got your back. Your move, sweetheart."

The chat closes and I'm left to ponder.

CHAPTER 33
CLASSIFICATION: STRIKER

My hands are numb, and my trigger finger is a bit slower to the pull. The freezing evenings in the tunnel are getting to me. The darkness doesn't make it any better. Double Tirade's windy glow by my side provides me with some light, but I find myself cautiously taking every step.

A warm gust of wind comes flying my way. It's almost soothing. I turn the corner, and shivers run down my spine as if I were hit by a bolt of lightning. In my direct line of sight is a slumbering dragon. It's larger than the red one, blue with spikes lined straight down the back. The wings are coated with ice, while its legs are powerful reinforced muscle.

"Striker to navigator. What grade dragon am I looking at?"

"An A Frost Dragon."

I bring up the profile to get a better analysis of my situation.

A-grade Frost Dragons are known for their nearly impenetrable armor casing and have the ability to instantly freeze a striker with their frozen breath. Typically they are found sleeping and will not engage unless disturbed. Weakness: The soft underbelly can be used as a vulnerable spot.

A takedown of this magnitude would edge me right below Tyrant in the standings. Even after all my efforts, I've only managed to regain my third spot. But I'm not foolish enough to believe that I can single handedly takedown an A frost dragon when it took the three executioners to take down a B+ fire dragon. The days of me selfishly rushing into any situation, half hoping to die and half hoping to survive,

are gone. With constant upgrades to Tirade, I am beginning to feel life has purpose. Plus, I have the civilians to think about. I can't let them down again.

I activate the distress code and pull up the territorial map. It seems Chaos and Ivy are closest to my location. Tyrant is further down and, knowing him, most likely won't answer. My only hope is to gain assistance while we have the element of surprise.

Seventeen minutes pass by leaving me time to set up Flutter bombs surrounding the giant beast. My bella rockets are primed and ready, and I have my P90s aimed at the eyes. Tirade is ready to unleash her wind attacks. I check the map again to see Chaos making her way to me, and Ivy trudging along behind her.

Another five minutes pass by as I stare at the beast, asleep, not knowing what's about to hit it. It's almost criminal what I'm doing. I mean, it's just here minding its own business, yet I am here about to ruin its day. But this is what must be done. The tunnels need to be clear so we can progress on to the next area, that much closer to the safety of the Oasis.

Dangerous thinking once again. I'm starting to make a habit of this.

Chaos sidles up alongside me, silent as ever and I point at the massive beast. I indicate the plan, and she nods. Nightfall is upon us, and the beast opens its eyes.

I unleash a barrage of P90s into the face of the beast. It roars. Chaos has just finished placing her defensive unit 5.5 when the dragon unleashes a destructive ice blast upon the shield, dissolving it in one blast. The defensive unit is completely fried. The two of us unload our energy-imbued ammunition into the creature but have zero effect. I pull out my scimitars and stride forward, my grappling spears' cords wrapped around the dragon's neck. They pull me in just as the dragon opens its mouth to feast.

What a dumb move.

A massive rock flies past my vision, smashing the dragon's head into the icy wall with an explosion.

I land on the neck of the dragon and jam my scimitars into the soft, fleshy eyes of the beast. It bellows out in agony, flapping its wings and causing an ice snowstorm that sweeps Chaos and Ivy up. Tirade counters with her own windstorm, slowing the ice storm a little. Chaos manages to use her owl, which drags her out of the ice storm and drops her on the back of the dragon. After turning her sniper rifle into a giant war hammer, she slams the back of the dragon, cracking its ice.

The Frost Dragon catapults itself out of the tunnel and heads into the sky. It twists and turns in a blind fury to get us off. I latch onto Chaos, who slips and nearly falls off. The grappling spears keeping us secure, and we hold onto each other as the dragon does all kinds of aerial maneuvers blind.

Eventually, it thrusts itself into the wall of a nearby mountain, dislodging the grappling spears and throwing us both off. As we tumble to our deaths, Chaos activates her thrusters—but with the two of us, it only manages to slow our descent. I contemplate all the things I'll never get to do, causing a rumbling in my stomach. Just as I'm about to relieve myself from the fear of dying. I remember the meteor dash.

Tapping my boots together, I focus my energy to my feet. I plant them on the air as though I were on ground. Slowly, in a mix of wind and heated air pockets, our descent slows down. My legs are burning up; meteor dash isn't meant to be used to stop at such high speeds. I crouch my legs and push downwards towards the ground. It feels like I'm flying, gliding, and falling all in one. It's a painful sensation, but one that I'll gladly take over dying. We crash land into a large pine tree that softens the blow just as I run out of energy.

I twist to put my back against the fall, holding Chaos atop of me. I land on my back with a loud crunch.

Several moments pass by in silence; I'm breathing heavily.

"We're alive..." says Chaos.

"You mind getting off me?"

She moves, and we hear another crunch. Something is broken. Something important.

Chaos, fully alert and functioning, swings her war hammer and patrols the perimeter as she was trained to do. I stay leaned against the trunk of the pine tree. My failed attempt to stand tells me that my back is somehow damaged. It's only a bittersweet idea to feel my legs, which are in severe pain. They seem to be burning up, as if they were falling meteors.

The freezing cold isn't making things any better. Every breath I inhale shoots pain into my lungs to the point where I try to slow down my breathing. I try the healing technique but my energy is nearly depleted. I close my eyes, exhausted.

I awake with a splint on my legs and some kind of shoddy device on my back. Whatever it is, I'm laid down flat on Chaos' undergarments. I glance over to see her trying her hand at lighting a fire.

"Having trouble?"

"No, don't worry. I'll get the fire going."

After another ten minutes in pitch black, she gives up and summons her owl, who sends down a small lightning bolt that sets the wood on fire.

"That was some smooth thinking out there. I thought we were dust for sure. What was that air maneuver?"

"Meteor dash. First time using it. Has some serious aftereffects though."

"Well, it gets the job done."

She moves closer into the light. With her helmet off, she looks almost like a model. Something one sees in the naughty movies. "Play Toy," I think it was called.

Who am I kidding... I've seen the entire "Play Toy" series.

"We need to stay warm if we're going to survive the night. Especially you. You're in pretty bad shape. But with that healing technique you have yet to teach me, you should be able to walk in the morning."

She gently grabs my arm and comes closer. The scent of sweat and leather mixed with her natural scent intoxicates my being. Blood rushes to my member, which throbs and grows hard.

Naturally she notices and gives me a sly smile.

"Not bad... not bad at all."

She pulls down my undergarments and grabs my member.

Who am I to protest?

I wake up in the morning feeling just as exhausted and beaten—though somehow fulfilled. I suppose sex with a beautiful woman will do that to you. While looking around, I notice that Chaos is nowhere to be found.

Must be checking the perimeter again.

Thirty minutes pass, and I eventually hear her footsteps. She comes back with a C-grade Were Rabbit. A grotesque-looking thing, but edible.

After cooking it up on the fire, I attempt to heal my severe wounds. I manage to restore my back to about 65% and my legs to about 23%. Just enough to walk, I suppose.

I move to caress Chaos, and she recoils as if I were some kind of viper.

"What are you doing?"

"We could go for round four?"

"I think not. That was then; this is now. I don't date Strikers anymore. Just pretend last night never happened."

"It was literally last night. I didn't even get to perform the way I wanted to."

"It was a fine performance, although I did most of the work. Now get up. Comms are down by the way. The dragon has caused a massive snowstorm, and I'm not sure it will end anytime soon."

"So? We can stay here until this blows over."

"You can stay here. I'm hunting that dragon."

And with that, Chaos takes several steps back into the wilderness. I struggle to my feet and activate my battlesuit's assembly. I somehow feel used, like a piece of meat. Shaking off that feeling with great effort, I make my way into the wilderness in an attempt to catch up to her.

"Guess she isn't named Chaos for nothing." I whisper.

CHAPTER 34
CLASSIFICATION: POLITICIAN

All the precious electronics in my truck are going haywire, from the multipurpose units to the mines. If I hadn't kicked all the other politicians out of my vehicle, I would be sure one of them had been tampering with my stuff. The three wide screens of my console illuminate, and I'm met with the image of a female cyber elf. Her face has an alluring blue glow, while the horns atop her head tell me she was born in the cyber realm, rather than converted. She might even be their equivalent to royalty, based on how she is dressed. Her glowing blue eyes tell me she is the source of the electronic disturbance.

Just as I am about to speak, she cuts me off.

"You have yet to procure the Crypto Pyramid. Did we not illuminate to you how important this artifact is? Or are you that dim-witted and slow?"

"No, your grace. We have encountered certain difficulties. With the vast number of tunnels filled with mobs."

"What does that have to do with us? Find the pyramid before it is activated."

"My reach is not like it is on Marda. Tracking down the RRA on this planet has proven to be difficult. But once I arrive in the Oasis, I assure you I will find them."

"You have another week. Then there will be consequences."

"As you wish your grace. Where, might I ask, is my brother?"

"You may not! What you may do is take the knee and receive your blessings."

I lower my face to hide my disdain for this creature. She will be one of the first cyber elves I overthrow when I become one of them.

While I take the knee, something I have only had to do in front of the IGF bigwigs, I remember what I am fighting for. A fit of violent coughing begins.

The cyber elf's lips curl into a grotesque smile, revealing sharp canines. I clench my fists in an effort to stem my fury.

"Before I change my mind, here."

She tosses a vial with pink liquid through the middle computer screen. It nearly lands on the floor, but I catch it. Dumping the contents into my mouth, I realize I must look real pathetic right about now. Addicted to some unknown substance from the cyber realm. I manage to save a bit of it for analysis.

With a surge of electricity, she leaves. Now that I am on a stringent time limit, I realize how dire my situation really is. I have heard of computer-related deaths, which I presume to be due to the cyber elves. It only makes sense. Their reach is far greater than I thought. Now that my life may be at stake, it is time that I take a closer look at these deaths. Additionally, I will need a competent navigator under my thumb to analyze the contents of this vial.

I pull up my screen to see the list of navigators in the top 10 and cross reference them with those connected to either of the murders. To my surprise, Vex's navigator has recently cracked the top five. Right at the edge at number five: a certain miss Allison Ravenguard. From a once prominent family in the Venusian Oasis to a bottom-feeding family in a one year. *Interesting. Her mother is sick.* I can certainly funnel extra credits her way to keep her mouth shut. With a sick mother, she will be tied to me like a tapeworm. After doing my due diligence and going over all the top ten navigators, I decide Allison is the best bet. Apparently, she has had relations with one of the murder victims. Another way to apply pressure.

There is a soft knocking at my door. I look at the screen to see it's Allison. My high-tech cameras reveal all. She is dressed in a t-shirt with grease stains and jeans. At least Vex had the wherewithal to dress for the occasion. I press the button to open the truck doors, allowing her entrance. From my most comfortable chair, I beckon for her to take a seat.

"I'd rather stand."

"As you wish."

"May I know why you have chosen to summon me now? Vex and Chaos are both missing after their battle with a dragon. They are presumed dead. I'd much rather use my time to navigate their search."

"I see. This won't take long."

"Good."

"I'll get straight to the point. I want to hire your services."

"My services? If so, you must go through the proper channels and send a requisition form to the IGF, who will send a compliance form to my supervisor, who will then receive an acceptance letter from me. The whole process should take about a month."

I chuckle. "I don't do forms."

"And I don't do shady off-the-book jobs."

"Is that so? Not even for your sick mother."

"What does she have to do with anything?"

"Well, the medication you've somehow managed to scrounge together for her is keeping her alive, but is it healing her? Sounds to me like it's simply suppressing her symptoms while providing an abundance of side effects. What if I were to say there might be a way to improve her condition, maybe even cure her of what ails her?"

"Then I'd say you're lying. There is no cure for what she has."

"Not yet, at least."

I hand her the remaining liquid in the vial.

"Is this enough for a full analysis?"

"Perhaps."

"Is it or is it not?"

"What if it is? I'm not going to join forces with a shady politician like yourself—one who cuts funding in one area only to fill his pockets with credits."

"Tell me about Jacob."

"He died recently. What of it? You're wasting your time. I won't work with you."

"For."

"For?"

"Yes, you're not going to be working with me... you'll be working for me. There is a difference. And I find it odd that one day you and Jacob were having disputes, and the next day he died."

"You yourself ruled that a case of cybernet overload. Happens to 0.00000000001% of all navigators. It's a minimal risk compared to the strikers. Are you insinuating I had something to do with a naturally occurring death? Or are you implying that you're incompetent and made a mistake in judgement?"

Clenching my fists, I realize she has turned the tables on me. It's not the way I expected the conversation to go. For a navigator, she is rather feisty and confident. A dangerous combination.

"Your frequent tardies are troubling. What has you so caught up?"

"I'm having stomach problems. Have been for a while. Could be the junk you feed us to keep us fat. Not sure, I'm no blacksmith. Listen here, you."

"It's Inquisitor Morange to you."

"Well, Inquisitor Morange. You have simply wasted my time when I should be assisting in the search for Vex. I thank you very much for that."

"Allison, before you go. Know that I will be keeping an eye on you."

"If you have nothing better to do, then sure. Watch till your eyes bleed."

And with that she's gone. Not what I expected. Not what I expected at all. As I pace back and forth in my truck, I contemplate my options—of which I have very few. I come to the conclusion that I will not let my emotions get the best of me. I still have the better part of a week. In the meantime, I will make use of the civilians.

"Great citizens of Marda, I am here today with my hat held low and my head even lower. It is my greatest concern that we are burdening the IGF unnecessarily. Now, some of you will say that this is their job: to clear the way for us. But can you not find it in your hearts to volunteer to assist in the elimination of the monsters that walk the tunnels? The faster we clear the tunnels, the better."

There is some grumbling amongst the cowardly people of Marda. Naturally, an entire planet of bankers, accountants, and other number-pushers would hesitate to take a hand in their own freedom.

"You mean to tell me not one of you would relish the idea of putting a bullet between the eyes of a C+ Frost Yeti? Or take down a Wildawere? We had a great planet and were a great nation. But now it is time to think about our future. We must endure and pursue on. The best way to do that is to expedite the process by assisting in the eradication of these beasts."

More cowardly grumblings.

My words have seemed to have fallen on deaf ears. Their fear far outweighs my superior oratory skills.

Stupid civilians.

I return to my truck, where I see a few of my politician *friends*.

"What do you lads want?"

"We want back in your truck, where you have your own private food replicator and top of the line facilities. What can we do to get back in?"

"Convince the masses to gather around a thousand volunteers to enter the tunnels and assist the strikers in eradicating the beasts. Do that, and I'll think about it."

Upon arrival to the navigators' quarters, I realize they have built a grand office, with many cubicles and carpeted floor. Quite welcoming for a makeshift office. I'm filled with the scent of greasy food and milkshakes. The aroma lingers in the air, causing me to cover my nose.

The supervisor lapdog rushes over, violating my personal space until my multipurpose unit pushes her back with its anti-gravity field. She backs up against a computer, making it tumble.

"Watch what you're doing." I say.

"S... sorry Inquisitor Morange."

"You should be."

"May I know why you are here?"

"I'd like to see the malfunctioning computers, the ones that caused the deaths of our beloved navigators."

"We disconnected both and placed them in the back."

"That won't do. I will need you to reconnect them to the common server so I can run full-length diagnostics."

"I don't think that's a good idea. It could infect the others."

"I do not recall asking your opinion. It would be best to keep such words to yourself."

She manages to nod and waddles towards the back of the tent. After a few minutes, both are plugged and logged into a guest admin account. One of my units connects to the computer and begins uploading the spyware and keylogger. It will take some time for it to fully infect all the computers, but I make sure to start with the top ten navigators.

There must be something tangible I can use on these navigators' computers. Not to mention Allison's demeanor, which is way too domineering for her to be a simple button pusher. She might have other dealings and has gained personality points.

I walk past the various cubicles to see what each member of the navigator team is doing. Some are playing an online RPG called Rogue Quest, others are playing online volute, while some have chat windows open. Must be nice, to be able to multi-task to the point where you're fooling around all day. Most of them have their strikers' visual feeds reduced in size, barely visible. I shake my head.

What a pity. Such undisciplined navigators we have here. Their eyes should be glued to their strikers' screens.

"You, come here." I point and indicate for the supervisor to come closer.

"Yes, Inquisitor Morange?"

"How goes the search for Vex and Chaos?"

"Word travels fast. It's been 24 hours, and there is a large snowstorm. We have deemed them deceased. It's a sad day, but people die every day. As the saying goes, it's just truly a shame that it had to be two of our top three."

"Hmmm, I see."

That idiotic Vex had to go and get himself killed. I thought him hardier than that.

CHAPTER 35
CLASSIFICATION: STRIKER

The snowstorm threatens to blow me off my feet, and video and audio communication are still down. As we continue our venture deeper into the wilderness, we have met Tundra Bears, Snow Falcons, and Frost Snakes. But no dragon. I caught up to Chaos to try to get her to change her mind but she only berates me for being a coward.

I simply think I'm being cautious. My memory of what the last dragon did to the encampment still fresh, I can only imagine what destruction this one can cause. As we push farther into the forest we see a large cavern followed by what looks like a blood trail.

Say what you want about Chaos, but she is an excellent tracker, Either that, or her instincts are really up to par. Dragons love caves and treasure; they also love their sleep. Our hope is that this dragon is asleep guarding treasure inside this cavern. A big hope, but I'll settle for just asleep.

We push forward into the cavern. There are icicles jutting from the ceiling. The blood trail stops suddenly. I look up just in time to see the dragon descend upon us like we're flies in a spider's trap. By rolling to the side, I manage to dodge the blow. A large crater of ice spikes surround the Frost Dragon.

It lashes out at me with its tail, connecting with my stomach and sending me crashing into the cavern wall. Chaos smashes her war hammer on the ground, creating ripples, but the dragon freezes the attack with its icy breath. Its left arm grabs her and tosses her into the ceiling. Icicles and rubble fall on her as she tumbles to the ground.

I rise to my feet sluggishly and send Tirade out. She taunts the dragon, drawing its attention to me with a howl. I meteor ahead with my scimitars, covering the distance with one jump. My legs are burning, but still I push forward. I manage to cleave the chin of the Frost Dragon. It catches me in the air with its claws and slams me into the snowy ground. The Frost Dragon looks down at me, blood still leaking from its eyes.

It coils back to unleash another wave of frost breath. Just when I am about to meet my demise, Chaos swings her war hammer from the side, catching the creature on the lower jaw. She follows this up by launching herself into the air with her thrusters and slamming the war hammer onto its head repeatedly. Her owl springs forth, summoning lightning upon our foe, which convulses.

And with that, the once-majestic beast is dead.

We speak our last words to the worthy foe and now must figure out a way to get it back to the encampment. Both of us breathing heavily, bloody, and drained, we get into a pseudo-argument.

"Maybe if we just take the head, the scavs can come back for the rest," says Chaos.

"Yeah."

"What's wrong with you? Don't tell me you're still upset about earlier."

"All I said was yeah. How did you come to that conclusion?"

"I can taste the heaviness in the air."

"Sure."

"Whatever, like I said, it was a one-time thing. Nothing to worry yourself over."

I hear loud clapping from the entrance of the cavern.

"Wow you guys really did it." The clapping stops. "Really took down the dragon of the west. We've been tracking that thing for a while."

"Curses. I recognize that voice," says Chaos.

"And I recognize yours. Hello, Chaos. Good to see you're back on Venusian like old times. I certainly hope I'm not interrupting a lovers' quarrel. But we can do this the easy way or the hard way. Either way, that dragon's head is coming home with us."

"Damned if it is," I say.

"Vex..."

"What?"

"I don't want to see you get hurt. Just give him the dragon head."

"Nah, not happening."

I meteor dash forward only to see the hooded figure sigh and raise his right arm, which is glowing bright blue. He holds his palm up and a beam of blue light washes over me. My entire body freezes in place.

Defeated again. Pathetic.

As I defrost in the hot spring water, my bones are still chilly. My arm is stiff, and my chest is damaged. But my physical pain pales in comparison to my mental pain. My ego is bruised in ways that I cannot explain. Now, I know, I'm on this whole enlightenment journey with Tirade, but one cannot completely destroy their ego. They can only grow it to the point where it is used as a shield, not as a weapon. I am not there yet.

Although Chaos is nowhere in sight, I know she is nearby. Her scent still lingers. From the looks of it, I'm at the Venusian Oasis, filled with natural hot springs and palm trees—a far cry from the snow filled tundra. My battlesuit is piled to the side. It has been cleaned and treated for any imperfections. A nice touch. I lean my head back against the stone of the hot spring,

"Someone is enjoying themselves," says Chaos.

"Yeah, I guess you could say that."

"Where have you been?"

"After checking up on you, I went and got my sniper hammer enchanted. I was inspired after seeing what those wind scimitars of yours can do. I don't think you've truly unlocked the true powers of those weapons."

"I agree. There are eight runes on their blades, and I've only activated three of them."

"Something to look forward to."

"Who was that guy?"

"That guy... he is someone from my past. When I lived here. We grew up together.

That's all you need to know."

"Seems pretty powerful."

"Yeah, he has climbed the ranks of the Planetary Division. He's ranked tenth. That's the equivalent of thirty ranks higher and more powerful than rank one of the Eclectic Division."

"What's your point?"

"My point, Vex, is that whatever you do, don't let him goad you into a duel or a tournament. He will chew you alive and spit you out just for fun. He's a sadistic fuck."

His voice cuts in. "Here I thought I was a gentle one. I mean, I was your first."

I already feel myself burning up as the rage builds up from my feet to my head. I rise from the hot spring water and press a button on my screen. As the suit assembles, I take a good look at Chaos' first.

He's wearing a blue hood with blue-and-silver medium armor. On his back are war axes, and his striker badge says number ten. He has a mysterious allure about him, which troubles me the most.

I will not back down. My honor must be avenged. But not now. When the time is right.

"I'm Vex, and you are?"

I stick out my hand to shake his, but he simply looks at my hand with disgust.

"I don't shake the hands of... dark elves. And they call me Ice Devil."

Biting my tongue to prevent myself from another Tiddly occurrence, I turn my attention to Chaos.

"Are you ready to go? We need to return to encampment and bring back the rest of the dragon."

"About that..."

"What she means to say is that I agreed to give her a twenty-percent finder's fee, and the remaining eighty percent is mine. My scavs are already taking back the dragon here as we speak. I truly appreciate you Eclectics luring it closer to the oasis, as we're only allowed to set foot a certain distance away."

"I see how it is. Cut me out of the deal, huh? Very well. Just point me in the direction of the camp, and I'll be on my way. You clearly know your way around this section of the planet."

"Vex don't be like that..."

"I know, Vex, it's just business."

"Mind yours, devil. I'm talking to Chaos."

She lowers her head and points me in what I believe is the right direction

I grab the hilts of my psionic scimitars and pack them away. I summon Tirade and jump on top of her.

Chaos rushes up to me and grabs my arm.

"You're not even going to ask if I'm coming back with you?"

"Nope."

And with that, I leave in a tornado of wind.

Two days have passed by the time I arrive back at base camp. Nightfall has come upon me. Suddenly my audio and video communication come back up.

"Vex to Tash, Allison, and Sansa. I'm back."

Allison is the first to respond.

"I knew you'd survive. I didn't care what anyone told me!" says Allison.

"Thank the Most High. I've been praying for you," says Tash.

"Cool beans," says Sansa.

It may not feel like a home, and they may not be family. But they're the closest thing to it. I have to do better. I must treat my troupe better.

CHAPTER 36
CLASSIFICATION: NAVIGATOR

After hearing the news that both Chaos and Vex are okay, spirits are lifted amongst the navigators. A large portion of the camp seems to be a bit chipper. The Eclectic Division has grown even more tightknit since the "Escape from Marda," as the civilians have come to call it. As my underground empire grows, my thoughts wander to all the possibilities. The civilians have rallied, and over a thousand have entered the tunnels to help eliminate the monsters there. With the demise of the dragon, things have become that much easier.

Vex seems to be in a mood. For the first time ever, he chooses to have breakfast with us. It's quite the sight to see him take a break from his usual brooding in the corner to see him brood up close. As always, something is on his mind. This time, instead of scheming on how to get to number two, he is plotting on how to get the number one rank. It's been a week since his return, and he has trained harder than I've ever seen him train. Tash has been working overtime on his upgrades, and Sansa has been up to something secretive. I suppose we all have our secrets, some more than others.

I look at the screen dedicated to one of my goons. He's having trouble wrangling a group of WereBears, B-grade nocturnal bears with a venomous bite. These exotic creatures will accrue a pretty penny. I check my personal credit account to see the large number growing larger by the day. Something about staring at the big numbers gets me wet. Just as I'm directing the buffoon to the tunnel exit, my computer crashes, then reboots. I stand up, looking around, to see a few other navigators doing the same.

My eyes lock on to Denz.

"Did your console crash too?" I ask.

"Yeah, what the hell man."

"This is the second time this week."

My supervisor makes her way over and investigates.

"Seems pretty normal to me. These devices are getting older by the day."

I think back to when this all started and recall that the first crash happened a few days after Inquisitor Morange's scan. Alarm bells go off in my mind.

Shit, shit, shit.

Basic keyloggers and spyware uploaded directly to the server can cause crashes whenever a user exceeds the cap. It is primitive, but very effective, and difficult to locate and delete. As the console reboots, I tap on it feverishly.

Come on, come on.

"Something the matter, Allison? You seem a little distraught."

"A little. I just don't like when I lose connection to my striker. Anything can happen these days."

"I understand. Things will be fine. Anyways, here is the food you ordered. A large basket of onion rings and fried filleted fish. Oh, and can't forget your strawberry milkshake."

"Thanks."

As I'm downing the milkshake, the console finally reboots. I search everywhere for any sign of a new program. Something sneaky. Anything. To no avail. Finally, I plop down in my chair with sweat pouring down my face. There has to be a way to track what he uploaded to the server. An idea pops into my mind—something I have been avoiding all this time. Contact with that cyber murderer. He is the only one I know capable of finding such high-level software.

I open up the chat, and to my amazement he is still online. The window shows that he has been active and online for two weeks straight.

Doesn't he ever sleep?

"Hey you, you've crossed my mind a few times," I type.

"Could have fooled me. It's been a few weeks."

"It takes time to process what you told me."

"Perhaps… or perhaps you need help with that keylogger and spyware you have infecting your console?"

"How do you know about that?"

"It burns like the fire in my heart for you. I miss you."

"You barely know me."

"Pardon? I know you better than you know yourself. Go ahead, quiz me on anything Allison related."

"What is my last name?"

"Easy, Ravenguard of the Ravenguard dynasty. A fallen dynasty of light elves living in the Oasis. Your mother is currently suffering from Ninten Sickness and is constantly on the brink of death. Your father is cheating on your mother with the helper you hired."

"What?!"

"Oh, yeah. You didn't know that. Next question."

My alarm bells are blazing like wildfire again. This man knows too much about me, and I know nothing about him. It's time for the tables to turn.

"Who are you?"

"Now you're asking the interesting questions. I am He Who Loves."

"That doesn't answer my question."

"It does, you are just not satisfied with the response."

"What do you want with me?"

"I want to be near you. Hold you. Love you."

"Have we met before?"

"Not in person. We can never meet in person. It's just not possible."

"Where are you from?"

"If I were to tell you, the heavens would fall from the sky and engulf you."

"You aren't making sense."

"I am. You just aren't understanding."

And with that that, He Who Loves logs off.

A new game pops up on my desktop called Eye Spy. I double click the file and open it to see it has logged all my actions since Inquisitor Morange was here.

That sneaky bastard.

I crack my knuckles and get to work. To my relief, Morange has yet to check the files accumulated. I cannot erase my files, or he will know I have something to hide. But what I can do is switch out my actions with someone else's— someone a lot more mundane. It would need to be someone who has a typing speed similar to mine, in case the supervisor is in on this. That means it has to be a top ten navigator.

Sorry Denz, but you are the only one I know that fits the bill.

CHAPTER 37
CLASSIFICATION: STRIKER

After a month of advanced training I am able to meteor dash with minimal overheating. This allows me to reach incredible speeds and angles with my upgraded P90s pain and suffocation. My strength has increased, letting me slice through even the toughest of material, and I have unlocked a fourth rune on the scimitars. It's an advanced suffocation bubble that traps my opponent in a large air prison. Swirling winds close in on my opponent shredding them at my whim.

It's time I test my battle skills on the one person I know that will gladly fight me.

I head over to Tyrant's tent where he has Ivy wrapped in his arms. I hate to admit it, but they do make a cute couple.

I knock on the side of the pole, and Tyrant stirs.

"What do you want?" he grunts.

"I'm ready for that duel that you owe me."

"Oh, are you now? Let's go. I've been looking to pummel you into the ground."

Ivy stirs and grumbles something about being big-headed men, but the gleam in her eyes shows that she wants to see this just as bad as anyone else. An official duel between the number-two-ranked striker and the number-three-ranked striker will be a sight to behold.

We move over to the front of the camp, where we do the official bow of the strikers with one fist laid across our chests.

A small crowd surrounds us: Tyrant's allies cheering him on, and a small group of soloists rooting for me.

Ivy comes in between us.

"This is an official striker duel that will only end when one party is incapacitated or submits."

We both nod our consent.

Tyrant is the first to make his move. He whips out his rocket launcher and fires it right at my feet. I dodge the massive explosion with my meteor dash and unleash pain and suffocation on his bulk. He raises his reinforced shield, causing my attack to charge his shield. He then sends forth a fire blast from his shield and runs towards me. I dash backwards, keeping my distance. Suffocation activates, causing the oxygen around his head to disappear. While he's clutching his throat, I fire several shots at his leg. He bellows as they pierce his armor like parchment.

Series ten bella rockets fly out of his suit, forcing me to run in circles firing on the rockets themselves.

Tyrant stomps on the ground and a stream of lava erupts from underneath my feet, catapulting me in the air. He sends his lava ram into my chest and I fly back, crashing into the group of soloists. I stagger to my feet, but Tyrant is already upon me.

Damn. He's quicker than he looks.

His monstrous fist comes crashing down on me as I block with both arms. I let loose my grappling spears, which pierce his neck and send bolts of energy into his body. He shudders and collapses on his back. It's at this point that the ram scoops me up into the air and is about to impale me when I unleash Tirade and leap onto her back midair.

The crowd erupts into applause at the dazzling display of acrobatics.

I land on Tirade and, standing on air pockets, she unleashes wind blast: a concentrated amount of wind energy that pours from her mouth, shredding anything in its wake. The Ram blocks Tyrant's body with its own, absorbing the entire attack.

We land, and I dismount Tirade.

Tyrant takes out his grenade launcher and fires several grenades in the air, then charges at me, dodging my P90 barrage in the process. Tirade activates taunt, freezing him in his tracks. I'm about to deal a devastating blow, when Tyrant activates his cancel technique, breaking the taunt. He grabs my left arm and breaks it immediately, grappling me into a chokehold. As I'm about to pass out, Tirade charges up another wind barrage, forcing Tyrant to release me and block with his shield.

I use this time to get back to my feet, catching my breath.

With my one good arm, I activate my healing technique and heal my other arm, bringing my energy close to zero.

Tyrant leans back. "Impressive. But this ends now."

The grenade projectiles he sent in the air lands on Tirade, causing her to dissolve.

We lock eyes and charge towards each other: Tyrant with his shield and grenade launcher, me with my two psionic scimitars. He fires his grenade launcher right at me while I activate wind wall and meteor dash simultaneously, catapulting me right at him. The projectiles bounce off my wind shield, flying back at him just as I barrel into his stomach, knocking the air out of his lungs. He drops to his knees as I land on my feet. I place both scimitars at his neck.

"Submit. It's over."

"You're gonna have to kill me, boy."

Ivy yells, "If you don't surrender, we're done."

He mumbles. "I surrender."

I give a sigh of relief. We can't afford to lose a top striker—but if I had to, I would have ended him right there and then.

I may not be the number 2 striker, but I am that much closer.

After a long night of celebrating alone in the scavengers' quarters, I see Sansa sneaking out of the encampment. Normally I wouldn't care, but I am trying to be a striker more involved with the comings and goings of my troupe.

Instead of hopping in her heap of junk, she skyboards towards the tunnels, which have nearly been cleared. There's just one last section to secure.

We reach the unknown section, where she gets off the sky board and pulls out a plasma launcher. Not as destructive as a rocket launcher, but much lighter and faster.

It still looks too big for her. I catch up to her just as we reach the unknown area of the tunnels.

"What do you think you're doing?"

"I'm hunting. Leave me alone, Vex."

"You're not authorized to hunt, especially not at night, especially not alone. Even experienced strikers don't do that."

"So? You won't help me; I have to help myself."

"You're not even wearing a battlesuit. You'll die instantly if a monster so much as grazes you."

"I can't afford a suit. But don't you understand? I have to become a striker or die trying."

"Such a stubborn child."

"Whatever. All I know is that I wrote that letter and sent it off. They said I have one year to take down an A+ monster by myself to be upgraded to striker."

I'm not sure if it's the alcohol or the sob story she told me last time, but part of me wants to help her.

"Fine. But if we're going to do this, you have to do it my way. We will go hunting together—but not until I get you a suitable set of armor."

At that, she beams the brightest smile I had ever seen. Then Sansa grasps me by the stomach and rains down tears into my battlesuit. I hope it doesn't absorb the tears.

The next morning, earlier than usual, I woke up with a throbbing headache. But I am a man of my word. I head over to Tash to order a suitable battlesuit for Sansa. I figure something A+ will be suitable. Expensive, but worth the weight in credits.

I can't afford to lose another scavenger.

Besides, I have taken a liking to her. Kind of like how you get used to a birthmark. Ugly at first, but eventually it's grows on you.

I make my way to see Tash to find that her tent is closed. Although it's still dark, I had expected her to still be there. I then head to the blacksmiths' quarters, an area closed off to all non-blacksmiths. These days I'm feeling more rebellious. I activate my stealth and enter the banned grounds.

What's the worst that can happen?

I notice the massive tents are marked with numbers instead of letters. My presumption is that it's based on rank. I pull up her profile to see that she is now ranked ninth. I'm pleasantly surprised. Last time I checked, she was in the twenties.

Eerily enough, there is no one roaming the area. Everyone seems to be in their tents. It's an odd contrast against the constant hustle and bustle of the scavs, the late-night computer gaming of the navigators, and the constant late-night frolicking of the strikers. As I approach the ninth-marked tent I notice fancy tiles lining to its entrance. I knock on the side of the pole.

No answer.

You'd think by now I would have learned my lesson about entering people's tents without permission. But I guess not.

I enter Tash's tent to see her sitting down with her legs crossed and eyes closed. A hood covers her face.

"Tash."

No response.

"Tash!" I nudge her on the shoulder.

Her eyes open; they are pitch black. Tash removes her hood as she rocks back and forth. Her face and skin are a distinct red tint, with sharp rocks embedded throughout her body. Energy surges through her body at an incredible rate—to the point that I can see it through the rocks.

Instinctively, I pull out my P90s and aim at her head. My hands tremble at the thought that my blacksmith has somehow turned into an Arunkai. I don't know what to think.

She whispers, "Vincent. Do not fret, it's still me."

Her voice is so soothing, it lulls me almost to sleep.

"What are you?"

"It is one of the many secrets of the blacksmiths. But I suppose it is destiny that I tell you now."

"Please help me to understand."

"Lower your weapons, and we can talk."

I lower my P90s to the marble floor of the tiles.

"It's very simple, really. The Most High is a deity from the rift. And as such, in order to connect to our deity, we must subdue our inner elf nature and become more rift-like. There is so much I wish I could tell you about the rift, but this chip keeps me at bay. Not to mention the fact that it would make your hunting more conflicted."

"What do you mean?"

"I sense a great disturbance in your heart, Vincent. You are questioning the path that has chosen you and thus becoming weak in your pursuit of the hunt."

I lower my head. "That may be so. But what does that have to do with the secrets?"

"I can only tell you one right now. I have analyzed your blood, Vex, as many others have since you started hunting. Your blood contains the mutation, and HQ constantly reads reports on your actions, along with those of other strikers who have it."

"What mutation?"

"It's common knowledge amongst the blacksmiths and HQ, but as far as I know, you'll be the first striker to know this. The mutation is something some elves develop in early adolescence. It's why there is fluidity in changing classifications at age twelve, but we are initially graded at birth. This mutation comes from a diocarbon that is released on planets with rifts. It increases aggressiveness and focus, while also diminishing certain inhibitions. It's the same diocarbon found in every rift specimen. It makes you the perfect killing machine." She takes a moment to wipe away her tears.

"We track this mutation at birth, and it is one of the primary defining traits for whether someone is classified as a striker. The problem is that when the mutation gets out of hand, you have a chance of becoming a psychopath or a madman."

"Why... are you telling me all of this?"

"Because HQ is paying an especially close eye on you and your DNA. Your mutation seems to be progressing rapidly. You should have turned into a mad man or psychopath already. But you continue to grow stronger and faster. The meteor dash you pulled off the other day broke the record by far. Your legs should have been dust."

"I see. I must go."

"That's all you have to say?"

"That's all there is to say. I've just learned I have more in common with these beasts that I have been hunting for the past decade than I thought. I also learned that blacksmiths are using some rogue rift god in their quest to keep up with the dwarves. I need to process this alone."

CHAPTER 38
CLASSIFICATION: POLITICIAN

We have finally arrived at the Oasis. With only a couple days left on my deadline, one would think I'd be anxious. But a cunning mind can never be pushed off kilter. I have reconnected with certain colleagues in the Oasis. After hearing directly from me that the threat of the RRA is real, they didn't seem concerned. In fact, they almost dared the RRA to try their ploy. A rather disheartening response.

But this is due to an underlying problem, something I cannot quite put my finger on. It seems there is something else that stomps its foot onto the pulse of this glorious Oasis. I don't know what it is, but I will find out soon enough. I decide to pay a visit to an old friend. Someone who has information on anything and everything.

My retired navigator.

My multipurpose unit knocks on the door to a fancy villa.

He seems to be living well.

The grumpy old man opens the door, shaking his cane. He's wearing a grey robe and grey boxers. He squints at me.

"Is that Morange?"

He shoots an obscene gesture at me, then slams the door in my face.

We didn't exactly leave on the best of terms.

I press a few buttons and my multipurpose unit hacks the keypad. I enter to all kinds of sirens going off. My multipurpose units activate their lasers for noise violation, pointing at Harold's forehead.

"Journeyman Harold, don't make this more difficult than it has to be. Turn off the alarm."

I see the hurt and hesitation in his eyes, but I have no other choice. He's the only one I can trust to divulge the secret that seems have washed over the Oasis.

"Why are you here?"

"I have important business in the Oasis."

"This I know, why are you here?"

"Because I need to know what's going on in this bloody city. It seems everyone is keeping some grand secret that they're dying to tell."

"I can't tell you. Believe me, I would if I could." He then points to a blue mark on his neck.

It's some kind of ancient sigil, but other than that, it's anybody's guess. I examine it closer and nod my head.

"I've seen that before."

"No you haven't, not possible."

"It's an ancient sigil that ensures one's secrecy." A presumption, but not a far stretch. Hopefully, my bluff will work.

"Hmmm, perhaps you have. Then you know that this Frost Knight and his minions are slowly taking over the Oasis. An S+-grade Arunkai. Intelligent, cunning, and above all ruthless. He makes us wear these sigils that force us to keep certain secrets. It interferes with our universal chips and bypasses all its functions—essentially making us slaves. HQ is at odds on what to do, and the Planetary Division is staying far away from those that the mark consumes."

Trying to maintain my composure, I shuffle around in my seat. "I have heard some rumblings, nothing concrete." I'm careful to keep it vague.

"We're all prisoners trapped here. He knows we managed to hire your services and transfer you here with the Traveler's Cube. He knows that you will eventually come for him, and he knows that he will win. That's all I can say without this sigil turning me into ice."

I need more information, but I won't be able to extract it out of him while he is in this state of mind.

"I can remove the sigil. It's mainly why I am here."

"Really?"

His old eyes, lighting up with hope, will forever haunt me.

"Yes, hold still. My multipurpose unit will take care of it."

I press a few buttons on my wrist console, activating the lasers on low power. One of my units hovers over to Harold and does an analysis of the sigil.

It seems to be a living, breathing organism. Something akin to a parasite. I can remove the sigil, but the parasite has already attached itself to the brain. It won't be possible to keep him alive after the procedure.

After giving Harold my politician's smile, I assure him that everything is going to be okay.

"Now, I'm just going to ask you a few questions and everything will be fine."

"It's gone right?"

"Yes, it's no more."

He breathes a sigh of relief, hunching back in his chair.

"Where is this Frost Knight located?"

"His castle is atop a moving behemoth of a creature. It can usually be found circling the frozen tundra side of The Oasis."

"What are its weaknesses?"

"Weaknesses? Well, he seems rather arrogant. Arrogance can ruin armies and diminish victories. And he seems to fear the desert wastelands—no matter what, the behemoth does not cross the desert boundaries to the east."

"I see. What else can you tell me about this knight?"

"Watch out for his archers. They have deceptively long range and impeccable accuracy."

"Thanks." I'm about to take my leave when Journeyman Harold collapses to the floor, clutching his head in pain.

"You lied, you lied!"

"I suppose so."

A blue worm with legs squirms out from his ear. Just as my multipurpose unit is about to kill it, I scoop it up in my gloves and place it in the empty vial.

Will be useful for analysis.

I watch in awe as Harold's body, starting with his feet and moving up, turns to ice.

After deep analysis of the Frost Parasite, I deem them an A+ grade creature that tunnels into the brain of its host while it sleeps. The creature then controls certain aspects of the brain in order to ensure survival and privacy. This Frost Knight must have a grand scheme at hand if he is keeping the people of The Oasis under such servitude. My first step is to figure out a way to prevent the Eclectic Division from becoming food for these parasites.

The civilians are nothing but parasites themselves—at least the ones that refused to fight for the cause. In any case, I open the panel and log onto the navigators' database. With it, I check the extracurricular activities of every navigator on site. There are some gruesome things like monster porn and navigation on the cybernet—a subsection of the cyber realm—but not what I am looking for. I will have to graymail them later. Right now, I am looking for correspondence with unknown parties on Venusian. And voila. A certain Denzel Dc has had frequent communications with unknown parties on Venusian and Marda.

I cross-reference the conversation with the dates of certain known meeting times of the RRA, but things seem to be mis-matched. This Denzel Dc is supposed to be my key to finding the Crypto Pyramid. But something pricks the back of my mind. His record of employment is impeccable. He has zero tardies. Unlike a certain Allison and Janice, who both have frequent tardies, and are both in the top ten.

I get tingles as the computer shuts off and the mirror becomes distorted. A cyber elf returns. Hoping it is my brother and not the uppity aristocrat, I turn to the mirror to see a familiar face drinking green liquid from a wine glass.

"Brother, I cannot stay long. We both know you do not have much time. But it seems someone on my end is helping one of the Eclectic Division navigators elude your investigation. The thing is, this navigator is also the notorious Sugar Cane. I hope that assists."

"Yes, brother, it does. More than you can imagine."

And with that, he logs off from my console.

This settles it. A clear path to victory. It has to be someone with the demeanor of an underworld queen pin.

I summon Allison to my truck once again, this time with an inner knowing. Once again, she is cool, calm, and collected. As copacetic as can be. Smug little...

"Allison, good to see you."

"Why am I here again?"

"I suppose it's as they say. Ain't nothing sweet about Sugar Cane but the name."

Suddenly, her demeanor changes to something I know all too well.

"Nothing to say for yourself?"

"I have nothing to say. I'll let my lawyer do the talking."

"Oh, I'm sure they would be the best lawyer money could buy. Unfortunately for you, it won't get that far."

I pull out my high-grade shotgun and aim it at her head. "What if I were to eradicate you, right here, right now? How does that sound for a genius plan?"

"Now, not to spoil anything for you, but this isn't the first time I've had a gun pointed at my face. If you're going to pull the trigger, let's expedite the process." She rummages through her pocket, pulling out a piece of candy and popping it into her mouth.

"As cold as they say. Frigid even." I glare at her. I'm almost envious; I wonder how I would react under similar circumstances. I've never truly faced down the end of a gun knowing that my life could end at any moment. There has always been the notion that I had the upper hand. "You've grown since when we last spoke."

"Yes, that is true. I came to the conclusion that this underground shit will either end with me in the morgue or on top as a queen pin."

"Then work with me, not for me. Together we can accomplish great things. All I need to start is the location of the Crypto Pyramid. Think about this. When we take out the RRA, you can take over their side of the operations. Fulfill both sides of the transactions. That's at least worth ten times the income. What they pay you is peanuts."

I see her eyes light up. There is her greatest sin. For Vex it is wrath, for me gluttony, but for our dear Sugar Cane, it is greed. A deadly combination if there ever was one.

"How do I know you won't turn me in when you're done with me?"

"How devious do you take me for?"

"I take you for the mold that grows on walls. The kind you can't get rid of until it has infested your entire house."

"Well said. What do you want, a contract of some sort?"

"No. I want an investment."

"What do you mean?"

"I want you to invest half your fortune in my operations, with clear transactions for expansion purposes. I want a cyber trail between you and me. Then and only then will we be joint at the hip."

My heart skips a beat as I contemplate the thought of being intertwined with a mere navigator. Especially one as deceptive and ruthless as her. One that matches my wits, or dare I say, even might surpass them? But I am time pressed. Half my fortune is a small price to pay for health and immortality. When I become a cyber elf, I will have to find a way to deal with her as well. Simply another added to the list.

"Very well. I will begin the transferring of credits immediately."

"Excellent."

"Now, I'll have you do something for our cause. It will even help your precious Vexation as well."

I remove the worm, which doesn't seem like it will live much longer, and hand her the vial.

"Find out as much about this... parasite as possible. We will need to prevent them from infesting our people. And there is one more thing you must find out. Something about an Arunkai, a Frost Knight to be specific."

"Is that all?"

"Nope, one more thing. You need to find the Crypto Pyramid. We only have one day left to find it, meaning need you to use force on the RRA and retrieve it."

"I'm not a striker. I don't go busting down doors."

"I'll be with you. It will be fine. Just gather as many of the strikers under your employment as possible."

CHAPTER 39
CLASSIFICATION: STRIKER

My mind is a cloudy as ever. I feel as though it has been infiltrated by a small army laying waste to my calm-inducing hormones. It's been a week since Tash divulged certain secrets to me, and I have barely slept a wink. Where once I felt I was becoming in tune with Tirade, I have now grown to hold her in contempt once again. The constant barrage of warnings about being swooped-up and converted disturb me. But above all, I feel caught in a loop. Is this all I'm meant to do?

I refuse to turn into what they think I will. I will not become a psychopath, nor will I become a mad man. Above all, I will not become a cyber elf, forever lost in the cyber realm, destined to be a mere collection of code.

While joining the line for striker food, I realize that I forgot to check the oxygen levels and what's for the breaking-of-fast. Not that it matters, but I haven't seen or heard of Chaos since the dragon theft. She must be enjoying herself, reunited with her family and her first.

They say a woman never forgets her first.

I shake thoughts of Chaos out of my head, as they will only cause more fog. I walk up to the front of the line to see that the meal is lobster and potatoes. Quite delicious. That's when it hits me: They feed us so well because any day could be our last. The blacksmiths get a good meal because they are the lynchpin of the economy, while the navigators are fed junk to keep them sluggish and glued to the consoles. And then there are the scavengers with their muck muck.

I'm hyperaware now, but not to the point that I'd do anything about it. I mean, what can one lone striker do about the way the scavengers are treated?

The thing about trying to create change in any group is that it requires a leader. Someone who decides to take a stand and lead the group to newfound prosperity. Just because I was the first to find out about the Battle for Marda doesn't automatically make me fit to lead an entire group of strikers. Just because I stepped up for one fight does not make a leader. A leader can rally the troops and raise the banner, and the people will come. A leader is the prime example of the change they wish to see in the world.

I am not that.

Or at least that's what I tell myself.

So I take my lobster and potatoes past the leering eyes of the scavengers and take a seat with my troupe. The second time in my life eating in a group. Quite the feat.

I may not be a leader now, but who's to say that cannot change one day?

Baby steps.

Allison gives me a smile, Tash gives me a nod, and Sansa is tinkering with some round orb.

"What is that thing you keep messing with?"

"It's a personal assistance bot. It will lower your reliance on your navigator and assist in battle. Also..." She leans in close. "It's a recording device. It's so I can learn more about your fighting style."

"I see. When will it be up and running? You've been working on that for quite some time."

"Patience, Vex. It will be well worth it."

I turn to Tash, who is eating her steak and fries in silence. Although it's always hearty, there isn't much variety in what the blacksmiths eat.

"When will the new upgrades come out?"

"Tomorrow."

"Excellent."

Finally, I turn to Allison, who has been beaming a wide smile at me this entire time. As if my presence alone brings her the utmost joy.

"How is the communication system? And what part of the tundra seems lucrative? I'm ready to go hunting today."

It's been a while since I hunted, and I've been eyeing a new upgrade for Tirade. Maybe that will shut her up. Or at least get her to say something new.

"The comm system is stronger than ever. We finally managed to fix the kinks with all that ice and snow. In terms of hunting grounds, there is a Frost Phoenix Den, which some strikers have had trouble clearing—mainly due to interference from the Planetary Division. It seems there are a lot of duels going on for debated territory."

"Sounds like fun."

I grow quiet and dig into my food. The succulent taste of butter mixed with the lobster meat flirts with my senses, promising to keep me glued to my plate for the foreseeable future.

Although I am last to finish, the rest of my troupe waits until I am finished to get up.

I suppose that's a sign of respect. It's rather odd to me. But I appreciate the gesture, nonetheless.

Baby steps.

I stride into the Phoenix Den ready to take down anything that comes my way. It's a large nest atop a giant tree, similar to the Bee Rexes' hive. I'm met by a series of large blue eggs and the bodies of what I recognize to be planetary strikers. As I approach the eggs in stealth mode, I see a blue blur cross my vision. Suddenly an egg is missing. The blue blur returns, and another egg is missing.

My instincts tell me this is somehow a striker moving that fast. I turn my comms to the quietest setting.

"Striker to navigator. Bring up profiles of planetary strikers capable of exceeding my wind speed."

"Allison to Vex. Only one comes up. Rank sixty-one, codename Speed Demon."

"Rank sixty-one huh, should be easy pickings."

"Vex, keep in mind that the planetary division is an elite division. I'd say rank sixty-one is the equivalent to a top twenty-five striker in our division. They can take you out if you let your guard down."

"Copy that."

Instead of trying to aim at Speed Demon, I aim where I anticipate he'll be next. Judging by the missing eggs, he is simply taking the ones closest to the exit. I lift my wrists and launch both my grappling spears. The first one strikes what I assume to be a phoenix egg, while the second latches on to speedster's ankle.

His battlesuit is a sleek blue design with a popped collar. On his left side, a blue holographic shield covers his entire arm. His helmet is sleek as well, with blue holographic feathers at the side. He wriggles and wrenches, but to no avail. Just as I'm about to send electricity through the wires, he pulls out a blue sickle and cuts them. And with that, he is gone once again.

A blur.

"Lucky shot. Bet you can't do that again," says Speed Demon.

He goes back to taking the eggs, paying me little to no mind.

"Bet I don't have to," I respond.

I send out Tirade, who taunts him in place just as he's about to pluck another phoenix egg. I let loose a couple rounds in his leg to cripple him.

"The rest of the eggs are mine. Hobble yourself back to..."

He is gone in another blue blur.

Suddenly my head is dazed, my visor cracked once again.

"Did you just punch me?"

"That I did."

He's much faster than I am. The only thing that might rival it is my meteor dash— but that's only used for explosive bursts not consistent speed. Even with haste, I pale in comparison.

"Listen here, Speed Demon."

"It's Mr. Speed Demon to you, old man Vexation. I'm shocked that you broke my speed record for longest distance traveled in shortest time. Although meteor dashing is kind of cheating."

"I'm not calling you mister. Your profile says that you're 18."

"You will respect the speedster."

He moves at blinding speeds once again. I activate my shields; one of them goes down instantly as his fist connects. He follows this attack with another, causing another shield to disappear. The attacks are relatively weak, but he is so fast that the physical damage adds up.

After a barrage of fists to my chest, head, and stomach, I am beginning to feel some pain.

He rushes in, and I spray and pray by twirling in a circle and shooting in random directions, making it difficult to dodge. Some of the bullets strike gold, causing him to drop to one knee.

"Are you done fooling around now?" I ask.

"I wasn't fooling around. I was giving it my all."

"Oh, well... I expected more."

I turn around just in time to see a giant blue phoenix charging us. Not wanting to wait for it to finish, I meteor dash and slice off its head with my scimitars. The bird goes down easy as I land.

"Ohh, that was so cool, sensei."

"I'm not your sensei. I don't need any honorifics."

We watch as the body of the phoenix turns into an egg with reinforced ice plating.

"Striker to navigator."

"What am I looking at?"

"Vex, you need to destroy that egg ASAP or it will explode, taking out the entire tree. You along with it."

"Copy that."

I fire my P90s, which are dealing reduced damage. After emptying their energy bar, I switch to my scimitars while sending out my Bella rockets. The egg seems to be absorbing some of the damage. I watch as the egg continues to expand, threatening to explode at any minute.

I turn to the speedster with disdain in my voice. "If you assist, I will give you twenty percent."

"Just need you to put some respect on my name."

"Alright, alright, Mr. Speed Demon."

"Cool cats."

He pulls out his sickle and charges it with an enormous amount of wind energy. After one long minute, he slices the egg in half—revealing a smaller egg, covered in feathers."

"Striker to navigator. You can send in the scav."

"You see, sensei, you can rely on me. When do we start advanced hunting techniques? I'll admit that I have trouble taking down monsters. All I really have is raw speed."

"First tell me how you managed to cut through that egg with such ease."

"Oh that? That's a move my mother taught me. It takes forever to charge, so I rarely manage to pull it off in actual battle. But I'm able to cut through virtually anything with it."

"Teach me how to execute that move and I will train you on how to take down monsters that surpass your skill level. It all starts with striking areas of vulnerability."

CHAPTER 40
CLASSIFICATION: NAVIGATOR

I roll up in the truck to the meeting spot where we typically make the exchange. As usual, there are a handful of RRA members. Beads of sweat drip onto my shirt as I hop out the truck. I'm decked in my elite battlesuit, and it is about time I test out my training.

Inquisitor Morange and his multipurpose units are hiding around the corner, while I have a truck load of bottom feeding strikers ready to pounce. This is a hostile takeover. Either we walk away with their entire operation in the palm of our hands, or we die in the process.

"Hey Sugar Cane, that armor sure looks good on you."

"Don't try and sweeten me up. Transfer the credits as usual."

"Normally we inspect a product or two before we transfer the credits. Or have you forgotten how we do business?"

"Change of plans."

I lift my mp5 and shoot one of his members in the head. Before they can withdraw their lava weapons, Inquisitor Morange's bots have incapacitated the other three members.

"Last chance. Transfer the credits."

'Alright, alright. Take 'em."

The head RRA member transfers the credits to my account.

Chump change compared with what Morange deposited. It barely covers the cost of the new strikers.

"Now lemme go. You got what you wanted."

"What do you know about the Crypto Pyramid?"

"Is that what this is about? You want that damn thing back? I mean, it was you that led us to it in the first place, and we paid you handsomely for it."

"Tell me where it is now!"

"Do you even know what it does? It's a real game changer. It will make everything we've been fighting for worthwhile. You think I'm just gonna..."

Inquisitor Morange walks over to face the RRA member and shoots him in the leg with a high-powered shotgun. The guy wriggles around on the floor.

"You bloody shot me. You'll regret that. I'm not telling you jack."

Inquisitor Morange lifts the RRA member with some type of anti-gravity maneuver. He then presses a few buttons on his wrist console, and one of the V0-4 units fires two lasers into the RRA member's eyes. His screams of pain and agony are etched into my brain forever.

"Give us the location. These lasers can induce pain up to ten times what you're currently feeling."

"Okay, okay. Just no more of the laser stuff alright?"

We arrive to a location deep in the tundra west of the Oasis: flat lands and frozen ground as far as the eyes can see. There is total silence as we search the area for signs of life.

"He lied to us. We should have kept him alive."

"No, no one can lie under my lasers of truth."

"Then how do you explain this?" I ask.

"What if they are under some kind of stealth, or perhaps underground?"

"That is possible. How do we root them out?"

The inquisitor taps a few buttons on his console, and his multipurpose units scan the area. After about ten minutes, they find a mound of icy grass composed of various metals.

"Clever, very clever," says Morange.

The robots pry open the metallic latch and open the mound. One after another, we drop down into the underground bunker.

It takes some time for my eyes to adjust, but adjust they do. I'm met with dim lighting in a dark tunnel. There are two ways to go.

"I say we go left."

"I say we go right."

"Figures. Let's just split up. I will take strikers thirty-seven, thirty-eight, thirty-nine, and fifty. You take fifty-five, fifty-seven, and seventy-eight."

"Very well," says Morange.

He probably doesn't care that he has the lower-level strikers, due to his multipurpose bots. I'll have to get me one of those.

My goons and I progress further down into the tunnels until we see a bright light shining from a room to the side. In a star formation, numbers thirty-nine and fifty lead the charge followed by thirty-seven and thirty-eight, and then myself. We rush into the room to see a bunch of alliance members connected to the cybernet, the underground server for criminals. It's dangerous because the cyber elves can easily fry your brain if they catch you poking around on there. I've only been on there a few times to test my dodging skills, as they are called. But anything to do with the cybernet is bad business. With guns pressed to the backs of their heads, we disconnect the alliance members, careful to follow the right protocol.

Lest we kill them instantly.

The first member of the alliance wakes up from his cyber daze.

"Scaddlywags, you found us, huh."

"Yup."

"Look here, this isn't what it looks like. We're actually the good guys in this. We just want to cure the Oasis of the virus that is this Frost Knight and do a complete wipe of the credit system. Is that too much to ask? We aren't that rebellious."

"And what does the Crypto Pyramid do?"

"That I can't tell you. I'll die with that secret."

I riddle his console with bullets from my mp5. That will hurt any techy more than a bullet to the knee.

"No, not my precious!"

"You're making me repeat myself, and I hate doing that. What does the Crypto Pyramid do?"

"It's a multipurpose device unlike anything we have ever seen. With it, we can connect to the IGF/GF server and rid all the planets of the entire credit system."

"How foolish. Then what would be our medium of exchange? Things would go into anarchy."

"No, we would introduce our own monetary system, known as alliance dollars."

"So we are to turn in one dictatorship for another? How dull. Here I though the RRA was more than just some power-hungry nerds."

"Say what you will about us, but you need us to help you eradicate the Frost Knight. His sigil is as dangerous as it gets."

"Show me the info you have on the Frost Knight, and perhaps our organizations can team up in taking down the threat."

"I don't know... who's to say you can be trusted? What's to say you won't blow my brains all over this floor once you have what you want?"

"One thing I can guarantee is that I will blow your brains out if I don't get it. What I want is simple: the Crypto Pyramid and the information you have on the Arunkai known as Frost Knight.

"Ok, here's what we'll do. I will hand you the information, and you will escort me and my surviving members back to our final safe house in the desert. As for the Crypto Pyramid..."

Inquisitor Morange barges through the door, covered in blood. One hand holds his shotgun and the other holds the Crypto Pyramid. He gives me a knowing smile.

"Sugar slowing you down, Sugar Cane? Would have thought you'd be finished up here by now."

"Just about."

The man widens his eyes while the rest of the group lowers their heads.

"Information and don't kill us?"

"Enough negotiating!" I bellow.

Another RRA member screams, "Just give her what she wants!"

The guy electronically transfers the information to my wrist console. I do a quick check and see they have gathered a lot of information on the Frost Knight. Utilizing this information will give us a much-needed edge against our opponent. If this Arunkai is anything like the Queen Bee, it will require everything we have to take him out.

I'm about to take my leave when Inquisitor Morange raises his eyebrow. "Aren't you forgetting something?"

"No, I believe we have everything."

"No prisoners and no witnesses. Or do you not want to have true dominion over their operations?"

"I do…"

"Speaking of which, I have a list of their clients. All you have to do is show me how bad you want it."

I let out a sigh and walk up to the now-crying RRA members.

"Please… mercy."

"My pockets are all out of that," is my only response.

I pull the trigger and let loose a barrage on the remaining RRA members. Blood and brain matter scatter all over the place. Now that the deed is done, it feels as though I've splashed cold water on my face. This killing thing gets easier and easier the more I do it. This is all for a grand purpose. To bring my underground empire to fruition. With the right number of credits, I can find a cure for my mother.

Or at least, that's what I say for comfort. But I have to admit: A part of me just enjoys the carnage.

I wake up the next morning in my semi-comfortable bed. The fact that I slept so well is a testament to how adjusted I have become to this whole Sugar Cane thing. At one point, I would have been up all night after such an escapade. But I put on my grease-stained t-shirt, blue jeans, and running shoes, and I head to my cubicle as if nothing happened.

Although I got a full night's rest, I'm exhausted by the time second snack comes around. The chat messenger pops up on my console.

"You can't trust him."

"Who?"

"Inquisitor Morange."

"Tell me something I don't know. But he is a means to an end."

"I see—that's good. You miss me?"

"I miss when life was simple."

"I hear that." He pauses. "You look tired."

"Don't mind how I look. Why are you spying on me?"

"You thought it was kind of kinky before, I'm sure. A mysterious muscular elf behind the computer. Watching your every move and taking care of things that you could not take care of yourself."

"You mean the way you took care of Inquisitor Morange finding out about my extracurriculars?"

"I admit that I underestimated certain parties."

"So you aren't the unsurpassed hacker I thought you were."

My screen goes fuzzy, then it shows me a hooded elf with glowing purple eyes. In his hand is a purple cube.

"Big whoop. I can hack a single unit with one eye closed."

Suddenly every console in the facility overloads the minds of their users. Everyone else in the facility slumps in their chairs.

Sweat bullets streak out as I rush to check the pulse of the person beside me. I breathe a sigh of relief to see that she is still alive.

"What did you do?!"

"Nothing too difficult. I just put them to sleep."

There is a long pause.

"How is that for hacking abilities?"

"Wake them up now!"

"I just wanted to show you how powerful I am. No need to get testy."

"What are you? No elf should be able to do such a thing."

"Well, if you must know, I'm a cyber elf, and I love you, Allison. I'd do anything for you. Even break the rules and regulations of my people."

"Wake them up, please."

"As you wish, my love."

"Don't call me that."

"Why not?"

"Because you're a cyber elf. You're a creature forever doomed to roam the cyber realm, lost in code. Nothing more than a string of 0s and 1s. How can you even be real?"

"Good question. But I am real."

And then a dark blue hand reaches out of the monitor and grabs my wrist. I recoil at the tingling sensation and tumble out of my chair. Gathering my senses, I turn off the console and rush over to my supervisor, who is just waking up.

"I'm not feeling well. I need to be excused."

"Fill in the ten-page form for sickness, and you may be excused."

"But this is urgent."

"Not more urgent than my meal. Fill in the form, and I'll consider it."

I clench my hands into fists but take a deep breath.

She's lucky I don't go full on Sugar Cane on her candy ass.

CHAPTER 41
CLASSIFICATION: STRIKER

We have cleared out the monsters on the outskirts of the Oasis and as a result have gained entrance into the Oasis for the citizens. As usual, the Eclectic Division made camp near the city that hired us. It's been some time since I've been in contact with Inquisitor Morange. He has been styling me by dodging my calls on his direct line. There are few things in this world that I dislike more than being ignored.

I decided to pay him an improvised visit to his villa deep in the Oasis. It will have to be discrete, as the Eclectic Division is banned from entrance into the Oasis unless severely injured or as a native member. It's a pity that the planets we fight so hard to protect hold us in such low regard. The more I think about my situation, the more I desire growth. Honestly, I feel stuck. Trapped between a ledge and a brick wall.

I'm on the edge and I cannot afford to be pushed.

Dressed like a thief in the night, I proceed into the Oasis. As I push farther into the city, I am amazed by the large, flashing signs. From 24-hour dining restaurants to the 24-hour movie theatres, the entire city is a bustling marketplace. Dwarves and elves intermingle in such harmony—it's a pleasant sight. I turn the corner swiftly to let a group of planetary officers pass by. My hand is forever near my P90s, ready to protect myself at a moment's notice. If I'm caught or identified, I will be expelled from striker duty and relegated to a bottom level scavenger.

A fate worse than death.

I inhale the scent of fresh deep-fried squid with mixed vegetables, making my stomach growl. My hope is that this is a misunderstanding, and I will be welcomed with open arms. All those promises of advancement, of a fruitful career, of adventures into the rift. What else do I have left to hang my helmet on? I have also concluded that the Eclectic Division is simply a loop. I can't continue going on like this.

Travel, locate, kill. Travel, locate, kill.

While I inch my way closer to the villa, I notice a slew of planetary officers on these streets mixed in with the normal foot traffic.

Security is tight.

I sidestep into an alleyway and use my grappling spears onto the roof of the building. Pulling myself up, I reach the top of the building. The view was not something I anticipated, but it's absolutely breathtaking. The sparkling lights, the unique structures, the bustling crowd late at night. But above all, the air. The air after a heavy rainfall somehow adds a certain allure. I will never forget the clean, crisp air that fills my lungs with each breath. It's as if the Most High came down and blew a gust of wind into my lungs himself.

Heh, the Most High. I mean, if the blacksmiths get results and can turn into rift-like beings, then the Most High must exist. If only strikers had something to believe in.

I look down at the villa beside the Envidia Corp building now beneath my feet. It's peculiar that he would purchase a villa in such a busy neighborhood. I know if I were well-off, I'd pick somewhere quiet, off in the suburbs.

Different strokes for different folks.

With my feet charged and legs bent, I meteor dash off the building. By utilizing the height difference and the momentum of my dashes, I am able to cover the wide distance. When I land on the villa roof, I am met with a guard and his rifle. Swiftly I send forth my grappling spears into his chest, followed by a surge of electricity. Just enough to stun him.

Picking up his rifle, I make my descent down the side of the villa. By the time I reach the bottom, I see two guards patrolling in the distance. I activate my stealth mode and slink past them. Met with the villa's back gate, I climb over it and enter the swimming pool area. A guard is sitting reading "Play Toy 5" on paper.

Those come straight to your console these days.

I pass by him and slide open the back door. Entering the villa, I am met with the scents of vanilla and lavender. A sensual scent if there ever was one. Smoke wafts around my stealthed body, leaving me somewhat visible. On the couch are three naked women pleasing a large, bulbous fellow.

He nods at me and I nod back.

Lowering the rifle slightly, I push forward into the kitchen. This time I'm met with two men railing a blonde woman atop a kitchen counter. The scent and smoke seem to be disrupting my sensors, so I turn down the sensitivity.

Something about the air is intoxicating. It makes me want to strip my clothes off and join them. Nevertheless, I push further. The music playing is some type of fast-paced dubstep or techno. I never could tell the difference. I hear moaning and screams from the second floor. After I stumble up the stairs, I am about to poke my head up when I see the beam of a laser scanning for warm bodies.

It doesn't take a genius to know that this is one of Inquisitor Morange's V0-4 multipurpose units. As always, he keeps them at his hip, making him near untouchable. Lucky for me, I had come prepared for this. I received a special overload device from Sansa, who isn't a goodie-goodie like the rest of my troupe. I'm sure Allison and Tash would both be appalled at what I am doing.

I throw the metal ball over the steps and listen as it rolls to a halt. The laser locks onto it and is about to fire when I hear a whizzing sound and then smell fried wiring. I wait a few more minutes, lest I get burned to a crisp by the bot, and then poke my head out. The bot is temporarily deactivated for anywhere from ten to fifteen minutes. I estimate that I have nine.

I open the door to my right. It's an empty bathroom. I move on to the other three doors, all open. Finally, I come to the last door, right behind the bot. Rifle poised at eye level, I go to open the door, then pause. Sweat bullets rush down my forehead. I take out the second overload device and throw it in the room.

A few seconds pass, then the sound of a shotgun goes off. I rush into the room and hurl my grappling spears into the other V0-4 multipurpose bot, which is facing the door. I duck and roll just as it shoots a concentrated beam at my neck. As I manage to imbue the spears with a large surge of electricity, the bot frizzles out, then overloads.

Boom.

I go flying backwards into a closet as the shotgun shreds apart my battlesuit over my stomach. Another shot like that in the same spot, and I'm a goner. Jumping up, I aim the rifle at Inquisitor Morange's head.

"Drop the shotgun. If I wanted you dead, you'd be on the floor already."

"What the hell, Vex!"

"Quiet you." I grumble.

Looking at the silk-covered bed, I see one female companion beside him and another chubbier one still underneath the blanket.

"Why have you been dodging my calls? I left you at least ten messages."

"I was busy. I am an Inquisitor. I have certain palms I must grease and other kinds of upkeep to maintain."

"I see you're upkeeping your balls in these women's mouths."

The woman beneath the blanket squirms a bit. It irks me that she is hiding her face. The only one that gets to be hidden is me. But that can wait.

"What do you want? Why did you come here?" asks Morange.

"I want to know who this Sugar Cane person is. You promised me Sugar Cane, amongst other things. And I want my just due. I want out of the Eclectic Division and into a better position."

"That's not possible so soon. You guys need to clear this planet of the monsters and prove to the IGF that you're worthy. I can only do so much. As far as Runnymede goes, I haven't found Sugar Cane yet. All I know is that she is somewhere in the Oasis, and that her operations have expanded."

I point the rifle at the figure under the blanket.

"Tell her to stop doing what she's doing and to get out from under the blanket."

"I don't think that's a good idea."

"I didn't ask you."

"Vex, it really isn't a good idea."

My finger clasps the trigger.

"Three seconds or you're all dead. You're clearly in league with this Sugar Cane."

"You don't know that."

"I'm not as stupid as you think I am. Someone of your talents could have easily narrowed down the list to a few navigators in my division. The fact that you're not even giving me a list of names shows me you're hiding something."

"Okay, okay. I'm coming out."

I know that voice all too well. I am used to hearing it without seeing anyone. Allison pops out from beneath the covers with a high-powered mp5. The bullets rain down on me just as I activate my shields.

I'm aiming the rifle at Allison's head when the door barges open and in storms a group of planetary officers. I turn my stealth back on and crash through the window. After landing on my side, I get up and make a beeline for the east entrance, full well knowing that Sansa is waiting for me at the west.

"Vex to Sansa."

"What's up? Did you find what you were looking for?"

"Yes, and then some. I can't return to the encampment. Allison is Sugar Cane, and she's in league with Inquisitor Morange."

"Heavy shit."

"Yeah."

"What now?"

"I have to get out of the city. I know you have your sights set on being a striker, so it's best that you stay away from me. I'll be branded a renegade and hunted down just like my father."

So it was in the beginning, so it will be in the end.

There is a long pause.

"Sansa to Vex."

"Yeah?"

"I'm coming too. I can't devote myself to an organization with such corrupt officials. The question is, where do we go now?"

"I hear the RRA has a final base somewhere in the desert, east of the Oasis. That's our best bet."

"Sounds like fun."

Breathing heavily, I draw a sigh of relief as the clunky yellow car pulls up beside me. How she found me so fast, I don't bother to ask.

As we zoom off towards the east entrance, I realize I am leaving behind everything I have ever known. I am betraying a cause I had devoted my entire life to. Not to mention the fact that I am choosing to join the losing side in a revolution. But what choice do I have?

On the bright side, at least I have this young sprout to keep me company—a kid who reminds me of myself in so many ways. The music catches my ears, and I turn it up.

"Silence" by Popcaan comes on. It's a song about being careful who you trust.

Tell me something I don't know.

CHAPTER 42
CLASSIFICATION: NAVIGATOR

The following morning, I lie in the silk sheets and contemplate everything that has just transpired. It's not like Vex and I were close. At least, not as close as I would have liked. It's a shame that we will lose another strong striker, but he must be hunted down and killed for his little escapade into Morange's villa.

What was he thinking? Barging in like that?

I suppose thinking things through was never his strong suit. But give me a break. Breaking into the Inquisitor's villa to have a little chit-chat about backhanded deals?

Fool.

Things may not be going as planned, but they are going the way they need to go. My hand is firmly around the underground smuggling ring, while my needs are being satisfied by a powerful man. Just what I needed. He may not be as young as I would have liked, but there are times where a woman has to compromise. Especially in this case. Now that our destinies are further intertwined, he will be more likely to be subservient to my demands. Or should I say requests? To be lying in bed with the one who is supposed to be investigating your illegal activities—what more could I ask for?

Yet somehow, my victory seems bittersweet. I never wanted it to result in Vex being excommunicated. Not to mention that Tash will be completely devastated when she hears the news. I suppose I should be the one to tell her. Word travels fast these days.

I rise and get dressed. While putting on my dress, I feel a little discomfort in my lower back. That old man Morange has the vitality of an ox. I put on my heels and wobble my way down the stairs.

Blasted shoes.

I see Morange, a few of his colleagues, and their pleasure mates sitting around a giant onyx dining table marked with an IM in the middle. The ivory lettering is a nice addition to the glorious onyx. There is a healthy heaping of scrambled Frost Ostrich eggs, steamed broccoli, and Marda toast. A relatively healthy breaking-of-fast, as Vex would call it. Quite the change from my usual deep-fried variety.

Look at them, all one big happy family

Morange beckons me over to a seat beside him and his pleasure mate, a slim brunette with hazel eyes. She's still wearing the black collar from last night. He tried to put one on me, as well.

"I'm no pet, and you don't own me." were my exact words.

Something tells me he rather likes when a woman is somewhat defiant. Or at least, when she puts up a fight to his whims and fancies. I take my place by his side and analyze the table. I recognize the plump fellow as the governor of the Oasis and one of the pleasure mates as a famous model. I presume the other people are similarly noteworthy. Suddenly I am made aware of my situation. I feel as though I am inadequate.

Simply a navigator for the Eclectic Division.

Or the underground queen pin whose grip on the smuggling ring has tightened.

"So, Sugar Cane. When can we expect a shipment from the depths of this Frost Knight's lair? I'm sure he has some exotic creatures on his moving territory."

I dig my nails into Morange's thigh to show my displeasure.

"First, we need to figure out this sigil thing, which is spreading amongst the population. These worms have proven to be quite the conundrum." I say.

The governor lets out a belly laugh. "A tiny brain-controlling worm. How fearsome. Have you noticed that it only affects the common people?"

"Yes, we have noticed certain trends."

"That's because of the encryption on the chips. The common people have the crappy T1 chips, while the elite and IGF members have the T3 and above. Meaning there is no threat to anyone of value."

"That is…"

"Splendid," Morange cuts me off.

"So, there you go. Hip-hip and hurrah, you can now facilitate an excursion onto this Frost Knight's territory. I want him off my planet and my hands on what treasures lie deep inside his ice castle."

While I eat the healthiest meal I've had since I was a child, I listen to the conversations between these so-called elite. One of the models dribbles and drabbles about her servant stealing a necklace. Another drones on about how she's now reached 30 and is out of her prime. She will have to retire soon. Morange is engaged in a heated debate with the governor about which game is more stimulating, Rogue Quest or volute.

Does anyone even remember I'm here? Do I really want to be part of this family?

After finishing my meal, I say my farewells to each member of the group and make my way back to the encampment west of the Oasis, a place where I feel more comfortable. Besides, I have to tell Tash and Sansa what has happened to Vex.

When I arrive at the encampment, there seems to be a large crowd gathered in the blacksmith quarters. My intuition acts up, telling me that something has gone horrible wrong. Rushing over to the crowd, I push my way through with all my might. Upon reaching my destination, I am met with the horrific sight of Tash's mangled body attached to some kind of mechanical device. Her throat is severed, and her wrists have bled out.

Clearly a suicide.

I push past the onlookers and grab the note from one of her blacksmith colleagues. It reads,

My greatest fear has come to fruition. To be abandoned and neglected by the one I had sworn an oath to. The one for whom I had devoted my entire career to maintaining his armor. His weapons. To healing him in his time of need. Through thick and thin, a blacksmith's bond to their striker is unrivaled, as dictated by the Most High. I could never just find a new striker, for that would be like finding a new limb. As such, I have chosen to give *myself to the Most High and take my chances in the afterlife. My faith is strong, and I know that this is the path laid out before me. Signed, Tash, the one who was abandoned.*

A curse on Vex and his foolish actions. Look what a mess you have caused. I will see his head on a platter if it's the last thing I do. I feel a tear beginning to form, but I stifle it.

The only thing sweet about Sugar Cane is the name, I remind myself.

"Allison to Sansa."

No response.

"Allison to Sansa. Kid, respond, this is urgent."

I march over to the scavengers' quarters where Sansa's tent is. Most of her stuff is there except for her battlesuit, her gear, and her vehicle.

Sansa must be on some kind of isolated hunt. Silly child. I keep telling her those are dangerous. Not even Vex ventures off completely isolated...

That's when it hits me. He may have taken Sansa with him. My only hope is that I'm wrong. As much as I hate to say it, my true family was my troupe. As dysfunctional as we may have been. Tash was the quiet, insecure sister, Sansa the uppity youngest sister and Vex a strong male figure. Even Runnymede was like a perverted uncle who did what he had to do to survive.

I lower my head and contemplate my next move. I must adjust to this new life. One among the elite, wielding an underground empire. It's what I wanted, right?

What use is it to gain the world in your left hand, only to lose your family in the other?

CHAPTER 43
CLASSIFICATION: STRIKER

o the dismay of the guards at the eastern gate of the Oasis, we phase travel through the massive metallic doorway and into deserts unknown. We are immediately met with a sandstorm that threatens to upend us. They call the desert side of the Oasis Dead Man's land. It's known for its S-grade beasts, and for its lack of water, food, and anything remotely resourceful. It's entirely possible that I am leading Sansa and myself on a wild duck hunt: a journey straight into the palms of death himself. Even if the RRA reside in the desert, the chances of finding them are next to none. But better to take those chances than to stare down the barrel of every striker in both divisions.

I sit here in the blistering heat, waiting for something besides mounds of sand. We continue to drive east for days. How this vehicle manages to drive for so long is a mystery to me. But I'm grateful.

For the first time in days, I speak.

"They'll make monsters of us." I pause. "IGF doesn't like stray strikers roaming about. A kill code will be placed on both our heads, and assassins will come looking."

"I knew the risks were high when I decided to join you."

"Why did you?"

"I told you. I'm not going to be part of an organization with corrupt officials. If everything you told me is true, then it sounds to me like this Inquisitor is up to no good, and he is well-connected. Vex, this is bigger than the two of us. We can back a revolution and become heroes in the process."

Her wide-eyed enthusiasm somehow stirs something in me. "I never took you for a revolutionary."

"I'm not. But the chance to overthrow a corrupt ruling body and become a hero? Now, I'm all about that! My name will forever be in the history books."

"I'll settle for surviving this hell hole. I honestly don't know what to look forward to. All I ever wanted to be was the number one striker. It's all I ever knew."

"Yeah, well, you know…"

The car feels as though it's being lifted into the air. I look outside to see a rising mound beneath us. I grab Sansa from the driver's seat instinctively and bail from the passenger's side door. We go tumbling out of the car onto the sand.

I look up to see a massive Sand Wurm swallowing the car whole, along with our provisions. It's identifiable by its large brown scales and the six-teethed flaps it has for a mouth. The stench it emits is horrendous. Sand falling from its body seems to shroud the creature, making its vitals difficult to identify.

I go to my comm unit to speak to my navigator, only to remember there is no navigator to speak to.

I grip my P90s with fervor, and my blades are ready to unleash havoc. But it's Sansa who makes the first move. Fluid as water, she pulls outs her compact plasma launcher and fires three plasma balls into the head of the beast. The Sand Wurm wriggles back and forth, seemingly unfazed. If anything, it's more enraged than in pain. The beast spits green acidic liquid in our direction, forcing us to run.

It burrows under the sand only to upend us, causing us to fly into the air. I meteor dash, unleashing pain and suffocation upon it. The P90s shred through its armored skin with ease. Sansa rushes in with some makeshift plasma blade and slices at the tail end of the creature. To my surprise, she cleaves through the creature with little effort.

Together we make quick work of the Sand Wurm, but the damage is done. The car is gone, and we're stuck in the middle of the desert. No provisions, no communications, and while being hunted down by the IGF's top desert strikers.

Fun times.

As we progress through the desert, the blistering heat begins to take its toll. Having two suns was all fine and dandy when we were in the tundra and mountains, but in this vast wasteland of a desert, it's the last thing I want. We continue to slog our way east in hopes of finding elven life. Dehydration kicks in.

Sansa collapses.

I look at her unconscious body and roll my eyes. Part of me wants to just leave her there, let the wild take her. But my better half decides on summoning Tirade with what little energy I have left.

I place Sansa on Tirade and continue walking east. I see something in the distance—an object protruding out the mound of sand.

My heartbeat increases as my hopes rise.

A well

In the sloppiest manner, we make our way to the well. I lick my parched lips at the thought of quenching my thirst with crisp, clean water. As my hands grip the metallic bucket, I peer inside to see—nothing. My hands tremble as I press the button to lower the bucket into the well.

Time comes to a standstill while the bucket lowers. I listen for the precious sound of metal submerging into water, but I am met only with silence.

It's still good. There will be just enough for us to drink.

My vision is now blurry, my mouth sandpaper.

As the bucket rises, I anticipate water, even if the bucket is only half-full. But I am met with a serpent coiled within the container. My hands reach swiftly for my P90s, but just as I withdraw them and take aim from the hips, the serpent uncoils itself to extend towards my neck. Its fangs pierce through my armor. I peel the serpent off me and dash it against the wall of the well. Unleashing pain and suffocation I empty both clips until my energy is completely depleted.

It matters not. Desert Serpents are the most venomous of snakes.

Within a few minutes, my eyes roll to the back of my head, and I drop to my knees. While I convulse, my life flashes before me. Images of abuse and betrayal.

I'm left with one final thought.

Downed by a mere D-grade serpent. How vexing.

The End

"Sometimes it's the closest people around you that do you the worst." – Negus Lamont

REVIEW + OTHER WORK

I hope you enjoyed this novel, and I would love to hear your feedback. Please leave an honest review on Amazon, Goodreads, etc. Reviews help very much, both with the rankings and in making me a better wordsmith. The next novels in this series will be:

Striker Y, released summer/fall 2020.
Striker Z, released winter 2020.

If you want to keep up to date with releases and other goodies, please join my e-mail list:

E-mail List Signup

https://www.neguslamont.com/subscriber-freebies

✉ E-mail: neguslamont@gmail.com